Emily Maguire is an Australian novelist, essayist and English teacher. Her articles and essays on sex, religion, culture and literature have been published in newspapers and journals, including *The Sydney Morning Herald*, *The Griffith Review* and *The Observer*. *The Gospel According to Luke* is her second novel. Her first, *Taming the Beast*, is also published by Serpent's Tail. She lives in Sydney.

Praise for *The Gospel According to Luke*

'Maguire is an energetic, often powerful writer who has once again shown us her hunger for more than most of us can chew comfortably' *The Australian Literary Review*

'Maguire has nailed it… [she] can dramatise ideological difference with realism and sympathy for all of the characters concerned' *Sydney Morning Herald*

'A powerful tale of faith and fanaticism' *Big Issue*

'*The Gospel According to Luke* presents the fundamental conflict of our times with precision, intelligence and a deep sympathy for believer and non-believer alike… Maguire reminds me of Dostoevsky in her ability to set aside her personal opinions to create convincing characters… one of the most profound contemporary novels I've read in years' *Catholic Herald*

Praise for *Taming the Beast*

'A hard-hitting debut about modern adolescence' *The List*

'The Australian novelist eschews the obvious child abuse narrative for a more complex look at the nature of violence and sex in this emotional rollercoaster' *Herald*

'In short, this might not be the novel to recommend to your primmer friends. But it's far too well-written to be discarded as shock-smut' *Arena*

'If you are seeking weight loss, this novel will give you far better results than any Atkins/South Beach/Cabbage Soup diet… By the end of *Taming the Beast* – through which I forgot to eat – I felt terrified, feverish, and green at the gills. And utterly awed' *Big Issue in the North*

'A disturbing and dark examination of obsessive love, with ferocious, unflinching sex and troubling, intense and bloody violence' *Bookmunch*

'Like Susanna Moore's *In the Cut* and Barbara Gowdy's *We So Seldom Look on Love*, this is an uncompromising look at sex, desire and unrequited love… Carefully narrated, this is a brilliant meditation on sex and power' *City Life*

'I was very impressed by *Taming the Beast*… Without being prurient, Maguire heads into extraordinarily dark psychosexual territory, withholding any easy answers' **Matt Thorne**, *Independent*

'This book explores the affect of the affair and its long-term implications through the woman's eyes' *Australian Times*

'It's a bleak, uneasy book, albeit powerfully written. It is also shockingly compelling' *Observer Magazine*

The *Gospel* According to *Luke*

Emily Maguire

First published in Australia by Brandl & Schlesinger Pty Ltd
in 2006

First published in GB in 2007 by Serpent's Tail,
an imprint of Profile Books Ltd
3A Exmouth House
Pine Street
London EC1R 0JH
website: *www.serpentstail.com*

ISBN 978 1 85242 990 4

Printed and bound in Great Britain by
CPI Bookmarque, Croydon CR0 4TD
This book is printed on FSC certified paper

10 9 8 7 6 5 4 3 2 1

PROLOGUE

Luke begins preparing for Sunday's sermon on Monday morning. He scans his bible, picking passages which relate somehow to world events or local concerns. There are always a few; the Bible has something to say about everything. It's the instruction book that people are always exclaiming they need and don't realise they already have. Luke decides on a scripture, prays about it, studies it, thinks hard, reads what others have said about it. He puts the Bible aside and gets on with the rest of his week's work – interviewing ministry candidates, inspecting the building site, proofing advertising copy. But the passage is always on his mind. He notices everything, seeking a connection. He searches for illumination in every face.

By Tuesday he is wild with joy or crushed by despair. The text is ridiculously abstract, contradictory, irrelevant. Or it is brilliant, vibrant, containing the greatest wisdom, inspiring the greatest, most profound thoughts that have ever entered his mind. He is humbled by God's great wisdom in guiding him to this scripture or frustrated at his own obtuseness in misunderstanding God's will.

On Wednesday he considers dumping the passage and picking a new one. It is the only way. This will never work out.

On Thursday he realises the passage is not the problem. It never is. He walks for hours, talking to himself, to the trees, to the Lord, trying to find the words that will make the story as alive to his congregation as it is in his heart.

Friday, he writes it all down, prays, puts it aside while he doorknocks another five streets to spread the word about the youth centre opening next month. When he reads the sermon again on Saturday morning he knows exactly what needs to be fixed and he does it easily and joyfully. He reads it to himself, over and over, adjusting his tone, altering his gestures, slowing down this section and speeding up another. He cannot sleep with the fear he will forget it all if he does not repeat it just one more time.

Sunday morning, early, he stands in the church alone and preaches to the retreating darkness. His heart beats too fast, he feels queasy and unsteady on his feet. He wishes it was eight already. He wishes it was over. He wishes he had never been called to do this, to submit week after week to this torture, this crushing self-doubt.

And then suddenly, it is okay. He can see in their faces that they want to hear what he says; they are attentive, rapt even. When he is self-deprecating they laugh affectionately; when he is raw and transparent, they cringe and look away, but just for a second. Their eyes always return to him, searching for the truth they know he will give them. By the time he is finished, he is bathed in sweat and love. It is the only time all week he does not feel lonely.

Sunday is Aggie's only day off, but she goes in to the clinic anyway, because, seriously, what else is there to do? Malcolm and Will spend Sundays sleeping late, going for brunch at some chic inner city café, then making love in the antique four-poster bed Aggie gave them when they set up house together. The bed had spent eighteen years in the service of her parents and then ten years as a spare bed which was slept in only once, by Aggie's ex-husband, the night before he left her. So she was pleased for the bed; it must be delighted to finally be used as a love nest after all those empty years.

So Mal, Will and the bed are together on this Sunday, and

although Aggie's own bed is sinfully comfortable, it is also depressingly large for just one woman. Even an unusually tall woman like Aggie. She cannot bear to lie in bed, contemplating the size of the empty space all around her. Instead she goes to her office where there is almost no space at all.

Malcolm's desk is crammed into one corner, Aggie's into its diagonal opposite. A couch for waiting clients and three rotating stands holding pamphlets about disease and pregnancy and dangerous pleasure, take up the rest of the main room. There are two small rooms out back: one is for confidential counselling sessions, and is just big enough for three folding chairs, and the other is a combined kitchen/laundry/toilet, which is not hygienic— but what can you do? It's not like the government is throwing money at sexual health clinics in these times of ultra-conservatism and right wing paranoia.

So Aggie spends Sunday in her tiny locked office, answering e-mails, reading last month's journals and health reports, drinking coffee and eating cornflakes from the box she keeps in her filing cabinet. She realises that not a single living person knows where she is or what she is doing. She realises she never has to tell anyone where she's going or what her plans are or why she is eating dry cereal instead of going next door for a sandwich. Is this independence or isolation? Powerful or pathetic? She would like to ask her mother – that expert in power and independence – but has no idea where she is or how to find her. Aggie bets her mother is not sitting alone in an unheated office reading about genital herpes.

To get the party started, rocket fuel. They spend a couple of minutes searching for a big enough bowl, before giving up and mixing it all in the kitchen sink. They can ladle it out with their glasses. It's a toxic mix: white rum from Rex's place, Jim Beam Black Label and Johnnie Walker nicked from Steve's old man, two casks of moselle purchased with a pile of scrounged-up change and half a case of Guinness that Honey stole from her step-dad while he was sleeping. If he finds out she took it, he will rip her hair from her skull.

It's a lot of booze for three sixteen-year-olds. Honey thinks they might die if they drink it all. But then some others arrive, friends of Rex's, slightly older guys who have pot and cigarettes which they distribute to Honey and the boys in exchange for access to the lethal brew. The blokes are all over Honey, which she is used to, because she is kind of hot, plus she is the only girl in a room full of boys, so what did she expect? But she is there for Steve and he knows it. He pushes the hair out of her eyes when she bends her head to suck back on the bong. She hands him cigarettes lit between her lips. At some point, she kisses him and it's like pushing her tongue into the neck of a rum bottle.

Honey loves parties like this. Someone's parents' house. Communal booze and drugs. Touching and laughing and kissing. No sense is talked. No unanswerable questions asked. Music videos playing and the radio on and a CD blasting and some German thrash metal band screaming from a computer which is flashing pictures of women in leather collars being assaulted by Alsatians and men in masks. Honey is cool with the noise and the porn and the smell. A lesser girl would feel intimidated.

The boys are shouting at each other, but Honey cannot follow the argument. Something about cars or maybe boats. Engines, anyway. Steve's hand is inside her shirt, his tongue in her ear. On the TV, a girl rides a mechanical pony, her face twisted in ecstasy. At least, Honey thinks it's ecstasy; she has never experienced it herself, just seen it on others a whole lot. Her glass clicks against her teeth and the booze dribbles down her chin, making Steve laugh.

Time has passed. Honey is on a bed, in the almost dark and Steve's wispy blonde fringe is in her eyes. Someone is pounding on the door. 'It's locked,' Steve shouts, his voice cracking with the effort. 'It's locked,' Steve whispers, breathing hot rum in her face.

'You and Ricky broke up, right?' Steve is removing her jeans.

'Aha.' She struggles to stay awake.

'So you're single, yeah?'

Honey says she is and his teeth flash white in the moonlight. She closes her eyes, aware of hands and moans and pounding on the door, in her head, on her skin.

She wakes up. Steve is gone and her thighs are sticky. She jumps up; her head hurts. Fast, she opens the window behind her and yaks into the darkness outside. She hears the splash as her vomit hits the ground below. Her throat and vagina burn.

Blankness, blackness, a dizzy walk through empty halls and rooms. Then she's smoking a cigarette in the living room. More boys and a couple of girls have come. They stare at Honey as though she is still naked and vomiting.

The rocket fuel is gone, but someone has produced a case of beer. It's Toohey's New, her mother's brand. It is funny to think that Honey's mother is probably, at this very moment, also drinking a Toohey's New and smoking a Winfield Red. Probably, Honey's mother also has just been fucked, but that is really sick and Honey does not want to think about it, so she starts a conversation with the boy beside her. She tells him her name is Mary; he kisses her hand and says he is Jesus.

All around her, people are shouting, their faces caught between laughing and crying. She thinks it's three in the morning, but the numbers on her pink plastic Swatch keep blurring, so she can't be sure. Steve is asleep, his head on her stomach, his mouth open. He looks like he fell and landed that way. He looks like it hurts to sleep.

PART ONE

1

Luke knew the question was coming. He'd been interviewed by the city dailies, the local weeklies, several university papers, a teen pop magazine and even a local small business journal, and sooner or later, the question always came. It was coming now, from the sweet red-headed reporter from *Parenting Monthly*.

She was apologetic, this one. Aware that the question was awkward, perhaps even rude. She shuffled in her seat, tucked her hair behind her ears, frowned as though she was about to deliver terrible news, and then nodded to herself and plunged in. 'And what is your, ah, ethnic background, Mr. Butler? Are your parents recent immigrants or...?'

'I'm afraid I can't tell you.'

A line appeared between her eyebrows. Her pale cheeks turned pink. 'Oh. I'm terribly... I didn't mean to be— it's just our readers are from diverse ethnic backgrounds and I thought it would—'

'Kerry, please, you misunderstand me.' Luke smiled and touched her hand. 'I'm not refusing to answer, I simply can't. I haven't the slightest idea where my parents are from. Or who they are. I was raised in a children's home.'

'Oh, oh!' She clutched at his hands. Luke continued to smile although he was squirming in his skin. This was why he hated telling his story. It was always met by raised eyebrows or satirical smiles of disbelief or this smothering, gasping pity.

'Could you do me a little favour?' he asked.

'Of course. Name it.'

'Could you not make a big deal out of this in your article? It's just that I don't want my personal story to detract from my role here.'

'Oh, but…'

'It's sort of private. I don't know why I told you, I just… well, I'm new at this being interviewed business. When I get asked a question, my instinct is to answer it. I should have said "off the record" or something, right? Or "no comment?" I'm not used to being secretive.'

His words were true; his manner though, was a lie. Luke did not feel polite or apologetic. He felt frustrated and impatient. These darn reporters rarely wrote a thing about the mission of the Christian Revolution or the nature of the Youth Centre they were supposed to be publicising. It was all about Luke's 'olive skin and deep brown eyes', his 'astounding youth', 'dark good looks', and, of course, his 'tragic past'.

Pastor Riley said this was a good thing. What he referred to as Luke's 'charisma' would get the teens through the front door, and what was happening inside would ensure they stayed. And then as they danced and sang, ate and drank, played football, tennis and basketball, took cooking classes and mechanics workshops, formed friendships with each other and trusting bonds with the leadership team, the Lord's message would get through, and young hearts would be changed.

So Luke smiled and charmed and shook hands and answered awkward questions. He held information nights for parents and good-naturedly shrugged off the flirtations of suburban mothers and the silent suspicions of suburban fathers. He led city councillors and community leaders through the brand-new, six-million-dollar centre and defended the Christian Revolution's purchase of twenty-one acres of prime real estate in the heart of Parramatta's central business district. He hung out in movie theatres and game arcades, handing out brochures, spreading the word, and yes, it was undeniable, being mooned at by teenage girls who seemed to get a crush when a young man so much as looked at them.

It was frustrating. Having graduated top of his Christian Revolution Ministerial College class; having done the requisite year as a roving missionary, during which he was responsible for more conversions than any other missionary in the history of the Christian Revolution; having spent eighteen months as a fundraiser, and in that time received more and larger donations than any other fundraiser; having served four years as a Junior Pastor, in which he tripled the under twenty-five congregation; and having dedicated more than half his life to ensuring the success of the Christian Revolution, Luke felt he deserved to be treated as something more than a glorified spokesmodel.

Patience, he told himself for the thousandth time. Patience. God had gifted him with this opportunity and he must patiently endure the trials required. God had led the Elders to appoint Luke as Senior Pastor of this unique, exciting, world-changing centre, and what kind of ingrate would he be if he blew it all by refusing to get out and charm the suburban masses for a couple of months?

'I'm afraid I have another appointment in ten minutes.' He tried to look genuinely sorry. 'Can I take you on the grand tour before you go?'

'Oh, yes, please. I'd love that.'

The reporter would agree to anything now, he knew, because she no longer saw him as a precocious young minister but as an abandoned child. *Use everything you are for His Glory*, Pastor Riley said. So Luke swallowed his discomfort and let the woman hold his arm and murmur soothingly while he led her around the centre.

His joy in the gift he'd been given overtook his uneasiness as he showed the reporter around the brand-new Northwestern Christian Youth Centre. The complex consisted of a three-hundred seat auditorium, two meeting halls, a recreation room, a lecture theatre, an industrial kitchen and ten self-contained cottages which would initially house the five-person leadership team and allow for guests and growth. The main auditorium was fitted with state-of-the-art sound, lighting and media equipment, and the recreation room had computers, game consoles, a wide-screen television and a DVD player. In the grounds were a tennis court, sports field, picnic and barbecue area, and under the building was security parking for one hundred and twenty cars.

As they walked, Luke talked, making sure to pause often enough for the reporter to make notes. What's unique about the NCYC, he said, is that it's a church which is not a church at all. There would be no sermons, ever. In fact, the centre would not even operate on Sundays – if you want to go to church, hook up with your parents, right? Here (he spun around on the vast back lawn) we'll have sausage sizzles and rock concerts. Over here (he ran fast, ahead of the reporter, making her laugh and pant) we'll have football matches, mini-Olympics, water fights and funfairs. He showed her the rooms for Bible studies (all singing, dancing, acting, eating, laughing Bible studies), workshops, one-on-one counselling, small-group meetings, dance classes, cooking classes, guitar lessons and computer games.

'And make sure you let the caring parents reading your magazine know that from nine in the morning to ten at night, six days a week, we're here to take care of their precious children', he told her. 'All our pastors and volunteers are trained in first aid and the centre is under constant security surveillance. Parents need never hire a babysitter again! Drop the kids off on a Saturday night, we'll entertain them, keep them out of trouble and maybe teach them a little something about God. Everyone wins.'

The reporter smiled, touched his arm, shook her head. 'Wonderful,' she said. 'Just wonderful.'

'Nine to ten, Monday to Saturday,' Luke repeated, making sure she got that down in her notebook. 'We're here for the kids.'

2

The frosted glass doors of the Northwest Christian Youth Centre opened onto a tree-lined semicircular courtyard. Teenagers in jeans and brand-name sports jackets stood in groups of three or four, talking and laughing in the winter sunshine. Soft rock music wafted into the courtyard through speakers built into the walls. A cart loaded with cans of soft drink and baskets of chocolate bars and fruit stood to one side. The only indication that this was the headquarters of a bunch of nut job fundamentalists was the bronze lettering on the far wall which read: *Start a Revolution, In His Name.*

Aggie approached a table covered in glossy pamphlets and pastel coloured information sheets. *Get Jiggy For Jesus!*, *Safe and Sound – Our Security Guarantee*, *The Christian Revolution – A History*, and *NCYC – This is Not a Church!* lay alongside *The Truth About Safe Sex* and *How Far is Too Far?*

The leaflet that had inspired Aggie's visit was not on the table. Clearly, the propaganda designed to recruit children to the cult was different from that intended to stir up hatred and prejudice in the general community. Besides, these freaks knew as well as she did that had they told a bunch of teenagers that Aggie's office was 'distributing pornography to children', those children would have been queuing up around the block to get some.

A girl of about twenty in a fluffy fuchsia jumper and a swinging blond ponytail bounced up to the table. Her name tag said: *Hi! I'm Belinda.*

'Welcome to the NCYC. Are you interested in signing your kids up to one of our programs?'

Aggie refused to feel insulted. So what if she looked old enough to be the mother of a teenager? She had more important things to worry about than anti-wrinkle creams and sun-spot concealer. She smiled down at the girl, who, like everyone out here, was at least half a head shorter than Aggie.

'Actually no. I was hoping to speak to the manager.'

'The manager? Oh, well we don't really have a manager. Each member of our Pastoral Team is responsible for various aspects of the Centre's operation. For example' – the girl pointed to her name tag – 'I am Belinda Swan, and I oversee the *Learn & Praise* program, organise the *Girls Only* and *Teen Spirit* groups and act as Personal Assistant to the Senior Pastor. I'm also the unofficial cleaning lady, laundress and kitchen hand. Not that I mind. It's all God's work. Even scrubbing pots. Right?'

'So this Senior Pastor… he's the boss?'

Belinda giggled. 'Technically, I guess. But he'd turn red as a beetroot if anyone called him that. He's our leader, sure, but–'

'Is he in?'

'I'll check if he's available. Your name?'

'Aggie Grey.'

Belinda nodded, taking a mobile phone from her belt and punching the keys. 'What is the visit regarding– Luke, hi. There's an Aggie Grey here to– yes, yes… you've been… yes, all right, I will. Bye.'

She returned the phone to her belt before looking back up at Aggie. 'Pastor Butler said to tell you he's been looking forward to meeting you. He's in the kitchen. Just go on through these doors, straight to the end of the corridor and it's the last door on the right. I'd show you the way but I have to stay here to meet and greet.'

Aggie thanked her and made her way through the courtyard. She noticed a few of the teenagers smiling at her as if they knew her, but she was pretty sure she had never seen any of these kids before. Freshly-scrubbed, expensively-dressed teens rarely ended up in Aggie's office. Not because they never needed help, but because they had somewhere better to go to get it. These beaming girls would flash the family health fund card and see a top gynaecologist for free. These clear-skinned boys had fathers to ruffle their hair and slip a packet of condoms in their top drawer. They were just kids, as much products of their unchosen upbringings as the illiterate and the abused, but Aggie felt the knot in her stomach tighten all the same.

She pushed open the frosted glass door and stepped inside the building. She stopped, momentarily stunned by the immediate change in environment. There was no sound here except for her own breathing and the distant hum of the air-conditioning. The air itself was warm and clean, and the atmospherically dim lighting illuminated only white walls and black doors as far as she could see. She headed down the corridor, aware with every step of how loud her footsteps were. They were not loud in the way that stiletto heels clicking against tiles are loud, but in the way that a giant's footsteps are loud, even when that giant is attempting to move lightly across the carpet in her rubber-soled sneakers.

Unavoidable loudness was one of the problems associated with being abnormally tall. Another was that she couldn't catch public transport with any level of comfort because if she got a seat her legs did not fit, and if she stood up she was glared at by the other standing passengers as if she *meant* for her armpits to be exactly level with their noses. To save the awkwardness, she drove or walked everywhere. She also went automatically to the back in movie theatres and learnt to smile and not scream when people said *How's the weather up there?* or *You must be great at basketball*. It wasn't all bad though; sometimes, being enormous was a great advantage, like for instance, when you had to walk alone into hostile territory and intimidate the shit out of some fundamentalist fucker. Then it was pretty sweet.

Aggie paused outside the kitchen door. The tinkling of a teaspoon in a teacup and a tuneless humming were not typically the sounds of one's enemy preparing for battle, but this was not a typical war. She took three deep breaths, imagining a piece of string running up her spine and through the top of her head. She pushed her shoulders back, sucked her stomach in and touched the top of her head to ensure her hair was not sticking up too alarmingly.

She pushed open the door and was greeted by a smiling boy with dark curls and a blinding lime shirt, holding aloft a yellow teacup. 'Hello. Tea or coffee?'

'Neither, thanks. I'm looking for Pastor Butler.'

'You've found him.' He motioned toward the enormous timber table that stood between them. 'Pull up a pew. I'm just brewing a pot. Sure you won't have a cup?'

Aggie stayed in the doorway. The boy in front of her couldn't be older than twenty. He was either playing a prank by pretending to be the boss, or he really was the boss. Either way, it was too ridiculous.

'You're in charge here?'

'No, no, no.' He carried the pot and a cup to the table, then slid onto the bench behind it. He motioned for Aggie to join him. She stood her ground.

'Can you tell me, please, who is in charge?'

The boy pointed to the ceiling. 'God, of course. I'm just doing his bidding. Now please, Aggie Grey, sit down. Let's talk.'

Aggie sat down because she felt ridiculous standing in the doorway looking down on this tea-sipping kid. He smiled; she did not.

'You know who I am, so I'd appreciate it if—'

'Luke Butler. Senior Pastor.' He put down his cup and offered her his hand, which she shook the way her father had taught her: fast and firm. Luke Butler did not look surprised at the firmness of her handshake; he matched it with his own. Aggie nearly said that he was strong for a kid, but remembered all the times she'd been told she was 'strong for a girl' and so withdrew her hand wordlessly.

'So,' he said, wrapping his hands around his tea cup. 'So.' He held her gaze, smiling as though he had a great secret he couldn't wait to tell.

'I'm here to talk about the leaflets.'

'Yes, I thought you might be.'

Aggie had intended to start by explaining the mission and history of the Sexual Health Advisory Service, but his calm arrogance irritated her. 'Your leaflets contain false allegations and are defamatory. If you don't stop distributing them, we will press charges.'

Luke Butler's smile remained. He topped up his teacup. 'You deny carrying out the activities listed? Encouraging illegal activities such as drug injection and under-age intercourse? Promoting homosexuality and promiscuity? Distributing pornography to children?'

'We encourage and promote nothing except health and safety. If you believe any of our activities are illegal, you're free to report us to the relevant authorities. You are not free, however, to distribute defamatory literature. It stops immediately or you'll be hearing from our lawyers.' Aggie was impressed with how that came out. *Our lawyers.* As if they could afford even a cleaner!

He sat back in his chair and ran both hands through his curls. 'Better get your PR staff involved too, then. Imagine how much fun the tabloids will have with this.'

Aggie knew he was right. Middle Australia would light up the switchboard of every talk-back show in the nation when it got out that a sexual health counsellor had dragged a courageous young pastor to court. She could see the front page of *The Daily Telegraph*: A gritty photo of dirty teenagers with messy hair and tight jeans facing off a clean-cut, lime-shirted bunch of Christian soldiers.

Aggie shrugged, bluffing. 'Maybe. Maybe not. If we can communicate to the community the importance of what we do, then–'

'Forget communicating to the community for a minute. Communicate to me. Tell *me* why you believe you should be allowed to continue operating.'

'Listen, you arrogant prick. I'm not justifying the validity of my work to you.' Aggie stood up. 'If the harassment doesn't stop, I will call the police. Then I'll call a lawyer. And you may have the *Telegraph* and the talk-back shock jocks on your side, but I can stir up every progressive in the country if I call in the ABC and the *Herald*.'

He stood and came around to her side of the table. For a moment Aggie thought he was going to hit her, but he only placed a hand on her shoulder. This was even more alarming to Aggie, who had been hit often but held by the shoulder rarely. She was so tall; it was awkward for a person to hold her there, and yet this boy did. 'I'm sorry I upset you,' he said.

'No, you didn't. It's fine.' She could not move back because of the table; she shrugged, but his hand would not be displaced.

'I didn't know you'd get so upset. I was just… I hadn't meant to be arrogant. I only wanted to understand why you do what you do. You seem like such a nice–' His hand fell, and he stepped back. 'I just wanted to understand how such a nice person could be in the business you're in.'

'This isn't about me, Mr Butler.' Aggie stepped sideways and made for the door. 'Stop the leaflets or you'll hear from our lawyers.'

'Let me show you out,' he said, but Aggie's long, fast strides left him finishing the sentence from the kitchen while she had already reached the front doors.

Malcolm was out the front of the office smoking when Aggie returned. She pulled a face at the disgusting cigarette in his hand, but he was already grinding it into the ashtray and so did not see.

'Thought this week was quitting week?'

Mal followed Aggie inside. 'Quitting at home week. Next week I'll stop smoking at work, and the week after that, I'll stop altogether.'

'And does Will know about your three-step program?' Aggie asked. Will had been on at Mal to quit smoking and lose weight almost since they'd met. It was bad enough, Will said, that Mal was fifteen years older, without having to worry about him dropping dead prematurely of a heart-attack. Will's fears were behind the stash of chips and lollies in Mal's desk drawer, the gym bag thrown onto the filing cabinet every Monday morning and taken home unopened every Friday night, and now, the cigarettes kept in a drawer alongside peppermints and deodorant spray.

Mal put a finger to his slightly smiling lips. 'You don't tell him about the smoking and I won't tell him about the smoked salmon at the Red Cross fundraiser.'

'I was drunk and it was dark.' This was true. It was also true that she had known after the first bite that the tiny cross-shaped sandwiches contained salmon, and she had not only swallowed the morsel already in her mouth but had proceeded to eat five more sandwiches. Mal, who was vegetarian only when Will was looking, had been delighted to smell salmon on Aggie's breath. She was the only person he knew who was more sanctimonious about her intake of animal products than Will.

'No excuse for slaughtering innocent salmon, Ag. None at all.'

Mal took a Mars Bar from his desk and unwrapped it slowly, lovingly. Then he grunted and half of it disappeared in one bite. He chewed with his mouth open and moaned with exaggerated delight. If it wasn't for the receding hairline and middle-aged belly anyone would think he was fourteen years old.

Aggie wondered if Mars Bars still had animal fats in them. It had been many years since she had last checked and the big manufacturers were more environmentally responsible as well as health-conscious these days. But then, Mal only ever carried on like this when he ate something Aggie couldn't. Not couldn't: wouldn't. Chose not to.

She took a soy protein bar from her desk drawer and bit into it with theatrical relish. She chewed and swallowed, pretending it did not taste like cardboard soaked in vinegar and Nutrasweet.

'Do you want to know about my meeting with the Bible Basher or what?'

Mal mumbled something through a mouth full of chocolate and caramel.

Aggie returned the protein bar to her drawer. She wasn't hungry enough for the taste not to bother her.

'The Senior Pastor is, like, ten years old, dressed like something out of Young Talent Time. He talked tough, but he's just enthusiastic about his shiny new grown-up job, I think. If he doesn't settle down in a week or so, we'll go over his head. Send a letter to the head office threatening legal action.'

'Why wait?'

'Goodwill. We have to live with them just across the street. No point getting into a legal stoush if it's not absolutely necessary.'

'Aggie Grey talking about goodwill toward fundies and eating smoked salmon at balls,' Mal said. 'Your mother would disown you.'

Aggie snorted. As if it was even possible for her mother to disown her. As if her mother – trekking through some South American jungle with her travel writer lover, using her rare e-mails home to inform Aggie of the political and social conditions of whatever country she happened to be in, and her even rarer phone calls to quiz Aggie on the social and political conditions in Australia – as if her mother could be any further from *owning* Aggie in the first place.

Aggie did not say this to Mal who was her mother's friend first, having met her a decade ago during a Gay Rights Rally in Canberra and named her as his personal hero for having the courage to leave her husband and child to live in a lesbian relationship at the age of thirty-five. Even having been best friend and workmate of that abandoned child for close to seven years had not changed his mind about Carrie Grey's courage and personal integrity. 'She is not responsible for anybody's happiness but her own,' Mal would lecture. This was true, but it also showed a harsh disregard for Aggie's father, whose unhappiness, which her mother caused but was not responsible for, had killed him.

3

Joe lived in the covered doorway of a long-abandoned drycleaners in the same street as Aggie's office. Joe was incorrigibly homeless. Over the years Aggie had known him he'd been placed in homes and hostels a dozen times by various religious and government social workers, but he was never gone from his doorway for more than a week or two. It had been a while since anyone bothered with Joe, and to be fair, he was hard to bother about. He drank, which was no surprise, but unlike many of the street alcoholics who drank for warmth and rest, Joe was a mean, filthy drunk. He drank and cursed, drank and threw bins through windows, drank and defecated on picnic tables. Joe was the first person Aggie introduced work experience placement kids to; meeting him killed any romantic notions about the nobility of homelessness or the warm-fuzziness of working with the destitute.

Aggie checked on Joe every night. If he was conscious she would ask him how we was and if he needed anything, and he would tell her to go fuck herself. If he was unconscious she would hold her breath and bend in close enough to determine whether he was breathing. She always hoped for an unconscious but breathing Joe; even the foulest of men were loveable when asleep.

Tonight he was on his side, his legs curled up toward his stomach, one arm stretched out in front. Aggie steeled herself for the stench of vinegar wine and unwashed flesh and crouched down. She knew something was wrong before her knees were fully bent: the stink was fouler and stronger than normal and his outstretched arm was convulsing.

'Joe?' Aggie picked up his arm and felt the warm stickiness of blood. 'Shit! Joe, can you hear me?'

She reached for her mobile, but then remembered the battery had died during an extended conversation with a potential donor. She yelled out for help, with no expectation of being heard. All the shops and offices had closed hours ago.

Joe gurgled and bile spilled out of his mouth and on to Aggie's leg. His arm continued to spasm between her hands; if she put it down he would injure himself further on the concrete. She glanced up and down the street, but it was late and no one walked through here after dark. Joe's convulsions had intensified and she was afraid he'd smash his skull open. Aggie kept hold of his arm and lifted his head up on to her leg. He was a dead weight but her office was very close. She thought she could make it there and call an ambulance.

'Joe? I'm going to lift you up, okay? It might hurt for second, but I promise it will be better soon.' Aggie slid out from underneath him. Immediately, Joe's head smashed onto the concrete. He reared up and fell down again, bashing himself into the ground.

'Have you called an ambulance?'

Aggie spun around. The boy pastor stood with phone in hand. She shook her head and he began punching the keys. While he talked to the emergency operator, Aggie set to work making Joe more comfortable. He was a small man, withered in the way of the very old and the addicted. Despite his frailty, he was heavy with unconsciousness and his convulsions made him difficult to move safely. Aggie managed to get his head onto her lap, but his legs continued to slam into the concrete.

'Slide over.' Luke Butler lifted Joe's legs and placed them on his own lap. The man lay like a plank across Aggie and Luke's laps, their four hands holding him still and attempting to soothe. 'Ambulance is on its way.'

'Thanks.' Aggie pulled a tissue from her pocket and attempted to stem the bleeding from Joe's elbow. The tissue was quickly soaked and useless, but Luke Butler pressed a handkerchief into her hands, and while she held that to the wound, he worked his right shoe off with his left foot, raised his shoeless foot up over Joe's legs and removed his sock.

'Hold the hankie there – it's much cleaner than this.' Aggie did as he asked, and Luke worked around her hand, binding the elbow with his thick black sock. 'Pathetic!' he said, chuckling. 'But it's better than nothing, I suppose.'

Sirens filled the air between them and they shared a brief, grateful smile. Then the paramedics were upon them, lifting their burden, firing off questions to which Aggie had few answers. One of the men noted her name and address in a book while the other strapped Joe to a stretcher.

'Thanks,' Aggie said again when the ambulance had gone. 'You saved me having to lug the old bastard down the street.'

Luke Butler smiled. 'You should carry a phone. It's dangerous around here at night.'

Aggie laughed, walking the few steps to stand under a street light. Blood on her hands, shirt, knee. Unidentified wetness on her lap, shirt, thighs. 'I know this area. I know the dangerous people. They don't hurt me. But yes,' she conceded, 'a working phone would have been helpful tonight.'

He startled her by grabbing her hand. 'You're all bloody.'

'Yeah. I got the messy end.'

He released her hand and stepped into the light. 'You sure?' Aggie saw the large brown stain on his white pants. She laughed and so did he.

'You don't seem bothered?'

'Nah. I'm used to it. I worked outreach for years. In the Cross mostly. Of course, I never wore white then. I thought my days of grime-proof dressing were done with.'

Aggie looked into his face. He wasn't old enough to have done anything 'for years'. But he had handled himself well with old Joe. She had to give him that.

She began walking and he kept step beside her. 'The Cross, huh? I bet you heard some sad stories working out there.'

'Some, sure. But I got to hear the joyful ones too. Sometimes I got to talk to folk who were heading down the path of promiscuity and drugs, and I was by their side as they committed to Jesus Christ and handed their lives over to Him to be healed. I can't tell you how exciting it is to witness that. How much better to point a person toward the light than to hand out protection against the dark.'

They had reached Aggie's office. 'Right. Thanks for helping. Go on home and get cleaned up.'

He looked at her oddly, his eyes squinting in concentration as though he were adding up a series of complex numbers in his head. After a few seconds he rubbed his forehead and smiled. 'What an amazing night.'

'Dramatic, anyway.'

'It never fails to astound me, the way God appears in the oddest – the most unexpected – places.'

'Joe's bowels are certainly an odd place for God to emerge from, I'll give you that.'

He looked confused again. 'Joe's– Oh! I see!' A brilliant smile lit up his face. 'Very funny. But no, I meant you, Aggie Grey. God's light is so strong in you right now. You glow with it.'

'Goodnight, Pastor.' Aggie began to unlock her door. His hand touched her shoulder and turned her around.

'I think you were sent to me, Aggie. By God. He sees what you're doing here; he sees that you have good intentions and a generous spirit. He sees your compassion and courage, and he wants you on his team. He sent you to me so I could show you the way.'

'I don't think so. I need to wash this blood off – and you really, really stink. Goodnight.'

'Oh, no, that's what's happened all right. I haven't been so sure of anything since I got my calling to the ministry. I'm all lit up by you.'

Aggie leant against the door, watching him watch her. He seemed to genuinely believe what he was saying. Aggie wondered whether he got these messages a lot.

He was looking at her expectantly. She didn't know what to say. His eyebrows started to move toward each other. His mouth straightened and two small lines appeared in the centre of his forehead. His eyebrows met over his nose, kissed and then parted again. Twice he opened his mouth as if to speak, closed it, pressed his lips together and sighed through his nose. He could have been just another terrified teenage boy, working up the courage to admit he kinda liked boys, or to ask her if it was true you could get AIDS from blowjobs.

'Look, I have to—'

His hand darted out, grabbed one of hers and held it tight. 'We're in the grip of something very powerful here, Aggie.'

'I'm not gripped by anything. Sorry.'

'I'm going to stop those leaflets. I was being stubborn. I was forging ahead with what I thought was right, and I wasn't paying attention to what God wants.'

Aggie swallowed air. 'And God wants you to stop harassing us?'

'I believe he wants me to help you find the way, and I can't do that if we're enemies.'

'No.'

'But you have to let me talk to you about Jesus. You have to give me the opportunity to show you the way.'

Aggie considered. An end to the harassment would be a relief, and would mean that at least one of the things on the to-do list she'd written fourteen hours ago would be completed. But was this the best way to achieve that aim? Shouldn't Luke stop the harassment because it was wrong, not because Aggie agreed to listen to a sermon? Was it ethical to allow herself to be used as a bargaining chip?

But then, how long had it been since a good-looking man – any man, in fact – had looked at her like she had something he needed?

'Okay.'

He licked his lips. 'Okay?'

'Yes,' she squeezed his hand and he jumped. His head snapped down and he inhaled sharply. He stared at their entwined hands with a look of total wonder. He pressed her palm with his thumb as if checking to see if it was real. His eyes met hers and he blinked several times.

'You're covered in poor old Joe,' he said, full of concern.

'You too,' Aggie said. And she went inside.

4

By the time Honey had thrown up her coffee, washed her face, reapplied her makeup and changed her shirt, she was running very late. The bus was long gone, so the only way she would possibly get to school on time was if she ran flat out the whole way. Since she was often running late for school, she knew all the fences to jump and backyards to cut through to get her there by first bell, but this stupid stomach bug caused her to spew her guts up whenever she moved at a pace above a snail's. So running, jumping and dodging were out.

She barely got to the end of her street before the nausea hit again. She looked around for a bush or tree to duck behind, but of course this being the concrete jungle and all, there weren't any. The best she could do was dive into the long grass of a vacant lot. She vomited painfully – there was nothing really to throw up, so it burnt like buggery – and then remained on her knees for a moment to recover her breath. From her position in the grass she could see the garbage strewn about: used condoms, broken glass and fast food wrappers strewn amongst the overgrown weeds. She realised her hand was resting on an old Crunchie wrapper and remembered she hadn't eaten since the Kit-Kat on the way home from school yesterday.

Honey stood and wiped her face with a baby wipe from the box she'd bought two days ago for this very reason. She took a deep breath, inhaled rotten vegetables and quickly lit a cigarette to block the stench.

As she reached the footpath, a white Monaro pulled up beside her. Honey knew the car pretty well because she'd spent half of last year spreadeagled on its back seat. Ricky Bashir stuck his head out the window and smiled in that creepy *I-know-what-your-tits-look-like* way that he had.

'Yo, Honey, wanna lift?'

Honey definitely wanted a lift. Ricky was about the last person she wanted to get a lift *with*, but she was sick and tired and late. She got in the car.

The drive to school was a short one, and so she only had to listen to a couple of minutes of Ricky's *I'm-so-fucking-hot-I-can't-even-believe-it-myself* bullshit, but it was more than enough. By the time she got out, promising she would definitely call him, she was thinking that she would rather walk for a day in the blazing sun, vomiting the whole time, than be stuck in a car with Ricky ever, ever again.

It was kind of funny how last year she wanted to be stuck in that car with him more than anything in the world, and now he made her sick, and nothing had really changed about him at all. He wasn't a bad bloke really; it was just that she stopped liking him when she met Steve and now when she thought about the way Ricky's sweat would drip onto her face during sex she felt really grossed out. Honey wondered if one day she would look back at Steve and feel sick. She liked him so much, but she had to admit that it was a real possibility that certain things – his habit of spitting on the footpath, or the yellow-headed pimples on his back, for example – would one day make her shudder.

But for now, he was still her man. She saw him waiting for her at the gate and felt a little shiver of fear. Not that he was scary or anything, just that he was always touching her, and this morning she didn't feel like being touched. She hadn't felt like being touched last night either, but she'd let him, because it had seemed easier than to tell him about the exhaustion and soreness. He was already all tense about the throwing up.

'Hey, Stevo,' Honey said in a bright, non-sick way.

Steve wasn't looking at her. He was looking past her shoulder at the road. His face was completely blank. Blank pale eyes, blank pale skin, blank chapped lips. Honey tried to kiss his cheek but he moved his face at the last minute, still not looking at her or changing his expression.

'Did I just see you get out of Ricky Bashir's car?'

Shit. Honey could not believe how totally stupid she was. All week she had been so totally stupid. Like on Monday, she forgot to bring the assignment on the Spartans that she had been working on all weekend, and of course, Mrs Delaney didn't believe that Honey had done it and left it at home, because who could possibly be that stupid – to spend all weekend working on something then not even bring it to school? And on Tuesday night Honey had put the frozen lasagne in the oven at six-thirty then gone to lie down a minute, because she was just so goddamn tired. But that was stupid, because she crashed out all together and next thing she knew Muzza was standing over her bed and she was covered in pieces of charred mince and rock-hard pasta, and her mother was yelling her head off because she'd had to spend her lotto money on hamburgers and chips. And now this. Getting out of Ricky's car right in front of Steve. She was definitely the stupidest person in all of Stupidonia.

'I missed the bus.' Honey slapped her forehead, showing Steve that she knew what a ditz she was. 'Ricky was passing.'

'Right.' Steve spat on the footpath. 'Did ya fuck him?'

'Yuck, no.' Honey laughed to show how ridiculous this was.

'Well, what am I meant to think, you ridin' around with that greasy wog. I bet anyone who saw youse would think you were fucking him again.'

Honey saw that he didn't really disbelieve her. He just had to do the macho thing or else she would think it was okay for her to go riding around with ex-boyfriends whenever she wanted. She rubbed his arm and smiled. 'I'm sorry. I won't get a lift with him again. I didn't think how it would look. I just felt real sick and–'

Steve's head snapped up. 'You said you missed the bus.'

'I did. I threw up for like, twenty minutes, this morning.'

Steve squinted at her. 'You still got that stomach thing.'

'Yeah. Gross, huh?'

'How long's it been?'

The way he was looking at her made her feel cold all over. She should never have told him about the vomiting. He was always thinking the worst about everything. She knew he was asking how long because he thought she had morning sickness or something stupid like that.

She stepped away a little, but he moved close again. 'How long?'

'I don't know. A week or something.' It had been nine days. But if she said that, he would definitely think it was more than a stomach bug.

Steve put his hands on her shoulders and looked at her hard. 'You know what I noticed last night?'

Honey tried to think. Last night they had hung out at Rex's place smoking cones and drinking VB. Honey stuck mostly to the pot because it helped with nausea. If Steve noticed she drank less and smoked more he didn't comment; he was pretty wasted himself. The only other thing that had happened last night was that they had stopped at the soccer field on the way home and had sex behind the toilet block, but they'd been screwing in empty parks and behind public buildings for months now, so there was nothing noteworthy about that.

'I noticed that whenever I touched you, you pulled a face. Like I was hurting you.'

Honey held his gaze, although this was really freaking her out. 'So sometimes you're a bit heavy-handed. Sometimes you're rough.'

'Rough like this?' He squeezed her left breast. It wasn't hard at all, but *God* it hurt. Fortunately, Honey was well used to pretending away pain.

'You're being weird, Steve. It's embarrassing.'

Steve took her chin in his hand. 'You're preggers.'

'No!' Honey jumped backward. 'Don't be stupid.'

'You're the stupid one. It's so fuckin' obvious. It's exactly the same as when Cassie was—'

'Right, you got one dumb slut knocked up and now you're the expert.'

Steve had gone all blank again, but this time his eyes were focused right on her. 'Get a test.'

'Don't be stupid.'

'Get a test.'

'You're fucked in the head, Steve. I'm not even talking to you any more.'

'Get a test.'

Honey turned away. 'Bell's about to go. I don't wanna be late for homeroom again.'

'Honey.' His tone demanded she stop.

'Gotta go,' she yelled and started to run. When she got to the girl's bathroom she had to sit with her head between her legs until the dizziness stopped. Then the tiny amount of liquid still in her stomach came up. Then she checked her undies for the blood that should have come three weeks ago. Then she started to cry.

5

Luke was supposed to be preparing a PowerPoint presentation about alcohol consumption, but his mind kept drifting. No, not drifting – jolting. He had dropped a pamphlet discussing the Christian approach to sex education into Aggie Grey's office earlier, and she had promised to read it and tell him what she thought. But that had been six hours ago. Surely she had read it by now? He reminded himself that patience was a virtue, and returned to his work.

He was busy formatting the word DRUNK so the text flashed like a warning, when he suddenly found himself wondering if those super tight curls of hers were natural. He laughed out loud at the absurdity of the thought and forced his mind back to the task at hand. But then, as he was typing up the Bible verses referring to alcohol use, he was suddenly laughing again at how when he'd walked into the clinic, Aggie had thrown her hands in the air and exclaimed: 'Ah, my brand new friend,' loud enough for everyone in the waiting room to hear. And he shook his head in wonder at how in the five minutes he spent at the clinic he had witnessed Aggie comforting a weeping teenage girl with a few whispered words; calming a raging parent whose son had been found with clinic-supplied condoms in his schoolbag; answering a relentlessly ringing phone; accepting a delivery of five boxes of something called *Sylk*;

entertaining the three kids in the waiting room with a risqué joke about John Howard's relationship with George W. Bush; and eating three cinnamon donuts. In amongst all that, she found the time to hear Luke's request, to accept the pamphlet, to smile and touch his arm and look right into his eyes, and tell him she would be sure to let him know what she thought.

'Hey, deep thinker, what's up?' Belinda was in the doorway, leaning on the A/V trolley. She had a habit of sneaking up on him when he was absorbed in some task or another, and she frequently entered his office without knocking. He had spoken to her about it before, but she always giggled and punched his shoulder as though he were joking.

He concealed his irritation with a smile. A small, closed smile, because he knew from experience that a broad, open smile would be interpreted as an invitation. 'I'm in cloud cuckoo land today, I'm afraid. I'm almost done, though. Why don't you set up the rest of the equipment and I'll bring the laptop in when I'm finished?'

Belinda pushed past the trolley and sat on the edge of his desk. He had the idea that she was trying to get him to notice her thighs, which emerged smooth and tan from her jean shorts. He noticed them all right and the only urge he had was to tell her to be a little more modest. This was a Christian youth centre, not a pick-up joint.

'Something's on your mind, Luke, I can tell.'

'Like I said, just a bit unfocused today.' He gazed intently at the computer screen.

'You want to talk about it?' She put her hand on his arm. She was *always* putting her hand on his arm. He never knew how to get it off him without seeming rude.

'Last thing I need is another distraction,' Luke said, not looking at her. 'You chuff off and get the room set up and let me finish here.'

Belinda patted him and sighed. 'You're a slave-driver, Luke Butler.'

He smiled tightly, typing furiously until the door creaked shut. Then he went back and deleted the gibberish he had typed and hoped that God would forgive him for the small lies he often told to rid himself of Belinda's attention.

It wasn't that he didn't like working with Belinda; he did. In fact, she, like every member of his ministry team, had been carefully chosen by Luke himself. He had pored over the academic records and fieldwork reports of every trainee Christian Revolution pastor in Australia, looking for the four Junior Pastors who would make his vision for the centre a reality. Each member of his team had to be a more-than-competent preacher, disciple and counsellor. Each would have to bring something special to the Centre so as to further Luke's vision of making it *the* place to be for the young Christians of Sydney. Belinda Swan was selected for the team because she had spent sixteen of her twenty-three years touring with her travelling evangelist family. Her entire education had been administered on the road by her parents, and therefore she knew her Bible better than anyone.

Kenny Driscoll had been chosen because he was a champion long-distance runner who had turned down a place at the Australian Institute of Sport to instead go to Bible college. He would head up the *Fit for Him* program. Leticia Stewart had graduated from the Conservatorium of Music with first class honours before earning the same distinction at Bible college. She could play seven instruments, compose for most of them, and she sang so beautifully it was hard to believe that the angels up in Heaven could do better. Leticia's skills were such that kids would be drawn to her sessions for the music alone; God willing, they would stay for the message.

Greg Delaney was the last member of the team to be approved, and the only one Luke had to battle the Elders over. At thirty-two, Greg was older than the others – but that wasn't exactly the problem. The problem with Greg was that he had what the Elders termed *a history*. He had spent the years from sixteen to twenty-eight drinking, drugged and fornicating. He was a self-confessed sex addict who, at a rough guess, had been sexually involved with over two hundred people. Not women. *People*.

But from the day Luke had found Greg collapsed in a smelly, soggy heap on the steps of the CR Church in Darlinghurst, he knew that God had big plans for the man. Luke had been with Greg every step of the way, supervising his rehab, praying for his salvation, assisting his entry into Bible college and helping him prepare for examinations. Greg had done his fieldwork under Luke's supervision, and Luke was convinced there was no better Junior Pastor in the nation. Greg had life experience. He had walked in the valley of the shadow of death – and the Lord had led him out. And while there was a lot to be said for the Belindas and Kennys of the world who had dedicated their entire lives to the Lord, there was more still to be said for the Gregs who knew on a visceral level what sin and temptation were all about. The Elders eventually gave in, but not before warning Luke that *one hint of impropriety* and Greg would be back handing song books to elderly city parishioners on Sunday nights.

Greg had behaved himself perfectly so far, as Luke had known he would. And Kenny and Leticia had set up ten programs between them, bringing well over a hundred new kids to the centre. And Belinda? Well, Belinda was every Senior Pastor's dream. She worked like a Trojan recruiting, programming and costing. She typed correspondence, met with parents, sweet-talked the Board of Elders and solved ninety-nine per cent of problems before Luke had a chance to worry about them. She made breakfast for the team every morning, took care of ordering all the kitchen supplies and co-ordinated the volunteer team who took care of laundry and cleaning. And she wore short shorts, low-cut shirts, clingy dresses and shiny lipstick. She knocked on Luke's door a hundred and twenty times a day, never waited for a response before charging in, then perching her bottom on his desk, touching, questioning, *bothering*.

And again, now, barely a minute since she'd left the room, her voice was assaulting him again as she knock-opened his door. 'Excuse me, Luke?'

He looked at her sharply. 'Problem?'

'That woman's here to see you. The one from yesterday?'

Luke was out of his chair before she'd finished speaking.

That morning, right after Luke Butler had left her office, Aggie had tried to contact her mother. After digging through the chaos of her desk drawers for twenty minutes, she had found the scrap of paper containing the ten-digit telephone number her mother had yelled down the phone at her when she last called five or six months ago. Aggie dialled it, and spent several frustrating minutes trying to communicate with the woman on the other end whose language was neither Spanish nor English but something which sounded a bit like both of those. Finally, after repeating her mother's name over and over, the voice on the end said: 'Mizz Grey gone long time,' and hung up.

Mizz Grey gone long time, all right. In eleven years Aggie had seen her mother maybe ten times, and had spoken to her over the phone, at best, once every couple of months. When they did speak, it was about one of three things: the struggle for gay, lesbian and trans-gendered rights, her mother's latest torrid love affair or Aggie's lack of same. Still, it was better than before. Better than when she was young and her mother spoke to her only to criticise and admonish, only to point out how disappointed she was that her one and only child was so very dull and drab.

Aggie, having taken after her father, was tall, heavy-boned, pale and frizzy-haired. Her mother, being a former Miss New South Wales, was slender, creamy-skinned and golden-haired. She tried to train Aggie in her own image, making her wear mousse and make-up from the time she was twelve. She dressed her in dark, straight pants and long jackets, told her to stand straighter, cover those freckles, never wear flats, don't walk so stiffly, don't smile so widely, don't laugh so raucously. Don't be so much like your goddamn father.

Aggie adored her goddamn father. He was huge and bald and red-faced. His skin was so creased and his eyebrows so grey that Aggie's seventh grade teacher commented on how lovely it was to see her grandfather taking such an interest in the school. Aggie knew her father was ancient, but he was playful and energetic and a thousand times more fun than his stern young wife. He sang in the shower and danced in the street; he laughed at least half-hourly, and with almost the same frequency, he told Aggie how amazing she was, how special, how absolutely incredibly perfect. When people said Aggie took after her father, she was pleased, even after she was old enough to understand that she had been insulted.

Still, Aggie tried to make her mother happy. She moussed and plucked and covered herself; she practised walking properly and talking nicely. When she was fifteen her mother warned her to stay away from boys because if she had learnt one thing in her miserable life, it was that messing around with boys when you were young and stupid could ruin your life forever. Aggie didn't really understand what was so miserable about her mother's life, but she stayed away from boys all the same. It was easy enough to do since no boy in all of Sydney was desperate enough to want to mess around with freakish Aggie Grey, with her splotchy skin and hair that looked liked pubes.

Then when Aggie was eighteen, her mother announced that she couldn't live a lie any longer. She was a lesbian, had always been a lesbian, had only slept with Gerard Grey as an experiment, had only married him because she was pregnant and afraid, had only stayed out of duty. Now that Aggie was an adult, Carrie was free. She moved in with a twenty-year-old herbologist called Venus, and told Aggie she was welcome to visit any time, but to make sure to call first in case they were in the middle of something, ha, ha, ha.

When Aggie walked in the front door the following afternoon, her father's brown plaid slippers kicked her in the forehead. He was hanging from the hallway light fitting, still in the pyjamas he had been wearing when Carrie had left the night before.

Aggie wore yellow to her father's funeral. Someone – she was too drunk to know who – told her that she was a brave girl, and that wearing bright clothing was a lovely tribute to a man who had brought such colour into the world. But that had nothing to do with it. Aggie wore yellow because it was her worst colour. She wore a short, loose, sleeveless yellow dress because her limbs were freckled, her knees and elbows knobbly, her body shapeless and her skin sallow. She did not, for the first time in five years, smother her face in Chanel foundation, correct her uneven lip-line with raisin lip pencil or smooth down her hair with half a can of mousse. She did not define her eyes with black mascara or wear high heels to elongate her chunky calves. She did not remember her posture. When her mother asked her why she would purposely make herself look so awful, Aggie laughed so hard that she threw up her father's whisky all over Venus' brown mock-suede boots.

But all that had happened over a decade ago. The two Grey women had since become friends, united in a cause. It had taken three years of thrice-weekly therapy sessions and a good ten years of teeth-gritting resentment, not to mention a couple of significant heartbreaks of her own, but Aggie now accepted that her mother was not to blame for her father's death, and that some women were just not cut out to be mothers at all.

As the years passed, Aggie was beginning to think that she too was missing that famous mothering instinct, and that had a man wanted her to have a baby at eighteen she may have done so and regretted it bitterly. This recognition had made her feel even closer to her mother. Not that she had told her this, since last time Carrie had called she'd only stayed on the line long enough to bark that useless phone number and to tell Aggie she'd fallen in love with the woman leading her tour group and would be accompanying her on a round-the-world trip to co-write a book on gay and lesbian-friendly travel destinations.

So, her unmotherly mother was wherever, doing whatever, Mal was at the bank trying to secure yet another overdraft for the clinic, and Aggie was sitting at her desk thumbing through a ridiculous Christian propaganda pamphlet and wanting to call up the boy who'd given it to her and tell him he was crazy and maybe so was she, because when he had walked into her office that morning she had felt something jump from the base of her spine to the pit of her stomach and then up into her chest, and by the time he had left, that something was in her throat, threatening to burst out of her mouth.

Her mother would have told her to stop punishing herself for her father's death by being attracted to men who would most certainly break her heart. Or she would have said: *Throw that disgusting trash in the bin, tell that freak you want nothing to do with him, then go home and treat yourself to a night of red wine and masturbation.* Mal would say: *You gotta be kidding me, the guy's a monster.* Aggie knew they were both right. She dropped the pamphlet in the bin.

Later, after counselling a fourteen-year-old who'd had more

lovers in the last year than Aggie in her whole life, she moved the pamphlet from the bin to her top drawer. When Mal popped in to say they'd been refused the overdraft so he was going home to talk to Will about investing more of his own money into the clinic, Aggie pulled the damn thing out of her drawer, put it on her desk, and stared at it. She flicked through it while on hold waiting for the electricity company to answer their phone so she could ask for an extension on the bill payment. When she was refused, she read the pamphlet cover to cover, kicked the underside of her desk with anger, felt better, and read it again, taking notes this time. Then she saw two clients, read over her notes feeling her indignation rise and her silly, twisted, self-loathing crush dissipate. By closing time she was ready.

6

Somewhere in the middle of Aggie Grey's verbal demolition of his *Family-Centred Reproduction Education* pamphlet, Luke was hit by a bolt of God's lightning. They were in the recreation room; Luke sprawled on a bean bag, Aggie sitting cross-legged in front of him. They both had coffee, but she had not touched hers because she had not stopped talking since she arrived. He had drunk half of his before leaving the rest to go cold, because to pick it up and bring it to his lips would mean looking away from her, and he could not seem to make himself do that for even a second.

She talked about her precious Secular Society and her Individual Rights and her Diverse Community. She argued the importance of a value-neutral model of sex education combined with comprehensive information and decision making tools. She shook her fists at him for condemning contraception use despite widespread disease, rampant teen pregnancy, over-population and hunger in Third World countries. She pointed an accusing finger at his chest, as though he was personally responsible for the six hundred thousand women who died from pregnancy and childbirth complications every year. When she talked about how natural homosexuality was, spittle flew from between her teeth and landed on his left shoulder.

All of this, and did he argue back? He did not! And was he silent simply because he was waiting for her to run out of steam so he could then sock her with all his brilliant refutations at once? No again! God help him, he was barely listening. He was thinking: I have never seen hair so curly; look at the way it moves in enormous clumps when she shakes her head and then stays there rather than falling back to its original place like every other head of hair in the world. Now I understand why Paul advised that women should cover their heads, for hair like hers would distract the most pious of men and tempt even the angels. And look at the way her eyes are green then brown then green again, and when she's really irate she squeezes them up tight and they look black. Her voice is so deep and strong, almost like a man's, but her throat is slim and white and almost certainly very, very soft.

And then God socked him in the chest. Hard. What was he doing, sitting there gawking at her while she spouted her disillusioned intellectual nonsense? God had not led Luke to Aggie in order to give him something nice to look at on winter afternoons! His mission was clear. He picked up his coffee and drained it, drawing strength from the bitter cold in his throat.

'Right, I get it,' he said, cutting her off mid-sentence. 'More coffee?'

She snorted. 'Were you even listening?'

'Of course.'

'Yeah? Summarise what I was saying then.'

'A summary, right.' Luke bit his lip and rubbed his chin, pretending to be thinking hard, aware that he was maybe playing up to her a bit, but deciding there was no harm in being light-hearted if it made her more receptive to his message. 'Okay, you think sex is great and everyone should do it as much as possible, with as many people as possible, in as many different ways as possible, without any consequences whatsoever.'

She laughed, picking up both their mugs. 'And I thought you

weren't paying attention.'

In the kitchen, Belinda was drinking tea and reading the newspaper. Luke noticed she'd changed out of her tiny shorts and t-shirt and into a long-sleeved shirt and jeans. He was thankful she was covering herself in time for tonight's group; it was hard enough for some of the boys to control their hormones without half-naked women prancing around. Luke had never personally had a problem with lust, but he thought that for men who did suffer from unwanted sexual urges, Belinda in tight shorts might be too much to handle. He made a mental note to chat with Greg and make sure everything was okay in that department.

'Hey, there.' Belinda looked up and smiled. 'I finished the presentation. It's all set up and ready to go.'

'Thanks.' Luke motioned to Aggie to go ahead and make the coffee. He turned back to Belinda. 'I'm afraid Aggie and I are going to be busy right up until the meeting starts, so if you could organise the seating in groups of six for me, that would be great.'

Belinda's smile slipped a little. 'What exactly are you—'

'Ask Greg if he'll help you out. He's in the library I think. Aggie and I will be in the rec room, so when Kenny gets in tell him he can use the television in my office to tape that doco he needs. '

Belinda giggled, which was odd because nothing funny had been said. 'Righto, you're the boss.'

Aggie passed a mug of coffee to Luke. 'Ready for round two?'

'Round two?' Belinda's voice was unnaturally high.

'One nil, my way,' Aggie said.

'Let's get back to it, shall we?' Luke took Aggie's elbow and led her towards the door.

'Ah, Luke?' Belinda was trailing them. Luke stopped and looked at her questioningly. He noticed she was looking at his hand on Aggie's elbow, which annoyed him so much that he maintained his hold even though it felt sort of awkward to be holding her like that when they were standing still in the hallway.

Belinda talked to Aggie's arm. 'What is it that you guys are busy with, exactly?'

'Sex,' Aggie said.

Belinda's neck snapped up. 'Pardon?'

Luke stifled his laughter. 'Sorry, Belinda, I didn't introduce you properly. Aggie is from the clinic across the street. We're seeing if we can agree on terms for a peace treaty.'

Belinda squinted at Aggie, then returned her gaze to Luke. 'Does Pastor Riley know?'

'I don't need his permission to liaise with our neighbours.'

'I know, but—'

'Right, I'll see you at seven.' Luke tugged Aggie's arm, and rushed her through the hallway and into the rec room, slopping coffee all over the floor in his haste to close the door.

'Did I say the wrong thing?' Aggie said, removing herself from his grip and laughing.

Luke sank down into a bean bag. 'Perfectly shocking. Belinda's going to need trauma counselling now, I think.'

'What is up with her?' She sat herself not *across* from his bean bag as before, but actually *on* his bean bag. Almost on him. 'Are you two involved?'

'Certainly not.'

'But she wishes, right? I mean, she follows you around like a puppy dog.'

'More like a guard dog.'

Aggie laughed, knocking his knee with hers. 'You don't like her?'

'No, I do. It's just that… She's my best Youth Pastor, I respect her knowledge and faith enormously, but she wants… I don't know, I suppose she wants to be married and thinks that I… We don't even know each other particularly well. I'm the Senior Pastor and that gives me a— well, a certain appeal.'

'You make it sound like you're a rock star or something. No offence, but you run a kiddie church.'

He considered the possibility that she was making fun of him, but discarded it in favour of the theory that she was genuinely trying to understand him. 'It's a status thing,' he explained. 'If you believe that love matches are made by God, then having God choose for you an ordained pastor is like an announcement to the world that you are purer and more godly than other girls. The problem is that some people think you can reverse the process – make a match with a minister and God will smile and agree. It can't work that way, but the girls – not to mention their parents – keep trying.'

Aggie gave a derisive laugh. 'Must be nice. All those women just begging for your attention and since you know you have your pick you can just take it easy, play the field?'

'You misunderstand.' Luke turned to her and held her mocking gaze. He felt it was very important that she understand him. 'A couple of years ago, when I was a Junior Pastor at the Darlinghurst church, I started to feel a bit sorry for myself, because it seemed everyone around me was part of a couple. I thought maybe the whole waiting for a sign from God thing was a metaphor that got taken too literally. I asked Pastor Riley – my boss, well, my earthly boss – I asked if he thought I could just choose someone nice for myself. I reasoned that surely God would want to reward one of his most loyal servants with love and companionship. I loved my work, I loved serving God, but I didn't feel fulfilled. I was so lonely. All these people around me, every minute of the day and night, and I was still so lonely, you know?'

'Yes. I know.' Aggie looked rapt, and he was sure now that she was not teasing him.

'Well, Pastor Riley really gave it to me. He said if I truly was God's loyal servant I would be thankful I had not been sent a companion. He pointed out that my sermons and group meetings attracted twice as many people as any other, and said that it was glorious God was reaching so many young women through me. He said I should be grateful for being single. That when God wants me to marry, I'll know about it.'

'God's plan or not, you've got time on your side. You're what – twenty-two?'

Luke laughed. 'Give or take seven years.'

'You are *not* my age.'

'Am I?' This made him inordinately happy. 'Well, you must understand then. Looking at thirty and wondering if the right person will ever come along.'

Aggie took a sip of her coffee; her eyes had a faraway look. She put her mug on the floor beside her and stretched her legs out in front of her. 'I do wonder if I'll ever meet *the one*. I wonder if there is such a creature. But as for marriage, well, been there, done that, and I'm in no hurry to repeat the experience.'

'You were married?'

'For about five minutes.'

Luke concentrated on keeping his smile going so she wouldn't know that his stomach had just dropped. God was really testing him with this girl. Not just a foul-mouthed, soft-skinned, pornographer. No, she had to be a *divorced* foul-mouthed, soft-skinned, pornographer. 'What happened?'

'The usual.' She raked her fingers through those gravity defying curls. 'I was eighteen and needy; he was thirty-five and opportunistic. My divorce went through the day before I turned twenty-one, and I considered myself lucky that I got off as lightly as I did.'

'I'm sorry.'

'Don't be. It was very educational. My next boyfriend, Matthew, was proud of all the disastrous relationships he'd had. He reckoned you grow as a person every time you make a lover hate you and can understand why.'

'He sounds like a dangerous man.'

Aggie looked at him with a small, sad smile. 'Aren't they all?'

Luke was going to protest that *he* wasn't dangerous, but then it occurred to him that she wasn't really speaking of *all* men, but of the specific sub-group whom she would consider partnering. Clearly, she did not think of Luke as a member of that group, or she would not have made that comment. He was pleased she felt safe with him, but at the same time, he wondered *why* she did. It didn't make sense that she trusted him because of his faith, since she was vocal in her dislike of Christianity in general and his particular strain of evangelism in particular. Her total ease with him was both gratifying and worrying. Wasn't she even *slightly* anxious around him?

'*All* men are dangerous, you say?'

'Sure. Actually, I should say that all *people* are dangerous once you get up close and personal. Just for me it's always been men. It's about love really, isn't it? The person you love the most holds the means to hurt you the most.'

'I wouldn't know, having never been in love.'

'I'm not just talking *in love* love. Any kind of love will do it. The parent-child thing can be particularly brutal.'

'I wouldn't know about that either.'

'About it being brutal?'

He had not known he was going to lift his hand and touch her hair, but there he was, touching it. Her hair felt much softer than he had imagined it would, and he was suddenly aware that he had been imagining how her hair might feel all day. He had expected it to be wiry and stiff, but it was soft and fluffy.

'Luke?'

He dropped his hand from her head and held it under its mate so it could not escape so shockingly again. 'Sorry.'

'No. It's…' She patted the tightly-bound hands. 'Did you not love your parents?'

'I didn't know my parents.'

'God, not at all?'

'I don't even know when I was born, really. Depends on whether I was two or three days old when I was found.'

'Fuck. Found?'

It was odd, but the squirmy, cringing dread that usually accompanied discussion of his past were absent and in their place a small happiness that this woman wanted to know him. He wanted that too, perhaps because he was certain she would never pat him on the head and call him a poor little lamb, though she might shake her marvellous hair and say the F-word. This was, surprisingly, fine with him.

'I was found sleeping peacefully inside an empty Foster's Lager box on Platform 2 at Granville Station,' he told her. 'The police never managed to track my mother down so I ended up at the New Hope Boys' Home in Redfern. Apparently the police named me before I was delivered to the Home, but nobody could ever tell me why they chose this name. The house mother suggested I might be named after some heroic policeman who died performing great deeds, because otherwise why would they give me such an inappropriate name?'

'Inappropriate?'

'Because I'm a darkie.'

Aggie looked at him hard. 'You're not even that dark. You're caramel. Anyway, so what?'

'Well, it caused a lot of disappointment. The couples wanting to adopt a little boy would choose from the information sheets which ones they wanted to meet. They'd skip over Hakim Ali and Yin Yip and Johnny Poulos and say that this Luke Butler sounds more their type. They'd say it was because my school reports were so good or because I was so athletic, but then when it came to meet me, these things were suddenly unimportant and they would choose some blond kid who couldn't even read and who preferred breaking other boys' bones to actual sport. It didn't take me long to figure out that the likelihood of me being chosen for adoption was minute, and that it became even smaller with each passing day. People like babies more than little boys, and they like little boys more than big ones, and regardless of age or size, people like light-coloured boys better than dark-coloured ones.'

'Not all people.'

'No, that's true. Some wanted a boy of their own ethnic back-ground, but no-one could be sure if I was or wasn't. I just had to accept that I wouldn't be leaving New Hope until they booted me out on my sixteenth birthday.'

Aggie put her hand on his knee. 'So you spent your whole child-hood there? God, that's terrible.'

'No, it really wasn't. Sometimes it was actually fun. I had my own little gang with the other boys who were never getting out. Like poor old Charlie who was Koori and told everyone his parents were just having a trip and would be back any day. And there was Dominic, who reckoned he was French, but no-one believed him because he was black and spoke Aussie and everyone knew French people were white and spoke wog. Charlie and Dom were the darkest and then it was a toss-up, depending on who had spent the most time in the sun, between Hakim the Leb, Johnny the Greek or me from Granville

Railway Station.

'Alex Morton was in our gang even though he wasn't dark. We made a special exception because the house fire which killed his parents and sister had burnt all the white off him. He spent half the time in a pressure suit and the other half plastered in bandages through which pus would ooze if he didn't change them often enough. The white kids rejected him, none of the prospective parents wanted him, strangers stared at him, and his skin was certainly coloured, and so he fit right in with us. Not that we were picky; safety in numbers is a good thing when you're an outcast.'

'It sounds horrendous.'

'Then I'm telling it wrong. It was fine. I was never beaten or locked in a closet. My basic needs were met, and when I got older I worked in the kitchen and garden for spending money. And I was well-liked within my group, sort of a leader, I suppose. It wasn't like a Dickens novel or anything.'

Aggie sighed at this and pressed both her hands to her face. When she touched his hands again he was aware of a moistness which might have been perspiration. It might also have been tears dabbed from her eyes. This possibility made him feel unspeakably awkward and so he kept talking, going on casually as though a stranger with soft hair and skin was not (maybe) weeping hot tears over him.

He told her how he had never wanted to lead the gang, it was just that he seemed to have a gift for arguing with racist teachers and beating the heck out of Nazi bullies, and this meant the other boys depended on him. But secretly, he never stopped wanting to be white. He spent the silent prayer time at the end of scripture class asking God to give him blue eyes and blond hair, or at the very least, skin that freckled in the sun instead of darkening. God never came through for him; he never got a single freckle, never a sun streak in his increasingly wavy hair. Of course, that was before he was a proper Christian.

When he was fourteen he was assigned *My Place* by Sally Morgan for his contemporary English text. He read it in one sitting, shaking inside and out for at least the last hundred pages. For the first time in his life he didn't want to be white. Or more precisely, not being white mattered less than not knowing what he was. He had always considered himself relatively fortunate to have been abandoned at birth. He knew that the boys at New Hope who remembered their parents, whether they were mourning their deaths like Alex or waiting for their return like Charlie, had a much harder time accepting their orphaned status. But now he was bitterly jealous of these other boys. At least they knew what they were!

Luke became fixated on discovering his ancestry. He wondered if, like Sally Morgan, he was part-Aboriginal, or if he was, as Hakim insisted, an Arab. He locked himself in the bathroom for hours at a time, comparing every aspect of his appearance to those of men of every possible ethnic background whose pictures he obsessively clipped from magazines and newspapers. His friends joked about his gallery of men, and liked to say that while Luke was busy searching for his roots, they were out in the world getting some.

The irony (he did not tell this bit to Aggie) was that of all the boys at Granville High, Luke was the one most girls would have been happy to give it up for. He knew this, but did not know why. When Luke looked in the mirror he saw hair like a Southern European, skin like an Arab, slim hips and long muscles like an Indian, black eyes like an Aboriginal boy. He didn't know what could possibly be attractive about all that. When girls stared at him in class or on the bus, he assumed they were trying to work out what he was. When they sent their friends to tell him they wanted to get with him, or when he found their love notes in his locker, he assumed they were chasing him because he was a novelty, the way all his friends wanted to get with the Austrian exchange student even though she was really fat.

Then on a perfect Spring day, a week before his fifteenth birthday, he was lying on the grass out the front of the State Library, reading about the racial breakdown and settlement patterns of the post-war migrant influx, when an Asian girl sat beside him and introduced herself as Mai.

Luke said hello, just to be polite, and returned to his book, lifting it up so it hid his face from the girl. 'What's your name?' she persisted.

'Luke,' he said from behind his book.

'You don't look like a Luke.'

That really pushed his buttons. He put down his book. 'What do I look like?'

'I don't know. But you definitely don't look like a Luke.' She smiled and crinkled up her nose. Luke noticed the sprinkle of freckles across the bridge. He had never seen an Asian with freckles; he thought they were reserved for whites.

'What does a Luke look like?' he asked her.

'Luke is a saint's name. You look too dark and dangerous to be a saint. You should be called Holden or J.D. or something like that.'

Luke laughed. 'What does Mai mean? Nutcase?'

'Flower.'

'It suits you,' he said, and immediately felt his face growing hot. 'I mean, you know, because it's an Asian name and you're Asian.'

'That matters you think? So what will we call you then? Is it Abu or maybe Muhammad? What shall we label you? I am Asian and you are what?'

'I'm not anything. Forget it.' Luke picked up his book, burning with shame and wondering for the thousandth time that summer why girls were always bothering him.

'I know what you are, Luke. You're the same as me.'

'What the hell are you talking about? You're a chong. I'm a wog or possibly a boonga or curry muncher. We're not the same.'

Mai smiled and leant forward as though she was about to tell him a great secret. As it turned out, she was. 'We have the same Father. Maybe you don't know it yet, but you are part of an enormous, inter-racial, multicultural family. And this family is the best one there is, Luke, because it isn't based on where you came from, but on where you're going.'

By the time the sun went down that day, Luke knew that where he was going was Heaven, and the family he belonged to was God's forever family. From then on whenever anyone asked him what he was, he answered with confidence and pride: 'I am a Christian.'

He was a Christian! Oh, God forgive me, I am a Christian, he thought. He was supposed to be talking to Aggie about God, not reliving his childhood while she stroked his hands and murmured comforting nothings.

'So that's it then. My entire life story. I bet you wish you'd never asked.'

'No, I… Fuck, Luke– no wonder you're alone.'

It was incredible. He had met her yesterday, yet she seemed to understand already what it had taken him many, many years to figure out: that having come into the world unloved and alone, he would remain so all his days. Like a man with no tastebuds trying to com-prehend chocolate, Luke had tried and failed to understand what it was that bound individuals together so tightly they would die rather than be wrenched apart.

This only applied to human love. God, of course, loved him so much that Luke almost wept with joy whenever he thought about it. God *was* love, and Luke knew this as surely as a person can know anything. This just made it harder to understand the deep love that human beings felt for each other. Compassion, he understood – humans were weak, pitiful things, tripping themselves up and then heroically struggling to their feet only to fall down again and again. Yes, compassion was easy, but to feel *passion* for imperfect, selfish, bio-logically driven creatures like himself – that seemed quite impossible.

'Do you still wonder about your parents?'

'Not really. Not any more. Since I found my Heavenly Father, I've stopped worrying about the earthly one.'

Aggie sighed; then she did something extraordinary: she lifted his arm, slid across so her body was pressed into his side and put her head on his shoulder. Luke could not have been more surprised, or more breathless, if she had punched him in the stomach. His hand took advantage of its owner's distraction and leapt back into Aggie's hair. Her curls swallowed his fingertips, and he wondered how he would ever get free of them.

Aggie began gently to stroke his leg, just above the kneecap. Her touch was soothing and he started to feel truly relaxed for the first time in he didn't know *how* long. Months, maybe years. There was just something about her warm breath on his neck and her firm, slow hand that made him feel at peace. He was thinking how easy it would be just to rest his head against hers and drift off to sleep, when shock-ing heat surged through his thighs and up into his groin.

Luke held his breath, closed his eyes and told himself not to panic. It wasn't like he'd never had an erection before. It was just that he hadn't had one in such a long time, and he had never, ever had one so close to another person. It was one thing for the teenage boys he counselled to have spontaneous erections – their bodies were swarming with hormones – but for Luke, a man of almost thirty, a man who had not even suffered a nocturnal emission for over a year, this was profoundly disturbing.

'You've gone all quiet on me. I hope I haven't depressed you.'

Luke cleared his throat. 'No. I was just thinking that the kids will be here soon.' He hadn't been thinking that at all, but now it had occurred to him, he realised that he *should* be thinking about it. That was his mission: the kids. Danny and Jack and Lisa and Fran and Bruce and Karen and Moira and Calista and Amanda and Ian and Danielle and Harry and Regina and Marianne and George and Marissa and Anna and Philip and both Stuarts – the dear, quiet chubby one and the tall, confident loud one – and Chris and Christine and Crystal and Charlotte and Matt and… that did the trick. He was back to normal again.

'I better go then.' Aggie lifted her head, giggling as he untangled his hand from her hair. 'It's awful, sorry.'

'No, it's lovely,' he said, because it was, and he couldn't have her thinking otherwise.

'I'm leaving before you tell me any more lies.' She smiled. 'I'm surprised to hear myself say this– but I had a nice time.'

'Why surprised?'

'Because I thought you would just lecture me about God the whole time.'

Luke felt the tightness in his chest. He was supposed to be talking to her about God. He was supposed to be leading her towards a personal relationship with Jesus Christ. His calling was to witness, preach, serve. The reason he was drawn to her so strongly was that God wanted her on his team, and He had to be sure that Luke got the message loud and clear.

'Okay, so I'll see you later?'

'Wait.' He couldn't let her leave like this. 'Do you know why you're here?'

'Because you asked me over?'

'No, I mean… why did I do that?'

She rolled her eyes. 'I don't know. Because you wanted to convert me with your family values propaganda? Because you wanted someone to drink coffee with? Because you cut open an orange and saw a vision of the Holy Virgin pleading with you to save my soul?'

'You think I'm a joke.'

'I think you're too bloody serious.'

He nodded, understanding that she was not making fun of him, that her sarcasm was a defence. Her professional persona was merely a protection from the cruelty of the world. Sometime in her youth – perhaps at the time of her ill-fated marriage, perhaps earlier with the brutal parent love thing she had mentioned – something had happened to make her feel lost and afraid. Because she was strong and resourceful she had worked out a way to survive whatever it was that hurt her so much, and because she was kind she had decided to work in a field teaching other lost souls how to survive. But it was a sad, hopeless struggle because all her supposed wisdom about the wild world just equipped her to trek deeper into the jungle. She needed him to show her the way out. No, that was pure vanity. She needed God to show her the way out; she needed Luke only to show her the way to God.

'Would you like to stay for the meeting?'

'I don't think so.'

'I'd love it if you would.'

Aggie looked over his shoulder, staring intensely at nothing. Luke was filled with a sense of urgency. He placed a hand on her shoulder and her eyes returned to his face. 'Please, Aggie, I'd like you to see what I do here. It would really be great if you could stay.'

'Okay.' Her expression was one that Luke recognised as resignation. She obviously sensed – although she was not ready to admit it on a conscious level – that God had a plan for her. Her serious nod, the way she looked right into his eyes for so long without blinking, the way she tenderly removed Luke's hand from her shoulder and squeezed it before letting go, all showed him she was accepting not just his invitation to stay for the meeting, but her fate as a servant of Christ.

Thursday nights were VIBE night, which meant thirty kids between the ages of thirteen and fifteen listening to a presentation about the topic of the week and then splitting into small groups to put together skits or write songs about the discussion. Tonight's presentation was about alcohol, and the kids had a ball creating scenes of drunk husbands beating wives, drunk boyfriends being sick on their girlfriends' shoes, and drunk drivers rolling their cars.

Luke always felt sad at how little needed to be explained. In fact, when it came to drink, drugs or sex, the kids often taught Luke a thing or two rather than the other way around. Tonight, for instance, he learnt that there were tablets one could take which delayed the symptoms of over-indulgence. As the thirteen-year-old telling him about it said, you could impress your mates by drinking hard all night, then just secretly throw up when you got home. Another girl told how her friend just stuck her fingers down her throat every two hours so she could keep drinking.

'Getting sick is far from the worst thing that can happen if you drink too much,' Aggie interjected. 'The first time I ever drank alcohol – and I was eighteen at the time – I went way overboard and ended up marrying the taxi driver who drove me home. I don't know of any tablet that could've prevented *that* disaster.'

The kids found this hysterical; Belinda shot Luke a look that clearly indicated she thought him insane for inviting this woman to participate. 'You're exaggerating,' he whispered to Aggie. 'I wish,' she whispered back.

When the meeting ended, at ten, Luke walked Aggie to her car across the street. Suddenly, it was a quarter to twelve. They laughed awkwardly and parted with a brushing of fingertips numb from the cold. Luke lay awake all night, unable to rid himself of the chill in his bones no matter how many blankets he piled on his bed, and unable to remember a single thing he had talked to Aggie about in the almost two hours he had stood beside her in the freezing night air.

The next night she came and helped with the preparations for the sausage sizzle. Every Friday night during football season the game was projected on the big screen and an indoor barbecue cooked up. It was the only officially organised activity without explicit personal development or Bible study aims, but Luke considered it one of the most important parts of the program. The casual, almost festive atmosphere of footy night bonded the group as friends, and some of the deepest, most satisfying connections he had made with his kids had been in impromptu chats after the game.

'I don't mind helping out,' Aggie said, scrunching her nose at the trays of raw sausages and steak. 'Just don't ask me to touch the dead cows.'

Of course, she was a vegetarian. A walking cliché – yet unlike any person he had ever met. 'The onions are all yours then.' He picked up a steak and tossed it from hand to hand. 'Personally, I love the feel of raw meat.'

Aggie made a gagging noise. He smiled, watching her determinedly disgusted expression from the corner of his eye, as he tore the strings of sausages apart with his fingers.

'That's the flesh of an animal you're playing with. One of *God's* creatures.'

'Mmm. Yet another reason to praise Him. Such delicious creatures he has given us.'

'There's like a hundred cows there.' Aggie waved her knife at the piles of raw meat, blinking her eyes fast to expel the onion tears. 'Surely you don't expect so many kids. Friday night is party night in teen land. It's getting wasted night.'

'Not for these teens.' Luke took the knife from Aggie, pointing her to the non-tear-inducing task of bread buttering. 'They all either grew up as Christians and would never consider getting *wasted*, or they grew up with New Age atheist liberal types who subjected them to adult ideas and behaviours and left the kids craving some wholesomeness and stability.'

She laughed. 'They're rebelling against their parents by being good?'

'Why not? Teenagers are natural seekers. They want truth and meaning, not relativism and ideology.'

'They'll find truth and meaning in football?'

'Some would say yes.' Luke laughed. 'But that isn't really the point of Friday night. Friday night is just for fun.'

And this Friday night was the most fun ever. On this Friday night, Parramatta beat the Broncos twelve-ten, their first victory for the season. Also, on this particular Friday night, Aggie Grey, the manager of a sexual health clinic that supplied condoms to homosexuals and arranged abortions and AIDS tests for minors, charmed fifty-seven teenagers, four Youth Pastors and one Senior Pastor so thoroughly that when she tried to leave at ten o'clock she had fifty of God's children begging her to stay. So she stayed and played charades with the younger kids, drank hot chocolate with the adults; talked to a gaggle of girls about their shoes and a gaggle of boys about their *X-Boxes*; promised Leticia that they would have lunch together one day next week; begged Kenny to use his boasted about mechanical skills to fix the clanking in her engine; checked to make sure every single kid had a lift home; stacked chairs, swept the floor, dried dishes, declined coffee, exclaimed her exhaustion, kissed Leticia,

Kenny, Greg and Belinda goodnight, and then stood with Luke in the open doorway pretending to leave for forty-five minutes.

'Maybe I would like some coffee,' she said, just after midnight. Back in the now-empty kitchen she told him about her parents, and he cried. She said that his tears touched her. And she touched his face. Luke felt as if she had gutted him with a rusty hook.

'I don't know if I can cope with this,' Aggie said, her fingertips lingering a moment on his chin before returning to the tabletop.

'With what?'

'This… this getting to know you, exchanging intimacies, watching you cry for me. Watching the way you are with those kids… You're so good. You're generous and compassionate and smart and kind and–'

'I can be meaner and stupider if it would help.'

'See!' Aggie lunged forward and jabbed a finger at his chest. 'You're being cute. You're joking. But the sick thing – the thing I find it hard to cope with – is that you *are* meaner and stupider. You are!'

Luke laughed, less amused than confused. 'I don't under–'

'You think homosexuality is a lifestyle choice – that's stupid. You judge and moralise and condemn people who are just trying to get by in this world, just trying to love and be loved. You think what I do is evil and wrong, you believe my poor dad is burning in Hell being punished over and over for being too weak and sad to go on, and you think my mum, my friends, people I love and respect, *good* people, should be condemned and imprisoned just because– Oh fuck it.'

She slumped back in her chair and ran her hands through her hair, her gaze fixed on the ceiling, her mouth pressed together so hard her lips were white. Luke sat silent, waiting until she calmed down and looked to him with more challenge than hostility in her eyes.

'I don't believe those things because I'm mean and stupid, Aggie; I believe them because the Bible says they're true. The same Bible that guides me in everything I do and believe. Your praise and your criticism are levelled at the same belief system.'

'That's crap.' Her voice was soft, but unrelenting. 'You are not your belief system.' Aggie lunged again, grabbing both his hands and holding them tight in her own. 'I knew what you believed before I met you. Knowing what you believed, I hated you. Yet, here I am, still hating what you believe, but unable to deny that I am dangerously far from hating you.'

Luke stared, silent, still, hot all over. One minute he was a servant of God explaining the truth of the Word to a well-meaning atheist, and the next minute he was a man being recognised as such by a woman. She had stolen his clothes, and he knew she would never return them because she liked him naked and squirming.

'Sorry, that was…' Aggie released his hands, and covered her face.

Luke sat, staring at her hidden face. His hands, his head, his everything hummed. He felt as Born Again as he had when Mai had confronted him outside the library and invited him to take his place in God's family.

She peeked through her fingers at him. 'I've really embarrassed myself, haven't I?'

'No.'

Her hands dropped away. 'No?'

Luke shook his head.

'Why are you staring at me?'

'I don't know.'

'Oh. Do you want to have dinner with me tomorrow night?'

'Yes.'

Aggie smiled. Luke had a devastating realisation. 'Oh, no! I have a conference in Newcastle; I won't be back till late.' He dreaded the long, drab day, with all those people wanting his attention and opinions and assistance, all those people who saw him as Pastor Butler and not as Luke, a man who could be loved regardless of his beliefs.

'Sunday night?'

His heart sank further. 'I'm preaching at the seven o'clock city service.'

'Come over after. I'll cook you dinner.' Aggie picked up her handbag, rifled around inside for a few seconds and pulled out a pen and a scrap of paper. 'My address,' she said, scribbling on the paper.

'You could come to the service.'

'No, I really couldn't.' She stood, bent, kissed his forehead. 'See you Sunday.'

7

Although she was almost thirty, Aggie had only ever slept with three men. The first was Kip McLean, the driver of the cab she caught home from her father's funeral. He talked non-stop the entire drive from the funeral home to her house, and she was thankful because she really didn't want to have to think about anything any more. Kip was thirty-five, twice divorced and only driving cabs while he saved for a fishing boat.

A week earlier Aggie would have been terrified of this big, weather-beaten man with his booming voice and green vines tattooed up his arms, but ever since she'd been kicked in the head by her father's dangling slippers, she had been fearless. She invited Kip in and he smiled slowly, picked up his radio and told base he was signing off. He roamed around Aggie's newly inherited house, drank gin from her newly inherited liquor cabinet and smoked a cigar he took from the drawer of her newly inherited antique writing desk. He asked her to go to bed with him, and she said yes because nobody had ever asked her before, and because she was lonely and angry and ugly, and because she had no-one to be good for any more.

Within a week, Kip McLean had moved in. Within six weeks, Aggie had married him. She loved him in that intense, needy, awestruck way that she had since discovered is characteristic of first love. But Aggie was not Kip's first love, and he was not needy or awestruck. He was affectionate, protective, charming and fun. He was also opportunistic, greedy and deceitful. When she felt him slipping away from her, she used a large proportion of her inheritance setting him up as a commercial fisherman, madly hoping his gratitude would re-ignite his love. He was indeed grateful, and for a few weeks he was as passionate as he had been in the first mad month. Then he shrugged helplessly, took his boat and a random pretty girl and sailed to Byron Bay.

Aggie did not grieve. The day after Kip left she threw herself at Matthew Rinehart, a dreadlocked anarchist from uni who had been asking her out ever since he discovered she was married. He moved into Aggie's house and introduced her to Tantra, deep ecology, anti-consumerism and hallucinogens. Matthew did actually love Aggie, but he had this thing about monogamous relationships being spiritual death. After six months, he told her he was becoming too attached to her and that he had to move on. Aggie was six weeks pregnant, which was hardly surprising considering Matthew had refused to use man-made barriers when making love. But he was gone, and she was alone, so she had an abortion and then a year later, after Matthew had come and gone again, she had another. He returned to her once more, nine months later, and she told him about the two pregnancies. He wept, saying he had never made anyone pregnant, and to have managed it twice with Aggie must mean that it was meant to be. Four months later he got another girl, a stunning raven-haired pianist, pregnant and although she too had an abortion, the fact he had implanted someone other than Aggie with his seed meant his belief in the predestination of their relationship was shaken. He left to explore the possibility of bliss with the other almost-mother of his most recent never-to-be-born child.

Aggie was alone for three years. Then she started working as a drug and alcohol counsellor at St John Hospital, where she met Dr

Simon Keating. He was twenty years older than Aggie, devastatingly attractive and very married. Aggie knew better than most the pain caused by infidelity and abandonment, but when Dr Simon Keating declared his passion and asked to move in with her she was so over-come with gratitude, that she managed to bury her guilt at being a home-wrecker. There were two years of crazy sex, exotic holidays, fancy parties and dinners and weekends spent taking his kids to the movies or Australia's Wonderland. Then one morning as he was get-ting ready for work, he announced that he had been having an affair with his wife and was going home.

Sometime later, Matthew returned, transformed from radical stu-dent to up-and-coming human rights lawyer. He wanted monogamy and he wanted it with Aggie. He moved back in, and this time Aggie really thought it would work. But after a year, he found a prettier woman to be monogamous with. He swore her looks had nothing to do with it – he fell in love with her *soul*, just as he'd fallen in love with Aggie's all those years ago at uni. He would love Tara even if she was as plain as anything, he said. He didn't say, *as plain as you*, but Aggie understood that was what he meant.

So that was that. Three relationships, intense and damaging. No one-night stands, no flings, not even a single date. She had not, like most women she knew, formed any theories about why men are the way they are, or what a woman should do to find, enthral, keep one. She did not believe men were such a generic bunch that a simple trick like never accepting a date after Wednesday or touching his arm when you said his name, would work for each and every one of them. Men were just like women: varied, likeable, detestable, human.

So it was not any philosophical or sexual political stance that led to her lack of romantic life, it was just that men did not ask out giants with frizzy hair and thick calves. And Aggie did not ask out men because she had never actually met one she liked enough to make the risk of humiliation and heartbreak worthwhile. Until now. The fascinating thing was that asking Luke to dinner had seemed a completely natural, risk-free thing to do. She hadn't deliberated or agonised, she'd just come right out and asked him.

She wasn't even nervous about his coming to her house, which normally she would be, because people freaked when they saw how huge it was. And she didn't have to worry about explaining how a young woman working practically for free could afford a three-story house in the better part of town, because Luke already knew all that. He had cried over her poor, rich father and he was not freaked out at all by who her mother was. She could show him her house with pride, knowing he would not be walking from room to room wondering about lesbian sex or gruesome death as Kip had confessed to doing.

The only problem was how to get through the weekend without going mad with excitement. She spent Saturday morning at the office and then did her weekly grocery shopping, taking care to choose the crispest lettuce and plumpest tomatoes for the salad she planned to make for Luke. She wondered if she should buy a steak or something for him, then decided that it would be worse than pathetic to cook something which turned her stomach just to impress a man. Even this man. He would love her vegetarian lasagne, she was sure.

At six o'clock she called Mal and told him she had a date tomorrow night and was going out of her mind with excitement. Mal was silent for a long time. 'Bullshit,' he said when she threatened to hang up if he didn't speak.

'Is not. I met a bloke; I asked him over for dinner; he said yes.'

'Well, I'll be blowed. You did warn him he'll have to clear the cobwebs out of the way before he can get it in, didn't you?'

'How amusing. So you wanna come over and keep me company?'

'Love to, Ag, but Will and I are on our way out the door. Dinner with Marsha.'

Aggie groaned. 'I hate her. She always tells me she could do wonders with my hair.'

'You should let her try. That mop of yours gets worse every day.'

'Fuck you.'

'And you wonder why you don't have any friends.'

Aggie hung up. She *did* wonder that and he knew it and tormented her with it. Aggie and Mal were accidental friends. They had met through his friendship with her mother and when he started running a homeless shelter he had hired Aggie as counsellor. She had worked for him ever since, following him from the lost cause of the shelter to the bureaucratic nightmare of hospital-based rehab to the freedom and stress of independent sexual health counselling. On the rare, drunken occasion he had told Aggie how he felt about her he had said it was her egalitarianism, passion and energy which appealed to him. She knew this was true, but also she knew he loved the fact that her mother was a famous, scandalous gay rights activist, that her pathetic love life freed her for heroic workloads and midnight vodka runs, and that, like him, she was ugly and awkward and grateful for any affection she received. And even knowing all this, she was indeed grateful for Mal's friendship. He was her first, best and only friend.

She didn't know why this was so. Throughout her school and university years she had envied other girls and women their friendships, blaming her mother for not passing on the seemingly secret rituals and traditions of women, the things that allowed them to bond and stay bonded. By the time she graduated she had accepted her inability to form close female friendship the same way she accepted that her hair would never look nice and that her father would never come back to life.

But then something remarkable began to occur. Standing guard next to paper-draped examination tables, squatting in vomit-filled gutters, stroking sweat-soaked foreheads, Aggie began to love other women. Holding the hands of women at their most frightened, most vulnerable, Aggie knew a closeness and kinship that could not be found in a thousand slumber parties or shopping excursions. But these were not friendships; the connection disappeared with the solving of their problems. These women brought their urgent, raw, visceral need to Aggie and she healed it and then they went away. She had never been able to make herself call up a woman and say: 'Hey, remember me, you squeezed my hand so hard during your after-rape medical that you broke three of my fingers? Now can you repay the favour? Can you sit and listen while I whine about my poor little rich girl life?'

Aggie loved women, empathised with them and yearned to help them, but she could not be friends with them. She didn't know why, she just knew that when she tried to talk to a woman about anything other than how she, Aggie, could help her, she forgot how to be comforting, approachable and non-threatening. She saw the expectation of reciprocity in the other woman's eyes and panicked. She never knew what to say if it wasn't: 'How can I help?' She didn't know the language of female bonding beyond pain and tragedy.

Last week, standing in a bank queue, Aggie eavesdropped as the woman behind her told her companion about her upcoming hen's night. *We're renting an apartment in the city*, she said. *We've hired a bartender. We went shopping for outfits on Saturday*. It struck Aggie that she never used plural pronouns unless she was talking about work. We meant her and Mal, the clinic, the business. *We* never meant Aggie and a lover or Aggie and a friend or Aggie and her family.

Except – she closed her eyes and hugged herself – except tomorrow night, *we* are having dinner together. Luke Butler and I. We.

8

Luke ordinarily enjoyed the state conferences; they gave him an opportunity to exchange worship inspiration and ministry plans with the other pastors, and they were always a great spiritual boost, feeling the joy and energy of all those servants of Christ crammed into one big room. He had been especially looking forward to this year's since he finally had a ministry of his own, even if it was a youth centre and not a church. But no matter how hard he tried to concentrate on the presentations and follow the discussions, his mind drifted again and again to Aggie.

She was brand new to him, yet he felt he knew her deeply. She was as much an orphan as he was, with her tragic father and her deviant mother both abandoning her when she was still virginal and unharmed, leaving her to be defiled and discarded by some rough fisherman. Luke was heartbroken at the loss of that lanky, awkward, freckle-faced girl, whom he knew he would have loved and adored and protected. It was too late to save that innocent child, but it was not too late to save the woman she had become. The fact he could not stop thinking about her, even while he tried with all his mental might to concentrate on the conference, was evidence that the Lord really did want him to save her. And when the Lord had made up His mind about something, resistance was futile.

During the dinner break, Luke tried to contribute to the

discussion at his table. He had been seated with the Youth Pastors which ordinarily would have infuriated him since he was a Senior Pastor who happened to oversee a youth centre and therefore belonged up the front with the other Senior Pastors. But tonight he could have been seated with a bunch of six-year-olds and he wouldn't have cared. He kept thinking *Aggie*. He ate, smiled, nodded, even offered up a relevant comment or two, but underneath it all he was thinking *she*.

'Well you're the expert, Luke. What do you reckon?'

He pretended his mouth was full, gesturing apologetically, forcing himself to concentrate. They had been talking about inner city youth ministry. Something about reaching out to the unchurched. Graham, the boy who'd asked the question, wanted to take his youth group into the city backstreets, have them preach to the down-and-outs on their own turf. Someone else at the table thought that was a mistake because of the Biblical injunction to stay away from sin. *Aggie* he thought. He faked a swallow, took a large sip of water, flicked through his mental database for a relevant scriptural illustration.

'This discussion makes me think of Peter,' Luke smiled, thinking not of Peter but of *her*. 'Remember how he forced himself to sit down and eat with all those unclean Gentiles, eating food which hadn't been prepared according to dietary law? Scripture told him this was wrong, but Peter felt called by God to reach out to the Gentiles. He realised that God hadn't got the old laws written down, and then sank into dumb retirement. God is active, involved. He sees what's going on down here and he knows that some things can't be solved in the way they would've been two thousand years ago. He calls us – calls Graham here – to a new understanding of the old laws.'

Graham beamed, the girl sitting next to Luke patted his back and told him she could understand why they'd given a youth centre to him. 'You're the real deal, Luke Butler,' she said. 'God is really alive in you.' But he felt heavy with guilt because his words had been empty of inspiration. He had played the dutiful leader and spat out an appropriate Biblical reference, but he barely knew what he was saying. God was alive in him, yes, but He was shouting *Aggie*.

He left the conference early, snuck into the Centre through the back gate and went straight to his cabin. He needed solitude. He needed to think about this extraordinary occurrence, this miracle of a woman. And as he thought about her, the way just knowing she was alive made him feel less alone, he was overcome with the desire to pray. Here in his dark and silent cabin he had found the connection to the Holy Spirit he had failed to find at the conference.

Suddenly he was inspired and the true meaning of his new obsession was stunningly apparent. He leant into the window, weeping into the darkness outside, letting his tears run down his cheeks, onto his throat and then his chest. *Lord, I thought I knew you, I thought I understood the way you loved your creation, but my knowledge was incomplete and shallow. But I understand now, I really do.* This *is how you feel about humanity.* This *is what it is to adore, to cherish, to* love! *a weak and sinful human being. In loving her, I finally understand how you can love the least of us, love me, and I thank you for this gift, this insight, this joy.*

Once a month, Luke gave a sermon at the main city church. The idea was to keep his preaching skills alive, and at the same time, reassure the parents of the NCYC kids that the man in charge of them was an honest-to-goodness, real deal, Christian Revolution minister. He enjoyed leading the service, but was less fond of the hand-shaking and conversation afterward. All those parents desperate to match him up with their daughters, and all those daughters standing too close, touching his back and forearms.

On the Sunday night he was to see Aggie, he spoke on the need for Christians to lead the community in tolerance towards ethnic minorities. Afterwards, Luke had six invitations to share the evening meal. Five of them were from the families of young women he knew were interested in courting him, and the other was from Belinda who gushed about the 'braveness' of his sermon and told him it inspired her to go and eat at that little Turkish place down the road even though it smelt funny. Luke turned down all offers with the truth that he had a previous engagement, and deftly avoided further questioning from Belinda by exclaiming on his lateness.

On the drive to Aggie's house, Luke sang along to the radio, admitting to himself that he was very excited about seeing her. He had missed her over the weekend, which was ridiculous considering that the previous weekend he had only known she existed because he was determined to shut down her business. How rapidly his world had been turned upside down. The feeling he had sought out his entire adult life, the feeling he feared he was incapable of experiencing, had all but consumed him – in a matter of days. But it was okay: he was remembering the Lord in everything he did and He would show the way. Right now, the Lord was showing him the way to Aggie's house.

When he was one street away, his anticipation manifested itself physically. This was the third such manifestation in as many days, not counting the one when she had rubbed his leg on Thursday, or the one on Friday night when he'd been talking to her in the car park. So this was the third time his usually well-behaved penis had responded to the mere thought of her. This was the only aspect of his calling to save Aggie which he found disturbing. If God wanted him to save Aggie – and Luke was certain He did – then why would he add lust to the otherwise pure mix of feelings he had for her? He pulled over to the curb and prayed, and after a few moments the offending organ deflated, leaving Luke to conclude that the lust was

Satan's way of trying to prevent him from winning another soul for God. Well, take that Satan! Luke laughed as he pulled back onto the road. Lust is vanquished through prayer, and I'm on my way again, making the journey I'm called to make.

Her house was enormous, taking up the entire corner block of her street. It appeared to be three stories, plus an attic, and the front garden was crowded with dark green shrubs, red and yellow rose bushes and wildflowers. Luke had never known anyone to live in such an imposing place, and he was abnormally nervous as he waited for her to answer the chiming bell. But then she opened the door and his anxiety dissolved.

She grabbed his hands and dragged him inside, kicking the door closed and talking non-stop as she led him up and down stairs, through low doorways and winding corridors. She told fantastic stories about the paintings hanging on the walls and the history of each piece of antique furniture. She was particularly proud of the old claw-foot bath which had once belonged to a convent. 'You can see the indentation,' she pointed out, 'from all those nuns' heads. They must have been short. My feet hang right over the edge when I lie in it.'

'You are uncommonly long,' Luke said, then realising she might interpret that comment as meaning he had been thinking about her unclothed body stretched out in the bath, went on: 'Tall. You're very tall. Extremely tall.'

'Yes,' she laughed. 'That's true.'

The walls were lined with paintings in gold antique frames. Luke was too ignorant to know if the art was good or bad, expensive or cheap, but what he did know was that sadness poured out of every picture. A small girl weeping into a bunch of daffodils; a black-cloaked woman leaning over the rail of a suspension bridge, the wind whipping her cloak behind her; a grey soldier, leaning heavily on his bayonet; a series of landscapes, each darker and more desolate than the last. No smiles or sunshine. No fluffy animals or stunning vistas. And tellingly, achingly, no photographs.

He asked her about it and she shrugged. 'I took them all down after Dad died. It was just too depressing. In every photo the only person who looked happy was him. Mum was always gorgeously sullen and I was always gangly and self-conscious, but Dad was... I used to have a wedding photo hanging over my bed, but I trashed it when Kip took off, and then when Simon moved in we had a picture of us together in the living room and a photo of his kids in the study. Matt and I had a lot of photos... It seemed pathetic to keep them up after he left.' She smiled. 'I suppose not having any photos is even more pathetic, isn't it? It's proof that I'm a total Nigel-no-friends.'

'The only photo I have up is of myself at my ordination,' Luke confessed.

'Hurray! I'm *not* the saddest almost-thirty-year-old in the world.'

They ate dinner on the back deck, overlooking a shimmering pool surrounded by palm trees and mounds of shiny black rocks. Well, she served dinner out there but Luke didn't eat a thing. He told her he was not hungry – which was only half an explanation. The rest of it was that he was captivated.

She told him about the time she had wrestled a knife from a strung-out junkie in a hospital waiting room, the time she had helped deliver a baby girl in the office of a homeless shelter, the time she had chased a mugger through Redfern and not only reclaimed her handbag but talked the guy into signing up to her rehab program. She told Luke about the television and radio interviews she'd done, the newspaper and magazine articles, the teaching and campaigning and lobbying. She had held training camps for youth workers, cookouts for homeless people and recreation trips for troubled teenagers. She had walked over hot coals – literally – to demonstrate to a group of heroin addicts how powerful the mind could be.

'Do you realise how incredible you are, Aggie?'

'No, I don't. Please feel free to tell me.' She laughed, tossing her head back and gulping wine.

By eleven o'clock, when they were sitting in her living room in front of a blazing fire – she sprawled on a brown velvet couch gulping red wine, he sitting upright in an overstuffed chair sipping lemonade – Luke had figured out that he had been giving Satan too much credit. The lust was from God and was just the cleverest thing ever. God *wanted* him to be tormented with desire, so that his work in saving her soul would be conducted with urgency. The sooner she gave herself to the Lord, the sooner Luke could give himself to her. He waited until there was a pause in her machine-gun chatter and then asked her if she'd ever actually been to a church service.

She drained her glass and placed it on the floor before answering. 'Weddings and funerals only. I can't stand religious people – present company excluded, though I have no idea why. I haven't made a new friend in ten years and here I am hanging out with a fucking minister.'

'God moves in mysterious ways.'

'See that's the kind of shit I can't stand.' Aggie stretched her legs out in front of her and her arms up in the air. 'Like when people say, "God healed me" or "God got me out of that burning building" or whatever. I mean, why is God so random? Why do some people pray and die anyway, and others boast about their survival, as if what? They prayed harder?'

'You're being simplistic.'

'Your religion is simplistic. It's do what you're told just because you were told, which is all fine and dandy, but what about those who weren't told? What about all those people in Iran or Afghanistan who are also doing what they've been told? No matter whether they have been good people or bad people, no matter whether they came by their beliefs through honest soul searching or through lazy acceptance, they will burn in Hell for eternity. Explain that!'

'If you're looking for easy answers—'

'You have no answers.'

He began to reach for her, stopped, folded his hands together and then realised he must look as though he were about to pray. He must look ridiculous. He unclasped his hands and rested them carefully on the arms of the big chair. He wished he could think of the right way to lead her to Christ.

'You want to know my theory?' She rolled onto her side, propping herself up on one elbow and regarding him with such intensity that he had to put his lemonade down lest he break the glass. 'People believe that stuff, because they need to feel the world is fair. It's like how kids who've been sexually assaulted end up with really bad self-esteem. It is actually less painful psychologically for them to believe that they are a bad person who deserved the abuse, than to believe that bad stuff just happens randomly. So when it's obvious to people that the world is unfair, that what goes around doesn't always come around, the concept of justice being served in an afterlife is a comfort.'

'Just because it's comforting doesn't mean it's not true. And you seem to be ignoring the flipside of that belief – the decidedly uncomfortable realisation that you will be held accountable for your own sins.'

Aggie's eyes widened. 'See, that's another thing: this concept of sin and innocence and guilt. Sometimes people do the wrong things for the right reasons. Like a woman might prostitute herself to get money to eat, or a man steal to pay for medicine for his kid. A lot of people are just trying to survive, you know? What kind of God would condemn these struggling, weak human beings for their transgressions?'

Luke *adored* this woman. She was insightful and compassionate, and what was truly uplifting was that her world view was so closely aligned with his own. She was more Christ-like than most of the Christians he knew; she was just missing the joy of knowing her Creator was in control of this seeming chaos. All Luke had to do was show her that this frightening, brutal world filled with small, struggling people who despair at the randomness of it all, is overseen by a loving God who has a plan so great that the mortal mind cannot conceive it.

'Huh! You have no answers! None!' Aggie leant forward and touched his knee, blinked at him, then sank back into her seat. She closed her eyes, opened them, narrowed them at Luke, laughed out loud. 'Okay. Say something.'

'You'll only ridicule me.'

Real sorrow filled her face. 'Oh, no, sweetie. I haven't meant to ridicule you. Sorry, sorry. Please talk to me.'

Sweetie. It was like a warm hand sliding into his own. Just a small term of endearment, like the *sweetheart* or *buddy* he used all the time at work. But coming from her mouth, combined with the deep feeling in her tone and the lament in her voice it was the nicest thing anyone had ever said to him.

'Luke?' Aggie leant forward to touch his knee again; this time she left her hand there and looked into his eyes. 'I really want to understand. What the hell did any of us ever do to deserve the pain we go through in this life?'

'You know Jesus was asked almost that exact question? People believed that those who suffered from disease or disability were being punished in some way, that they deserved their affliction, so one day after He had restored the sight of a blind man, his disciples wanted to know why the man had been born blind in the first place. "Who sinned?" they asked. And Jesus told them that no-one had sinned. He said that the man had been blinded so that the works of God might be made visible through him.'

'That's horrible,' she said. 'Like some awful puppet show. Aren't I wonderful to repair the puppet I deliberately broke.'

'No, Aggie, you mis–' He grabbed at the hand she withdrew from his knee. He held it tight. 'Think of filthy Joe or the prostitutes working Koloona St. Think of the addicted, the destitute, the mentally ill. Most people believe of them what the disciples believed of the blind man – that people so afflicted must have done something wrong, that they deserve their pain. But you know that isn't so and so you help them, and when you do – whether it is obvious to you or not – you are revealing God's love. You are doing Jesus' work.'

'Oh, Luke.' Her hands pulled free of his. 'You really don't understand how stupid you sound, do you?'

It was as if her fist had gone straight through him. He watched her pour and drink more wine; she was oblivious to the damage she had caused. He had forgotten how devastating ignorance and thoughtlessness could be. He went to the window and focused on her overgrown garden, lit by spotlights and a nearly-full moon. Its beauty filled the hole she had made in him.

'Enough God talk, okay?' Aggie was at his side.

'No. Look at the riot of colour that makes up our world. The yellow and crimson, the pinks, the indigo. At least ten different shades of green in this small area alone. In a few hours, the sun will come up and the sky will be purple, then gold, then clear pale blue. God could easily have made a grey universe, but He didn't. And it's not just the colours. What about the fragrance of flowers, the scent of freshly mown grass, of rain, the texture of sand or silk, the warmth of the sun and the cool relief of a summer breeze? All these colours and smells and textures are not necessary for our survival; they're gifts from a God who loves us.'

Aggie pressed her forehead to the window. 'You're scaring me.'

'It's awesome, I know, but you don't need to be afraid.'

'That's not what I meant.' Her face was hidden in its own shadow. 'The world is not devoted to human life, Luke. The colours of nature are diverse because getting or avoiding attention helps plants survive in different areas. Same with fragrance – it's an attractant or repellent. And the warm sun causes cancer and summer breezes turn into gales which rip houses apart. None of it is there for our convenience or pleasure. Nature has its own rules and we just have to enjoy what we can and shelter from what harms us.'

'Ah, but we have the senses to enjoy it, don't we? Since seeing the blush of a rose isn't necessary for our survival, God could have made us like tigers, able to see only in shades of blue. He gave us the capacity to take pleasure in our surroundings.'

'You're killing me here!' She spun around and took hold of his arms; her grip was inescapable. 'Our senses have evolved over time to give us the best possible chance of survival. We see colour so we can differentiate between food and poison. Our sense of taste confirms whether something's edible before we swallow it, and we have the ability to sniff out food and potential mates. We can hear a predator coming from a distance, and we know from touching if a surface will burn or freeze us, cause us pain or pleasure.'

Luke had heard these arguments often and debated them with people far more eloquent than Aggie, but he had never been so close to believing that a man was nothing but a dumb beast, driven by hunger and need. If God was the architect of desire then Luke would surely be warm in the arms of his good Christian wife at this very moment. Instead he was boiling in his skin because of the animal scent and touch of this infuriating amateur Darwinist.

He stepped back two paces, which was as far as the length of her arms allowed. He had to concentrate. Satan's most powerful weapon was science and he was winning souls at an alarming rate, recruiting those who sought to understand rather than trust. The arguments Aggie put forth at first gave comfort because they imposed order on a chaotic world. But beyond that initial relief at having solved all the mysteries was a pit of despair. If one believed that human suffering was logical but meaningless, nihilism was just a few sleepless nights away.

'Do you really believe,' Luke asked Aggie, 'that who you are, what you value, your desires – everything about you – is shaped by physiology which in turn is shaped by evolution? Flowers are not truly beautiful; it's just that your brain has evolved to experience pleasure when a certain pattern of light hits your retina. If you feel love for a person, you are merely reacting to your programming, selfishly looking to propagate your genes. Is that your view?'

'Hmmm,' Aggie said. She released him, returning to her earlier position on the sofa. Luke watched as she drained her wine and poured herself another glass. He found that although having her close to him was distracting and uncomfortable, having her choose to move away, having her not even look at him, stung badly. He would like it best if she wanted to touch him, but didn't because *he* put himself out of *her* reach.

'Aggie?' Luke sat across from her, willing her to touch his knee so he could brush her hand away.

'So, okay,' she said, not touching, not looking. 'I want to think that love is more than a selfish response to biological programming, but… if not that, then what?'

'G–'

'Don't say God!' Aggie reached, touched, laughed. All was well with Luke's world. 'Saying God is the same as saying biology. An overpowering, unstoppable force that makes us want what we want and feel how we feel.'

'But not a morally neutral force like Nature.' Luke touched her hand, but did not move it from his leg. 'God designed us and knows us better than we can know ourselves. He is the source of all love.'

Aggie pulled away. She took a large gulp of wine; some escaped her mouth and dribbled down her chin. She left the spill alone, giving Luke reason to think she might want him to wipe her face for her. He was still considering this when she spoke again. 'At the meeting the other night, when Leticia was talking to the kids about charity, she said the most important commandment given by Jesus was to "love one another", which sounds really nice when you're talking about being kind to homeless people or the mentally ill– but what about us?'

Luke thought *us* sounded as lovely as *sweetie*. 'Us?' he said, disappointed that it did not sound sweet coming from his own mouth, merely hesitant and awkward.

'Us,' she repeated, slugging down some more wine, adding to the red trickle on her chin. 'A couple of independent, opinionated adults who have no real reason to be friends or even speak to each other outside of a courtroom. Yet we– well, love is a heavy word, so let's say *care for* each other, will we? Let me ask you, Pastor Butler, why you care about me enough to spend your free time trying to save my soul? Is it because Jesus told you to?'

'No, Aggie, it's–'

'Because if that's the only reason, then you should go away. If you're just following orders from above, then bugger off!'

'How can you think–'

'Shit!' Aggie had missed her mouth altogether and the red wine was working quickly to imitate a stab wound on her chest. 'Shit, shit, bugger it!' She pulled at the front of her jumper. Luke realised that she was more than a little drunk. She had opened a second bottle of wine some time ago; he wasn't used to drinkers and hadn't thought anything of it. Now she was on her back, writhing around wrestling her jumper off. She hurled it over the back of the lounge with a 'piss off'. The wine had soaked through to her white t-shirt – which appeared to be a size or two too small – leaving a pale pink wet patch over her left breast. Luke had never seen anything so lovely as the outline of Aggie's nipple through that wet, pink cotton.

'Ahem.' She cleared her throat dramatically, and he, startled, met her eyes. He saw that she knew he had been staring at her breast, defiling her with his eyes. The hot acid sting of shame made him gasp. He couldn't remember the words to say.

Aggie arched her back, licked her sticky-with-wine-lips. 'Come over here,' she said, patting the edge of the sofa. Luke did not move. She repeated the request, slower and with her eyes closed and back arched. Luke excused himself to the bathroom where he washed his face with cold water and begged God to give him strength. Within minutes he heard the unholy sound of her snores. He thanked the Lord and sneaked out into the night.

9

When Honey was twelve, Marcus Selden, who was fifteen, told her that if she didn't swallow a guy's stuff when she sucked him off, it was like she hadn't done it at all. When she spat into a tissue, he felt nothing, Marcus said. This made her want to cry. All that spit and energy and neck pain for nothing. All those little ulcers where her teeth cut her gums, the stinging of her scalp, the grass-stained jeans – for nothing. So after that, Honey always swallowed. After a while, it didn't bother her. You could get used to anything.

But then one day in Year 9 when Honey was sharing a fag with a couple of seniors in the dunny, Haley Morris (who was seventeen) told her that semen had a whole lot of male hormones in it, so if you drank too much, you would grow hair on your chest. Clara Piper (who was younger than Haley, but whose boyfriend was, like, thirty) said that Haley was full of it. There were fuck-all hormones in spunk, but there was a shit-load of sugar, so if you were watching your weight – and who wasn't – you should spit it out. Honey was about to ask what their boyfriends thought about them not swallowing, when she was hit with the realisation that what Marcus had told her was utter crap. Not feel a thing, he said! Well what the hell was all that hair pulling and moaning and shit? Jeez, she was a twit. Thank Christ she hadn't said anything in front of Haley and Clara. They'd never speak to her again if they knew how stupid she was.

So Honey went back to spitting out and found that the boys she went out with liked it just fine. Ricky complained the first time, but she told him about the hairy chest and the putting on weight and after that he always had a tissue ready for her. But Steve was different. He said she didn't have to do anything she didn't want to, but if she loved him then why wouldn't she want to drink his stuff? And he didn't think she understood how horrible it felt to have a girl spit out part of you. How would *she* like it if *he* spit *her* stuff out because it was so gross? She almost said *what stuff?* But she got his point and she did love him and it wasn't so awful really. You could get used to anything.

Sixteen, up the goddamn duff. She nicked *Your Body: A Guided Tour of Womanhood* from the school library and sat on the disabled dunny with the book open to *Pregnancy: Do's and Don'ts*, a cig between her lips to calm her nerves. She wanted to know what *not to do* so she could do it. She made mental notes: excessive drinking, smoking, amphetamine use, heavy lifting, starvation. And then, in amongst the prescriptions for trouble-free pregnancy, she read the truth, finally, about swallowing.

Swallowing your partner's semen, the book said, *desensitises your body to his DNA, reducing the likelihood of rejection (pre-eclampsia).*

So that was it. If only she hadn't swallowed, maybe her body would have recognised Steve's stuff for the foul, poisonous invader it was. Maybe her body would have done what her mouth should have: spat that crap out. Then maybe she wouldn't be in this condition.

She dropped the book, and her ciggie, in the toilet and went to try and score some speed.

10

Luke woke on Monday morning to a new sensation. It was like his skull was trying to break free, like his guts were searching for a way out. And down there was the worst. Down there, his skin was so tight he was sure it would split. Even during his morning prayers, a time when he rarely felt anything but peace, his body battled to be freed.

He skipped breakfast, sure that nothing more could fit inside him. He stayed in the shower until the hot water ran out, and then he stood, head against the tiles, hands determinedly by his sides, and let the cold water run over his spine and buttocks until he was shuddering. If it had not been Monday morning, he would have knelt naked on the freezing tiles and prayed some more, but he was already late for the staff meeting.

They were waiting in the rec room. Belinda perched on a stool, her long brown legs crossed over each other, a folder open across her thighs. Greg sprawled across three giant floor cushions, looking as though he'd been there all night; Leticia and Kenny side by side on a bean bag, the way Luke and Aggie had been just last week.

'We missed you at breakfast,' Belinda said.

'I wasn't hungry.' His smile, too, felt tight.

'Must have been a great dinner last night.'

They were all staring at him. 'Great,' he said, because it was, he was sure it was, it was just he hadn't been able to eat it because *she* had filled him up already. *Oh, God, oh, God, I am so full.*

'You always get so darned spoilt after a sermon, Luke Butler. Talk about perks of the job! What was it last night? Another one of Mrs Stevens' roast chickens? Or was it Clarissa Fennel's beef stroganoff?'

'No, no.' Luke cleared his throat. 'I had a dinner appointment with Miss Grey, last night.'

'Oh,' said Belinda.

'Like, a *business* appointment, or…' Kenny shrugged.

'A dinner appointment, I said already. Now, what's on the agenda?'

'So, a date?'

Luke sighed. 'I had dinner with Miss Grey, at her home. She served salad and vegetarian lasagne. I talked to her about God, she raised the usual uneducated atheistic objections and I did my best to counter them. Any other questions or can we get this meeting started?'

They got the meeting started, but there were other questions. He saw them lurking in their eyes. He felt them inside himself, straining to get out.

He stood just inside the doorway, watching her. She was behind her desk, the phone cradled between her left shoulder and her ear. Or really the phone was buried in a mass of curly hair. Her skin, under the harsh fluorescent lights was raw looking. It looked as though she had tried to rub off her freckles with sandpaper. She was facing him, but her eyes were closed. She murmured into the phone and massaged her temples with her fingers.

'Hangover.'

'What?' Luke spun around. Behind him was a fat man in a navy tracksuit.

The man smiled and stepped past him. 'Reckons the light makes her head want to split open. I told her she'll get mugged sitting there with her eyes closed but she doesn't listen. Ha! Nice!'

Luke looked back at Aggie. Her eyes were still closed, and she continued murmuring into the cradled receiver, but she had extended one arm and raised a middle finger.

'So,' the man said, 'what can we do you for?'

'I'm… ah, I'm here to see, ah, Miss Grey.'

'No need for formalities, mate. It's just Aggie. And I'm Mal. Take a seat, she won't be long.' He scrunched a piece of computer paper and threw it across the room. It hit Aggie right on the top of her head. She opened her eyes, closed them, opened them just a crack, mouthed an obscenity at Mal, then, turning in her chair noticed Luke sitting against the wall. Her eyes widened once more. Cringing, she sat up straight, mumbled into the phone again and hung up.

'Luke!'

'Hello.' He couldn't help smiling; his face just fell that way when she looked at him. 'Rough night?'

'I disgraced myself. I'm so sorry.'

'No, I'm sorry. I shouldn't have just left like—'

'Whoa! Hold it!' Mal was striding toward Luke. 'You're the bloke who got her trashed last night?'

'Ah, I didn't—'

'Aggie! Why would you not tell me about this? This is—' Mal looked Luke over and turned back to Aggie, '—very nice.'

'Oh, shit,' Aggie said. 'Had to happen sometime. Right, Mal, this is my *friend* Pastor Luke Butler.'

'Pastor? Like, a minister?'

'Yes, I work just across the—'

'You're from over there?' Mal turned to Aggie. 'This is the fuck-tard who– But he's gor– Jesus Christ, woman, are you fucking insane?'

Aggie laughed, which Luke found irritating in the extreme. 'Settle down, Mal, all right?' She stood up, wincing and closing her eyes for a moment. 'Don't mind him, Luke, he's jealous.'

'I'm telling you, Aggie, I am going to kick your–'

'Let's go for a walk.' Aggie was beside him. Her hand was on his arm. Mal was still talking but Luke had stopped listening. Aggie was leading him out the door. She was saying she was happy he had come. She was reaching down and taking his hand.

'So that's your boss?'

'So he reckons.' She dropped his hand. 'My head is killing me. Can we sit?'

They sat on a bench at the edge of the reserve. Their view was of the carpark. Luke had many things he wanted to say, to ask, but he was distracted with wondering if she would pick up his hand again now they were sitting. He kept the hand closest to her limp and away from his thigh. It seemed very important that she touch it. The hand grew big and hot in the silence; he was aware of a splinter of wood under his index finger, a slight cramp in his upper knuckles, a need to scratch the fleshy pad of his palm.

'I'm sorry about last night.'

'S'okay.' He stared at her hand, relaxed and open on her right thigh.

'I don't usually drink so much.'

'I'm glad to hear that. It isn't healthy.'

'You're so strange.' She sighed.

She picked up his hand, and something broke open inside him. He breathed deeply of the crisp morning air. He smelt grass and petrol. He held tight to the warm hand. He breathed in the day and breathed out gratitude.

'Mal thinks I'm mad,' Aggie said. 'I mean, he thought that any-way, but now...'

'Is he...?' Luke cleared his throat. 'Is he in love with you?'

'What?' She laughed. Her arm jerked around a little, pulling his hand with it.

'You said, ah, that he was jealous. Just before, when I–'

'Jealous of *me*, sweetie.'

'Why would he be– Oh! He's– oh, you mean he... he's a gay?'

She dropped his hand. She slid to the far end of the bench. 'You don't have to sound so disgusted.'

'I'm afraid I can't help it. I've never had a homosexual eyeing me off before. You could have warned me.'

'Oh, for God's sake! Perhaps I should erect a sign: "Beware of the faggot." Then you'd know to wear protective clothing and carry anti-septic spray when you came to visit.'

Luke clamped his mouth shut and stared at his knees. He had to remember this was not her fault; she didn't know any better. He thought of Greg, who was the purest Christian he knew even though he used to perform abhorrent acts with other men. Deviance could be defeated, but anger and open disgust would not do it.

'S'cuse me, Sir. S'cuse me, Lady.'

An old man limped towards them. He was wearing a red baseball cap, brown sandals, purple jeans and an overcoat that probably used to be black. A hole in the front revealed a patch of curly grey chest hair.

'Could I trouble you for some change?'

Luke swallowed his annoyance at being interrupted. 'Well, I don't know,' he said to the man. 'What do you need change for?'

'God, Luke, give him some bloody change.'

Luke stood up and stepped close to the man. The stench over-powered him for a moment, but he used the trick he had learnt while ministering to the street people in Darlinghurst: look straight into the person's eyes and acknowledge the presence of Jesus Christ. He heard Jesus' voice, soft and a little sad: 'I say to you, what you did not do for one of these least ones, you did not do for me.' Now Luke was able to put his arm around the old man's shoulders as though the smell of alcohol and piss was as pleasant as chocolate and roses.

'Where you sleeping, friend?'

'Here n' there.'

'Your coat looks kind of worn out.'

The man nodded. 'S'why I need some change, see?'

'For a new coat?'

'For God's sake.' Aggie joined them, thrusting a five dollar note at the man. 'Here you go, mate.'

'Thank you, darlin'– Hey!'

Luke had snatched the bill away. He stepped in front of Aggie, ignoring her foot stamping protests. 'This is not going to get you a new coat. This–' he held the five dollar note in the air, '–is only going to get you a bottle of cheap plonk.'

The man sighed tragically. 'Warm as a new coat.'

'Yeah, I know.' Luke patted the man's shoulder. 'If I get you a new coat, and something to eat, will you promise me you won't spend this money on grog?'

'Yessir.'

'Okay?'

The man nodded.

'Just right across the road there, friend. You go right on in and ask for Greg. Say Luke sent you over for a coat and a feed.' Luke gave the man Aggie's five dollars and, bowing, the man headed off in the direction of the NCYC.

'You know he's going to spend that money on grog,' Aggie said.

'Yeah.' Luke sat down. 'Wouldn't you if you were him?'

Aggie sat beside him and put her head on his shoulder. Her hand was wrapped in his, just like that. 'You confuse me.'

'I'm sorry.'

'I like you too much.'

He pressed his face to her hair for just a moment. 'How can it be too much?'

'Don't be disingenuous.'

'I'm not. We like each other. That's good.'

'No, it's not. I like you so much, but you can never... you hate everything about me.'

'I don't hate, Aggie.' He returned his face to her hair. She didn't seem to mind. While he was thinking of nothing but the delicious way her curls tickled his nostrils, God filled him with inspiration. He sat up straight and turned to face her. 'There's a way to help him.'

She raised her eyebrows. 'The alkie?'

'Mal. There's a group in America— I met this man at a conference— they help people like Mal. This man used to be one of them, but God cured him and now he has this organisation— No! Aggie, wait a minute. Don't go! Hear me out.'

'Fuck you.' She was half way across the carpark already.

11

She forgave him, of course. Not because he deserved it, but because of the way he held her hand so tight, like he expected her to pull it away from him. The way he pressed his face to her hair, inhaling and thinking she didn't notice. His energy and compassion and charm and insight and humour and... and his beauty. Yes, that too. Beautiful people usually made her feel so ugly, but his beauty was generous; he made her feel pretty. He made her feel like a person a man would hang himself over.

She let him take her out to yum cha, where he greeted the hostess by name, ate three plates of chicken feet, and seven custard buns. They went to a movie, some awful American cartoon about a duck and a dog solving a mystery. He laughed loudly and genuinely throughout, and squeezed her hand too tight when the dog told the duck that their friendship was strong enough to overcome the species barrier. Three Saturdays in a row they ate dinner at her house; three times a week they ate lunch together in the park, or her office or his. She helped with his youth group almost every night and stayed up late drinking coffee in the NCYC kitchen.

She didn't want Mal to hate her, so she lied about her chaste and pure romance. Then she started to hate herself, so she told Mal the truth, how happy and lost and in love she was. He told her she was replaying the dysfunction of her childhood, falling for someone who would inevitably leave her. He reminded her that Luke was a bigot and a fanatic. She told Mal that Luke's goodness outweighed his occasional ignorant prejudice, and even as she said it she wondered what the tipping point was. Whether it would make the slightest difference to her heart.

Increasingly, she could not sleep after spending an evening with Luke. She was hotly aware of her skin. When she undressed she found her underpants were soaked through. She had rarely in her life felt the urge to masturbate and found now – to her shame – that she was horrible at it. She wore herself out trying to relieve the unfamiliar tension. She tried reading Anaïs Nin and Henry Miller and Colette, and applied the silver bullet vibrator her mother had given her last Christmas until the batteries went dead. Then she stayed in the bath with the shower nozzle massaging her throbbing clitoris until the water was cold and her fingertips were wrinkled. She continued to see him every day, and every night she tried but failed to convince herself that the large white hands between her legs were Luke's small brown ones.

Aggie sat on the floor of the darkened rec room, her back against the wall, and lit the candle propped between her knees. The light it gave out was small, but as the thirty teenagers around her lit their own candles, the room brightened enough that she could see Luke looking at her from the other side of the room. He held her gaze for a couple of seconds, then smiled and began walking slowly around the circle of candles.

'This is better, right? Before we couldn't see a thing, we were stumbling and dropping our matches, bumping into each other, swearing– yes, I heard you, Matthew.' There was giggling. 'But did you notice what happened when the candles started burning? First just one, then two, then five, then all of them? You lit each other's way, guys! Those who were having trouble finding their matches had their way lit by those who had already got theirs going. Now, we can all see each other clearly. Now the room looks so bright and lovely.' He stopped behind a girl with long red plaits. 'This is exactly what happens when we invite the Holy Spirit in. We not only get a guiding light for ourselves, but when others see our light they are inspired to find their own. And the more people who are filled with the Spirit, the brighter the world is.'

Thirty-one faces gazed up at Luke. The kids in front of him had to crane their necks and twist their bodies, but their eyes shone with a calm trust and admiration. Aggie too was unable to look away from him, and it made her wonder how many of these kids were inspired by his message and how many were, like her, enchanted by the beauty and grace of the man.

Afterward, as she helped him pick up the discarded candles and matchboxes, he asked her whether she had enjoyed the meeting. He always asked her this and her answer was always the same: The company was good, but the same couldn't be said for the content. Usually he laughed, but tonight he did not. He came to her, took the candle out of her hand and frowned darkly. 'Why do you keep coming?'

Finally! Aggie touched his angry face, thinking *finally*. 'For you, of course.' She stroked his face, thinking *please, please let this be it*.

'You don't get anything out of it at all?'

'I get to watch you—'

'No.' He drew back from her touch. 'I mean, do you get anything out of it spiritually? Are you getting any closer to God?'

'Luke, I don't believe in God. I can't get close to someone who doesn't exist.'

He scowled. 'He exists.'

'No, Luke. *We* exist. We're real. *I'm* real.' She held her arms out wide, sick with how much she needed him to touch her.

The anger melted from his face. 'I know.' He took her in his arms and pressed his face into the side of her neck. 'I know, I know.'

She held her breath as though not breathing would stop him moving away. Of course, it didn't. Of course, he stepped away almost immediately. But suddenly the light was out, and she could hear him breathing beside her in the dark.

Finally.

She heard a match strike. 'Does this candle exist?' His smiling face was illuminated.

She sighed and sank into the nearest chair. 'Yes, Luke, the candle exists.'

'And you know that because you can see it, right?'

'Yawn.'

He smiled, leant forward and then it was dark. 'Okay, what about now.'

'The candle still exists even though I can't see it. Just like God. Point well made— bravo. Bloody hell, Luke, I'm not twelve.'

'No, you're not.' His voice was sad. 'You don't get it though, you really don't. You want certainty and you'll never get that. Certainty is missing the point. Faith is about this. Just sitting in the dark, feeling confused and scared. Feeling like you just can't hold on any more. Like you're going to just— Not knowing if the light's ever coming back on, but hanging in there anyway. Just letting it be dark for a while.'

She reached into the darkness in front of her and found his face. She felt his eyelids, nose, chin, lips. His hand met hers as it travelled down his neck; he held her still. She said his name and he coughed, jolted away and then he was on the other side of the room and the light was back on.

'And just when you don't expect it…' He gestured toward the

bulb, but his eyes were on his feet.

Aggie picked up the candle at her own feet. She stood on shaky legs and said good night and sobbed harder than she had in years as she drove home. She cried herself to sleep, only to wake after an hour. Disoriented, headachy, mad, she grabbed the damn candle and pushed it inside herself. She rammed it so hard and fast that shards of hardened wax came off and stuck to her wet flesh. She gritted her teeth and rolled onto her stomach, impaling herself on to the crumbling wax, snapping it with the force. Unrelieved, pathetic, she collapsed on her stomach, the broken candle inside her, and cried until she could hardly breathe.

12

Toward the end of Belinda's *Christian Dating? There's no such thing!* presentation, it occurred to Luke that his relationship with Aggie had moved from the white zone of Witnessing to the blue area of Buddies, was currently placed in the yellow band of Special Friendship and was fast approaching the Red Hot Danger Zone of Intimacy. Seeing each other more than twice a week. Seeing each other without a group of friends. Talking on the telephone more than three times a week. An understanding that weekend nights would be spent together. Sustained touching such as hand holding or cuddling. The next step – according to Belinda's presentation – was kissing. 'And once the kissing starts,' Belinda warned, 'it takes a strong, strong person to call a halt. Better to catch things before they reach that stage. Better to prove to your special friend how much you respect them *and* how much you love the Lord by keeping those lips unlocked.'

Luke agreed with every word Belinda had said, and equally, he was convinced that he was stronger and more in love with God and more respectful of his special friend than the average strong, loving, respectful Christian man. If he could hold Aggie's hand, if he could touch her soft hair, if he could feel her breast pressing against his arm and her hipbone knocking against his and still not give in to the temptation to commit sexual sin against his own body, then surely taking her face between his palms and drawing her mouth towards his would not cause an unstoppable slide into sin.

So it was not fear of crashing into the Red Hot Danger Zone that had caused him pause. The truth was that he wasn't really sure how kissing Aggie would work. She was taller than him for a start. Also, he was wise enough in the ways of the world to know that the kissing she would expect was not the peck on the cheek or even the brief pressing together of lips type. The kissing she would expect would be open-mouthed, protracted and wet. He suspected that tongues would be involved, although he could not imagine what exactly they would do. And what about hands? Would they hang limp at their sides, or would they touch each other while it was happening? Luke thought he would like to touch her hair but wasn't sure if that was the sort of thing one did when kissing.

He decided he would kiss her next time they were alone together. No, alone kissing was going too far. He would kiss her in public. In the park or at the cinema. No, the cinema was dark; he might miss her mouth or place his hands somewhere inappropriate or get distracted by her scent. He had noticed that last night in the rec room – how the darkness had heightened his sense of smell so that he could hardly breathe with the thickness of her scent. Musky, damp, slightly acrid, the smell came back to him now, and with it, the dizziness of the night before. That smell could make a man forget God.

He would kiss her in the park then, in daylight on the bench behind the gum tree. He would go over after the meeting and ask her to take a walk with him. *Aggie,* he would say, *would you mind if I kissed you?*

He waited until the kids had filed out of the hall, then ran to his office to put on his good denim jacket and fix his hair. He wondered if he should go to his room and brush his teeth or if sucking on a peppermint would be sufficient. Out the window he could see that

Kenny had a game of rugby going with some of the younger boys and that Leticia and a few of the girls from this morning's group were cheering from the sidelines. Normally he would go and join them, but today was not normal. Today he was going to kiss Agatha Grey.

'Ah, Luke?'

He turned and smiled, even as his heart sank. 'Belinda. Great presentation this morning. I was thinking we could do something similar for the juniors? Maybe tone down the kissing stuff a little, talk more about the importance of having a broad range of friends.'

Belinda beamed. 'Great idea. I'll work on it this weekend and you can let me know what you think.' She sat in his visitor's chair, crossed her legs and looked him up and down. 'You're all spruced up. Going somewhere?'

'Yeah, I was just on my way out. Did you want something?'

'Actually, yeah… I, ah, I was hoping we could chat?'

He thought of Aggie's lips. Pale pink with deep red corners which flashed at you when she laughed or yelled or yawned. Now that he had made the decision to kiss her, it was excruciating to have to wait. He stifled a sigh and sat behind his desk. 'Of course' he told Belinda, who was his colleague and friend and, most importantly, his spiritual responsibility. 'What's on your mind?'

'Well, it's just…' Belinda's smile slipped into a grimace. 'It's kind of a sensitive topic, Luke, and I'm a little nervous about bringing it up.'

Luke resisted the impulse to roll his eyes. 'You should know not to be nervous with me. Come on, now.'

'Right, it's just… It's about Aggie Grey.'

'Yes?' Luke was pleased at the neutrality of his tone.

'People are wondering if–' Belinda raised her eyebrows. Luke stared back at her blankly, forcing her to go on. 'People are wondering about your relationship with Aggie. Wondering if she's your, ah, girlfriend?'

'Who's wondering?'

Belinda shrugged. 'Everyone who's noticed how much time you spend with her.'

'Aggie is not my girlfriend.'

'Right, okay. So, ah…' Belinda grimaced again.

'So, ah, what?'

'Luke, come on.' Belinda leant forward again. 'A month ago you had everyone in the community writing letters and printing banners against the woman, and now you spend all of your free time hanging out with her.'

'The campaign was never against Aggie. It was against the clinic.'

'Whatever. Point is, suddenly the clinic is okay and the woman who runs it is your best friend? What gives?'

Luke smiled at Belinda and clenched his fists under the desktop. 'The clinic is certainly not okay, and I'm shocked you would make such an inference. It became clear to me that we were going about things in the wrong way. Jesus taught understanding and peace, not aggression and righteousness. He was known for the company He kept. Prostitutes, thieves, people other religious leaders wouldn't go near – Jesus drew them close. He befriended the worst sinners in the land; he ate at their tables and drank from their cups. He didn't do that because He approved of their way of life. He did it to be the best friend a sinner ever had.'

'Surely you don't compare yourself with Jesus? He was without human weakness; His motives were always pure. You must recall what Paul said about bad company?'

'I am familiar with Paul's teachings, thank you, Belinda. And am most certainly not comparing myself with Jesus; I am simply try-ing to live by His example. We can talk all we like about how great God is, but it is through our actions that the unsaved judge us. By acting with compassion, tolerance, love, we *show* them the grace of God.'

Belinda smiled tightly. 'You're right, of course. I'm sorry for doubting you. It's just that people talk...'

'Wonderful. Let them spread the word. We welcome sinners. We *embrace* them.'

'Yes, wonderful!' Belinda rose from her seat. 'You're very good to be so kind to unfortunates, Luke. We should all follow your example.'

Luke laughed, though he felt hot with rage. 'Aggie is hardly an unfortunate! She's an extremely accomplished young woman. She is not an object of pity, I assure you.'

'So she *has* been saved?'

He was winded by it. How wrong-headed he'd been. How disgracefully self-deceiving. He looked hard at Belinda. She was wide-eyed, seemingly at the anticipation of having such wonderful news confirmed. Seemingly? Maybe it was real. Maybe he was being far too harsh on Belinda, who after all, was a dedicated Youth Pastor, a good Christian, a pure and chaste young woman who had dedicated her life to the service of Jesus Christ.

'Not yet.'

'Then I pity her.'

'But she will be. It's my mission.'

Belinda came around to his side of the desk, bent low and embraced him. He sat unmoving, allowing her small, smooth arms to press his head to her almost bare chest. Her breasts were soft and warm beneath his face, but he felt nothing. 'You're a good man, Luke.' Belinda straightened up, smiled down at him pityingly. 'If you say you're going to save her, then I believe you will.'

She left the room. Luke put his head on the desk. He stayed like that for an hour or more. When he lifted his head again, his vision was blurred and his temples throbbed, but his mind felt clearer.

'Ag, it's me.'

'I was just thinking about you.'

'I've been thinking about you too.'

'Good things, I hope?'

'I want you to sign up for introductory Bible study classes.'

She laughed. 'What?'

'Classes for people from a non-Christian background. We hold them at—'

'We've been through this. There's no way.'

'It's very important that you do this.'

Silence.

'Aggie?'

'Yes, that's me. Who are you?'

He was losing his surety. He closed his eyes and asked God to fill him up. 'I'm trying to help you.'

'You want to help me, then go get me some Singapore noodles from down the road. I'm starving.'

'This is serious. I've been neglecting my duty. Your soul is in—'

'Enough, Luke, okay? Drop it.'

He was silent. He needed her to be saved so he could give himself to her. That was selfish, he knew, but it was even more selfish to 'drop it'. Eternal life was more important than avoiding uncomfortable conversations. Her precious soul was worth more than amiable companionship.

'Are you going to say anything?'

'Why, Aggie?'

'Because I don't like one-sided conversations.'

'I mean why won't you open your mind to the possibility that I might actually know what I'm talking about. I truly have your interests at heart here.'

'I swear to god, Luke, I'm going to hang up if you don't stop this shit.'

'I don't mind the swearing, but can you please not blaspheme?'

Click.

13

How can anyone be so completely – ugh!' Aggie stalked the length of the clinic, glancing faux-casually at the NCYC each time she passed the window. She had been doing this for so long her legs were getting tired, but she thought it best to keep moving. Sitting down felt like giving up. 'He doesn't seem to have the slightest clue how to talk to other human beings. It's like he's been brought up by wolves!'

'Maybe if you did some work you'd feel better?'

Aggie pulled a face at Mal, who was intent on his monitor and so did not see her anyway. 'I have a client at twelve. Until then, I intend to pace.'

'Can you do it elsewhere? I'm trying to concentrate.'

Aggie stuck her tongue out. 'You're a shitty friend.'

'You're a shitty employee. Do some fucking work.'

Aggie sat on Mal's desk, pushing several thick folders to the floor. He swore. Aggie lay down, her head on his keyboard, her feet hanging over the edge. Mal poked her in the ribs. 'Get off my desk.'

Aggie spread her arms, knocking something cold and heavy off the desk and crumpling several papers under her elbows. 'I just don't get it. The chemistry is out of this world. Every time we see each other it's like… ah God, you've seen us together, Mal, don't you think he seems keen? He seems so– ah, I don't know.'

'He's a wanker; you're great and deserve much better. Now get off my fucking desk.'

'I feel like Luke's the one. Like this is meant to be, you know?'

'You said that about Matthew.'

That was true. But she had only said it because he kept coming back to her, and it seemed impossible that someone as brilliant as Matthew would keep returning to someone as dull as Aggie unless the hand of fate was pushing him. This was different; when she was with Luke she knew that they were destined to be enemies, but that she would easily tear the universe into shreds if it tried to stop her having him. Aggie told Mal this and he stopped trying to force her head off his keyboard and instead stroked her hair.

'However strong the attraction, it would never work long-term. His values are diametrically opposed to yours.'

'Not all of them. He's honest and trustworthy. He's a pacifist and believes that ending poverty is the way to stop terrorism. He's on the front line of the battle against racism and prejudice, and he is just so unbelievably compassionate. You know he–'

'Ag, he hates gays.'

'No, he doesn't. He loves the sinner and hates the– fuck, Mal, I know, okay? I know. But it's not his fault. He's a good man who's been brainwashed into believing these awful things. He's ill, really. He uses religion the same way an alcoholic uses booze. And Mal, I *know* addiction, right? I'm good with addicts. I just have to get him to–'

'Lose his religion?'

'Yeah.' Aggie sighed. 'How do I do that?'

'Auschwitz did it for me.'

'What? You were never religious.'

Mal snorted. 'I try and block out the memory, but I was a genuine guilt-wracked Catholic boy for the first decade-and-a-half of my life. I went to confession every single day of the year I turned fifteen, constantly terrified that a bus would hit me between my boyfriend's house and the church, and I would be condemned to an eternity in the fires of Hell. Then I learnt about Auschwitz, and I was instantly cured. I sat there in history class, listening to Sister Marguerite recite the list of diseases and tortures and extermination techniques, and I was just hit with this… this epiphany. Not only did God allow this atrocity to occur, but He would surely approve, since He Himself condemned fags and Jews to eternal torment. I decided that if God was on the side of Hitler, then he could shove his Heaven up his supernatural arse.'

'Hurray for you. Did you convert your mum too? She's the least religious old broad I know.' Aggie went to Mal's mother's for Christmas dinner every year and the three of them got shit-faced and competed to invent the filthiest substitute lyrics for popular Christmas carols. Mrs Addison had won last year with her rendition of *The Twelve Lays of Christmas*.

'Dad was the mad Catholic. When he died, Mum kept going out of habit until Father O'Brien told her she couldn't continue to take communion as long as she allowed me to carry on my *lifestyle* under her roof. She never took communion again. She still calls red wine "blood of Christ" sometimes.'

Aggie felt fortunate to have escaped the strange mythical education that the majority of Australian kids endured. Her father worshipped his wife, his daughter and money, in that order; her mother worshipped herself. Christmas was a picnic of Greek salad and crunchy baguettes at Bondi beach; Easter meant too much chocolate and three days of sleeping late. When Aggie's paternal grandmother died, the extended family took turns to read poems in her honour and then cast her ashes out into the Pacific. There was no talk of Heaven.

Aggie's wedding, too, had been strictly secular. A hired yacht, a celebrant from the yellow pages, a bunch of drunk fisherman and stoned uni students, a teenage bride who was simultaneously drowning in grief and flying high on sexual passion, and a groom who insisted that only the best would do for his wife, and so spent a great deal of her dead father's money on first class tickets for a honeymoon in Rome.

Religion was a big thing in Rome, and Aggie remembered how disgusted she had felt when she finally saw Vatican City after walking half a day through streets crawling with beggars. The place was filled with more priceless art treasures than she could take in. It was a golden contradiction of the vows of poverty. 'Evils pay well,' Kip said, in a rare sombre tone. He wouldn't answer any of Aggie's questions and was quiet for the rest of the day, but she knew he had gone to an Anglican boarding school and so figured that had something to do with it. From then on she noticed that whenever they passed a church he would look at the ground and walk faster, like a child desperate to escape the attention of a gang of bullies.

'I have to save him,' Aggie said.

'He doesn't want to be saved, Ag.'

'So I should just give up? Just forget I ever met him?'

Mal was silent, twisting her hair around his finger. After a while he bent over and kissed her forehead. 'Get up.' Aggie let him haul her to an upright position. 'Listen,' he said. 'Don't think I approve of this, because I don't.' Mal looked out the window towards the NCYC, shook his head, then looked back at Aggie. 'But I will say this: he's crazy about you, Aggie. He blushes like a schoolgirl when you so much as smile at him through the window. If you're determined to win him over – against my best advice, mind you – then I say just be yourself. His faith is unlikely to crumble under your poorly-constructed theological arguments, but if he loves you, he'll have to have those arguments with himself.'

Aggie hugged him. 'I love you.'

'Ag, be careful. It might work out, but it probably won't.'

'I have to try.'

'You sure this isn't just some kink? Getting hot over a minister?'

'You forget I have no religion. A minister is totally not taboo. A virgin on the other hand...'

'He's a...? That's it.' Mal held up his hands. 'Now I know you're insane. I'm getting out of here before you infect me.'

Aggie laughed. Nothing was solved, but she felt better. Malcolm said Luke was crazy about her, so it had to be true. 'Don't go, Mal, I'm having fun.'

He was putting on his jacket, struggling to stuff his too-large arms into the narrow sleeves. Mal kissed her forehead again. 'I have stuff to do, be back about eleven, okay?' He paused at the door and looked back at her. 'Don't call him until I get back. You need supervision with this one.'

14

Honey was late again, and it was totally not her fault, since that fuckhead Muzza had sold her clock radio for dope money and her useless mother had forgotten to bang on her door before leaving for work like she'd promised. When she did finally wake up at eight-forty, she found that there was not only no coffee or milk but there was not even hot water. She wondered how long it would be before they paid the bill this time. She was not strong enough to go three months without hot showers like she had last winter. She'd had just about as much as she could stand.

Honey made it to the bus stop in time for the nine-thirteen, which would have at least got her to school in time for second period, but then the nausea kicked in and the bus came and went as she was spewing behind the fence of the retirement home. She reminded herself that after today the sickness would be gone. After today *it* would be gone and she could get on with her life. No, not get on with her life − start a new life. The old one sucked. The old life got her into this disgusting mess. She would make a clean start. Stop hanging around with Steve and his lot. Stop smoking dope and stealing shit from Woolworths. Stop turning into her fucking mother. Clean start, new life, fresh chances. As soon as she got rid of the fuck-ing *thing* inside her.

It was an hour until the next bus, and by the time she got to school it would nearly be time to leave again because she had to be at the clinic by twelve. She decided to walk straight to the clinic. Even with stopping twice to throw up and once to dry-retch, the trip only took twenty-minutes. So what that she had missed the morning's classes? She knew education was the key to getting the hell out of here, but really, the importance of three hours of English and History was just nil when compared to the importance of not being another damn teenage mother.

When she got to the carpark she lit a cigarette and removed from her backpack the tampon box containing the cash Steve had nicked for her. She counted the notes and smoothed out the creases, thankful that Muzza was the kind of man who refused to touch 'disgusting women's things'. She slipped the money into her shirt pocket and tossed the tampon box on the ground. According to the girls' dunny experts you had to wear giant mattress pads for a week after an abortion. Honey didn't care if she had to wear them for a year; at least it would mean there was nothing in her except blood.

She wished suddenly that Steve was here, that he was the kind of boyfriend who would hold her hand during the interview and then stroke her face and tell her it was all going to be all right, and they were making the right decision and he loved her no matter what. But then, if he was that kind of boyfriend she wouldn't be here craving comfort, because if he was that kind of boyfriend he would've used condoms in the first place. And if she wasn't such a comfort-needing, spineless, sentimental little moron she would have made him. That was the truth when you got right down to it: she had only herself to blame, and she had only herself to hold onto if she was feeling scared. Which she wasn't. Much.

Honey finished her cigarette, dropped it on the asphalt and put it out with the thick glob of bile that had been lining her throat all morning. Head held high, chest out, shoulders back, she made her way across the car park towards the glass-fronted office with *Sexual Health Clinic* in bold black type on the door. As she pushed the door open, someone whistled and she turned, heart hammering in her chest, expecting to see Muzza or her mum or one of the teachers.

There was no-one behind her or anywhere close by. A lady with a pram passed by on the other side of the street and a kid on a bike cut through the carpark to get to the council reserve. No-one was paying any attention to Honey at all. It was nerves. Plain old dumb nerves. Something flashed in the corner of her eye, and she turned towards it as another flash blinded her. A yell rose in her throat, but then her vision cleared and she saw that the sun glinting off the side mirror of a white van was causing flashes of light as it drove slowly by. She took a deep breath and entered the clinic.

A woman behind a desk covered in three thousand pieces of paper stood up and smiled. 'Can I help you?'

'I'm Honey. I'm, um, I'm early for my–'

The woman squinted down at her desk, pushing aside folders and papers until she unearthed what must have been an appointment book. 'Right… ah, Honey Allende?'

Honey nodded, smiling a little, because the woman had pronounced her name properly. *Ayenday* instead of *Alendee* like most people did.

'You're the first appointment today. We can start now if you like?'

Honey nodded and followed the woman through a doorway behind the desk. 'Wait one sec. I've got to lock the door. I'm alone here until eleven.'

Honey sank into the nearest chair and looked around. There was nothing else in the room except for three more straight-backed wooden chairs and a small table that looked like it had been pinched from an old lady's living room. Honey was relieved that there weren't any posters on the wall. Once she had gone to a family planning

clinic to find out about getting the pill, and the posters about genital warts and herpes freaked her out so much that she had left
without seeing a doctor.

'Right.' The woman sat beside Honey, placing a box of tissues and
a manila folder on the table. 'My name's Aggie. I'm a qualified counsellor, which means I'm trained to look at people's problems in an
objective way and help them find a solution they are comfortable
with. I will not judge you or lecture you, nor will I tell you what to
do. This meeting is completely confidential and so is any action that
you decide to take as a result of this session. Any questions?'

'Do I have to do this? This counselling stuff I mean? Can't I just,
you know, get it done?'

Aggie leant forward, resting her elbows on her knees. 'You can
do whatever you like, Honey, but you requested this appointment.
That indicates that you have something you want to talk about.'

'I thought I *had* to talk about it first. Steve – that's my boyfriend
– he said that they make you talk first, to be certain that it's what you
want. Even if you know what you want – which I really do, believe
me – they make you have this bit first.' Honey realised she was talking at about twice her normal speed. She pressed her palms against
her still-flat belly and took a long, slow breath. 'Anyway, I want to get
rid of it. So if it's not an absolute requirement, if it's not law or anything, can we just get straight to the… the procedure or whatever
you call it.'

Aggie frowned, tapping her nails against her chin. Stumpy nails,
shiny chin. Honey wondered if she was a lesbian. Steve reckoned that
women who worked in abortion clinics were lesbians, spending their
lives ripping the offspring from other women's wombs because they
were so bitter about not being able to get knocked up themselves.
Honey told him he was full of shit, because he pretty much thought
every woman with a job or a mind or a decent pair of walking shoes

was a lesbian. But looking at Aggie Grey you had to wonder.

'Honey, you know, we don't actually perform terminations here, don't you?'

'Oh.' Honey did not know that at all. If she had known they did not actually perform terminations here she would not be sitting here, she would be sitting in the place where they actually did perform terminations. 'Um, Steve said–'

'Your boyfriend?'

'Right. He said that, um, he said he's – well, not him, but a girl he used to… he knows a girl who got one done here once. He said if I just made an appointment–'

'There was a surgery next door, but it moved because of the protestors. It wasn't safe for the staff having everyone know it was there. We can still refer you, but not until we know you're genuine.'

'I'm genuine, I swear. I have to get rid of it and I want it done today. I have money. Cash.' She tapped her top pocket, to show the woman she was serious.

'I'll give them a call and see how soon we can arrange it. But I do need to go through a few things with you first.'

To Honey's relief, the questions were easy. Date of birth, had she seen a doctor, had she been pregnant before, was she making the decision of her own free will, did she have any allergies, had she ever been tested for HIV, who was her contact in case of emergency. When they were done, Aggie was true to her word, leaving the room and coming back five minutes later with a slip of paper bearing an address in Granville.

'They can see you at two. The procedure only takes about ten minutes, but the appointment will last three to four hours and will include paperwork, blood and urine tests, ultrasound and pelvic examination followed by the medical procedure and recovery. There'll be a uniformed security guard at the door, who'll ask for that appointment slip and get you to walk through a metal detector. He's there to make sure you and the staff are safe from nutcases, so once you get past him you can relax.'

Honey stood. 'That it?'

'That's it. You sure you don't want to talk a bit? You've got some time before the appointment.'

Honey started to decline, but the sound of glass breaking cut her off. Aggie ran from the room and Honey caught the words 'fucking cuntface fucker' and then something incoherent, and then a door opening and then: 'For fucksake, what next?'

Honey walked out into the main office. The front window was gone, except for a few jagged edges clinging to the frame. Aggie was standing amongst the shattered glass, looking out at the deserted street. She was holding a brick in both hands, and another was at her feet.

Honey felt as if she was going to cry – not that that was such a big deal these days. Bloody hormones. But still, this was maybe something to cry about, unlike ads for toilet paper or that thing in History class about the Aboriginal kids being taken from their families.

Steve and the guys broke windows a lot: cars, shops, houses, offices, whatever. They didn't do it for any reason except they were pissed and bored and it was fun for about ten seconds to hear the smash and then run until the blood rushed in your ears. But being inside and seeing that poor lady staring helplessly into space was not fun.

'Got a broom?' she said. Aggie turned and looked at her as though she'd appeared out of thin air. 'Dustpan and brush or something? To clean up the glass with?'

'Oh.' Aggie shook her head and kind of smiled. 'Don't you worry, Honey, you've got enough on your mind.'

Honey noticed a door next to the one she had gone through

before. 'So this'll keep my mind off it,' she said, pushing the door open and seeing a sink, fridge, mop, bucket, broom. She grabbed the broom and bucket and headed back out to the mess. Aggie was on the phone, so Honey got to work sweeping the glass into a neat pile. She was just finishing scraping it into the bucket when Aggie hung up.

'Thanks Honey. That was really nice of you.' Aggie took a deep breath. 'Police are on their way. Not that they'll do anything. Never do.'

'This has happened before?' Honey leant the broom against the wall and sat on the edge of the desk. The sweeping had made her feel dizzy.

'Not exactly. Usually it's graffiti or people standing out there yelling stuff. They've never–' She stared at the brick.

Honey felt so horrible and so useless. She didn't know if she should just leave, or if maybe she should go and pat her on the shoulder or something. She decided the best thing was to keep out of the way. She took a few deep breaths to clear the light-headedness, then grabbed the broom and bucket and carried them back out to the little storage room. When she returned to the office, Aggie was on the phone again.

'I'm telling you,' she said, her voice high and screechy, 'it isn't anything to do with Luke. No, I'm sure. Yes, I know it – Malcolm – no, Malcolm, it isn't him… yes, okay, okay, Jesus Christ! Okay! No, don't do that, Mal, please. I will talk to him, but I am telling you it isn't– Shit!' Aggie slammed the phone down and kicked the wall.

'You all right?'

She turned to Honey and smiled as though nothing had happened. 'Thanks for your help with the glass. You don't need to hang around here. You didn't see anything anyway so the police won't need to–'

'Aggie!' A man was running across the road, towards them. 'Oh, Aggie!'

Aggie opened the front door just as he arrived at it. The man threw his arms around her and rubbed her heaving back. 'Oh, Aggie, oh heh, heh, Aggie, shush. You're okay, aren't you? You're okay. It's just glass. Easily replaced. You're fine.'

Aggie lifted her head from the man's shoulder and looked into his face. 'I thought all this stuff was over with. I thought we were going to be left in peace.'

The man held Aggie by the shoulders and stepped back from her. Honey got a good look at his face for the first time. He was dark, but cute. 'You can't expect that, Aggie. It's never going to happen.'

'What?' Aggie pulled away from him, taking three fast steps backward. 'What the fuck does that mean?'

Honey wondered if she should say something. She could tell that something really intense was going on between the two of them and they seemed to be completely unaware that she was there witnessing it all. She looked at the empty window frame, wondering if she could just sort of step out without Aggie and the man noticing. She started edging toward it, and then everything went black.

Honey was lying on her back, in the dark. She was fairly certain that she had fainted. Someone was squeezing her left wrist. There was a hand on her forehead. A man said, 'If she doesn't wake up in ten seconds I'm calling an ambulance.' A woman said, 'Oh hell.' Honey opened her eyes and was rewarded with a smile from the cute guy. 'Ah, there you are, sweetheart. You had us worried for a minute.'

Aggie was on her knees beside the man, and her eyes were very red as though she had been crying for days. 'How's your head?'

'Fine. How long was I–'

'Barely two minutes,' said Aggie, 'but it felt much longer.' She stroked Honey's forehead. 'Stay here with Luke for a minute, okay? I have to go talk to the police. I'll be right back.'

'I'm fine. Sorry to be so much trouble.'

'This is not your fault at all. Just relax.' Aggie's voice wavered slightly as she turned to the man and said, 'Yell if you need me?' He nodded, placing his palm against Aggie's cheek and mouthing something that Honey could not make out. Then Aggie was up and gone and the man was holding Honey's hand again.

'I'd like to get up. Maybe go outside for a bit.'

'Slow, okay?' He leant over her, taking hold of her shoulders and helping her to a sitting position. His hair smelt like peaches, which would normally be nice since she was used to men who smelt like cigarettes and sweat and grease, but in her present condition it made her want to puke. Fortunately he stood up before the scent overpowered her. 'You okay?' he asked, and when she said yes he took hold of her from behind, his arms around her chest, and pulled her to her feet. Then holding her by the elbow, he led her out onto the street.

Outside, she pulled a slightly squashed cigarette packet from her backpack and lit up before offering one to the man, who shook his head with exaggerated force.

'You're anti-smoking, huh?'

'Yes, I am.'

'Me too. I'm quitting.'

'I can see that.'

'After today, I'm quitting.'

'Good for you. What's so special about today?'

Honey laughed, which hurt her head and throat. 'Nothing, at all.'

'I'm missing something.'

'Yeah.'

He squinted at her. 'Something to do with why you're here?'

Honey shrugged. He was cute, but not exactly a genius.

'Something to do with why you're here and also to do with why you fainted?'

She shrugged again, blowing smoke not exactly *into* his face but fairly close. The way he scrunched up his eyes and wriggled his mouth in reaction to the smoke reminded her of the look her grandmother got whenever she saw an ethnic person. Thinking of that made her feel bad, because Luke was ethnic and probably had people like Honey's grandmother screwing up their faces at him all the time, and so it was pretty mean for Honey to blow smoke in his face when he was just trying to be friendly.

'So do you work here?' she asked, stubbing out the cigarette before it was even half gone. It wasn't for his sake; she felt kind of woozy.

He laughed then. Laughed so hard that it was a full minute before he managed to answer her question. 'I work across the street.'

Honey looked across the street and finally got the joke. The entire block was taken up by the Northwestern Christian Youth Centre. She had known it was there, having walked past it a hundred times, having been harassed several times by its evangelising teenyboppers while she'd been waiting outside the Chinese takeaway down the street, and having read the very funny letters its members sent to the local newspaper protesting everything from sex education in schools to Harry Potter books in the public library. She had known of course, that the NCYC was responsible for closing down the Adult Bookshop that used to be on Hastings Road, and that anyone stupid enough to hang out in the council reserve on a weeknight would be preached to and lectured and begged to 'come inside and hear the word.' She knew about the goddamn NCYC but in her tension and fear, she had not given it a second thought.

'I have to go,' Honey said.

'Why?' Luke smiled and touched her arm.

'I have an appointment.'

'But I promised Aggie I'd watch over you until she got back. She's had enough drama today without me making it worse by losing you.'

'Did you smash the window?' Honey asked.

'No! Why would you think that?'

'Just something I overheard. Aggie was sticking up for you.'

He smiled and let out a little sigh. 'Ah.'

'Are you and her—'

'Friends.'

'Friends?'

'Close friends.' Another little sigh. 'Despite our differences.'

Differences. Like Aggie was ugly, white and at least thirty and Luke was gorgeous, of indeterminate ethnic origin and twenty-three at the most. But that was so shallow it was like something Honey's mother would think. He meant, of course, that since Aggie worked *here* and he worked *there*, there were a thousand or more differences large and small that most human beings would not consider it possible to overcome.

'You've got a hide showing your face around here!' A fat man with a red face charged towards them from the car park.

'Here's trouble,' Luke said, not sounding worried in the slightest. 'Hello, Malcolm, how are you this morning?'

The man came to a halt in front of Luke, glanced at Honey and then stuck his finger into Luke's chest. 'You have exactly thirty seconds to fuck off. Starting now. Thirty. Twenty-nine. Twenty-eight.'

'I'm afraid I can't leave just yet. Aggie has left this young lady in my charge until the police have finished inside. It would be terribly irresponsible of me just to walk away.'

The man turned his gaze on Honey again. 'And you are?'

'She's one of your clients, Malcolm, so be nice.'

'Oh,' Malcolm said, his voice dropping to a conversational level. 'Sorry you got caught up in all this. If I ever get my hands on the bastards who did this—' He looked menacingly at Luke, '—God help me, I'll kill them.'

'I don't know that God would actually help you if you—'

'That's it. Get the fuck out of here now.' Malcolm grabbed Luke by the front of his shirt, lifted him half a foot off the ground and then dropped him. Luke staggered backwards, straightened, held up both hands in a gesture of surrender and then turned to Honey. 'Come on, we'll wait across the street.'

'Oh, no you won't.' Malcolm grabbed Honey's arm. 'She'll stay here thank you very much.'

Honey shook off his hand and was immediately pulled to the side by Luke who put a possessive arm over her shoulder, holding her tightly against him. The two men eyed each other off, Malcolm clearly deciding whether it was worth the trouble to beat Luke into a bloody pulp. Honey started to say that she just wanted to leave, but then out of the corner of her eye she spotted the same van that had circled her in the car park earlier.

'That van was here this morning,' she said. 'I think they took a picture of me.'

Luke and Malcolm turned towards the van as a middle-aged woman in a beige linen sundress climbed out. She smiled as she approached them and thrust a piece of yellow paper into Honey's hand. 'Smile, dear, you're a star.'

Honey stared down at a photo of herself, taken less than two hours ago at this very spot. Above the photo, in a gothic-dripping-blood font, was printed *Baby Killer!!!* Under the photo it said: *Parents and Citizens beware! This child killing child was spotted entering the Holocaust Headquarters in Koloona Street wearing a Parramatta Heights Senior School uniform!!!!! Does she share a class with YOUR child?!!!*

Luke was saying something to the woman. Honey couldn't understand a single word. She was vaguely aware that only Luke's grip was keeping her standing. Malcolm seemed to have taken off as soon as the woman appeared. Honey stared at the crappy, grainy close-up of her face. You could see the pimple she had tried so hard to cover, but because of the poor quality print it looked like a black spot in the centre of her forehead. She looked like a Hindu. A blonde, pale-skinned, school uniform-wearing Hindu.

Her head began to clear and she was able to make out a few words of the conversation. She heard Luke saying 'compassion' and 'non-confrontational' and the woman saying something about Luke being blind and greatly deceived. 'Slaughter of the innocents' came up, as did 'infanticide' and 'legalised murder'. Honey knew these phrases were directed at her, but she had no real reaction, not until she heard the woman telling Luke that the photos were a legitimate means of lifting the veil of secrecy that had so far protected people like *her*.

'Like me?' Honey said, looking the woman in the eye and seeing cold superiority. 'There's a veil protecting me? Really?'

'Honey, you don't have to–'

'Not any more there's not.' The woman said, smiling – *smiling!* – at Honey. 'My camera is my weapon and I will use it to expose you and your type.'

Honey laughed in a way that sounded kind of crazy even to her own ears. She felt Luke's grip on her arm tighten, and his hipbone stabbed her in the side she was held so close. What had been support was now bondage, and she was grateful for it because she was just about angry enough to tear the eyeballs right out of this smug bitch's head. 'Aren't you a bit late?' Honey said, loud and fast and with too much spit, 'For exposing me I mean?'

The woman frowned and took a step back. Honey tried to move

towards her, but was held fast by Luke. 'Where were you ten years ago when my step-daddy was fucking me every day after kinder-garten? Huh? Huh? Where was your fucking camera when my current father figure was stealing all my shit to sell for drug money and then shooting up his fucking crap in my bedroom? Where was your fucking camera then, you stupid bitch!'

Everything went black, but she hadn't fainted because she could hear perfectly well. She could hear Luke telling her she was okay and the woman screaming that she didn't have to listen to that kind of filth. She heard the argument that ensued when Malcolm, Aggie and Luke insisted that the policeman charge the woman and the woman and policeman insisting that no law had been broken. And she heard the sound of her own sobbing, a raw, ugly soggy noise that seemed as though it could never be stopped.

15

Luke managed to convince Aggie and Malcolm that the best thing was to get the girl away from all the drama. He took her across the road and asked Belinda to sit with her in the rec room while he waited in his office for Aggie. He waited impatiently, pacing and biting his nails, unsure what he would say to her when she arrived, but certain that having her close again would soothe him.

He had been horrified to look out and see the broken glass across the road. Violence of any kind distressed him, but the thought that something might have happened to Aggie was unbearable. What if she had been standing near the window when the brick hit? If she had been killed, she would have died thinking that Luke did not care enough to call her back after that terrible phone call, instead of knowing the truth, which was that he had not stopped thinking about her wanting him to kiss her all morning. But he had been terrified to speak to her while he was in such a state. How could he have explained his predicament in a reasonable way when his body hummed all over at the thought of her?

All that was trivial compared with the fact that had she been killed this morning, she would have been assigned to an eternity of torment and pain. God had called Luke to save her soul, and he had failed miserably at this task, because he was more concerned with his own selfish, twisted desires than with Aggie's eternal life. It was just as Belinda had tried to tell him: until Aggie is saved she is an object of pity and compassion. Oh, God, if she had died!

And now there was the problem of the girl. Problem or solution? Was the girl God's reminder that Aggie was, after all, a woman who contributed to the murder of babies for profit? A woman who exploited lost crying children, manipulated them into paying to have their bodies ripped open, their wombs robbed.

But Lord, he prayed to the oak outside his window, *Lord, she is a lost child herself. Should I feel compassion or disgust? Do I condemn her or embrace her? And if what you want, my Lord, is for me to lead her to you, why, oh why, oh why, must I be tormented with such passion? Don't you know I am your faithful servant and would do anything you ask of me? Must you test me so? Please, Lord, I beg you, take away the desire that clouds my judgement. Please, Lord, help me to know what is right.*

'Luke?'

He turned and sighed. She was in the room with him, dishevelled, red-eyed, pale. She sank into the chair behind his desk and he, without a word, sat across from her.

After a minute, she said: 'Where's the girl?'

'With Belinda. Are her parents coming?'

'No.'

'Did you call them?'

'That would be a breach of confidentiality.' Her voice was husky, her eyes puffy. Her hair was sticking up all over her head.

'She's a child.'

'She's sixteen– and she's not your concern.'

'Aggie, a troubled girl *is* my concern. Her defenceless baby is my concern.'

Aggie closed her eyes and sighed. 'Luke, please don't be difficult. I've had a really bad day.'

Luke hated to see her so ragged, hated to have to add to the wreck of her day, but there was so much at stake here. Jesus may have associated with criminals but he surely wouldn't have supplied them with their victims and told them to have a nice afternoon. He surely would never have condemned a child to death because he had feelings for its killer.

'I'm very sorry you've had a bad day, Aggie, I really am– but I'm not going to hand a girl over to you so you can assist in the murder of her child. We can talk this through and work out–'

'I didn't come here for a discussion. I told my client I would drive her home, and I intend to do so. If you interfere, I will call the police and then I will call a lawyer.' Her tone was restrained, but everything else about her was wild.

'Aggie, please–'

'No. Go and tell my client I'm here.'

Luke couldn't look at her. He stood and stared out the window. The oak had no answers for him. He looked, instead, at the sandy brick wall of his apartment. If he leant out of his office window, he could actually touch the wall with his fingertips, and sometimes when he was working late at night, he would contemplate crawling through the window, rather than making the long cold trek around the block to the door of his little home. Today, he looked through his bedroom window and saw the room as Aggie would see it: bare, grim, cold. He thought of her home with its burgundies and golds, its rich velvet curtains, tapestry-covered furniture and deep shag-pile carpets. Despite its luxury and colour it too was a cold place, too large for one person and filled with things loved by a dead man. The only warmth in Aggie's home emanated from the woman herself, and he wished he could now take her back to his own room and let her breathe some of her fire into it.

'Fine. I'll find her myself. Thanks for nothing.'

'Wait!' Luke turned from the window, forcing himself to hold her gaze, although her eyes caused him considerable distress. 'Don't be angry. It's too much, really. Your passion and fortitude in the face of... I find you distracting at the best of times, but when you're all... fiery, like this I can't keep track of anything. I just don't...' He did not know how to go on, and so shrugged pathetically and waited for her wrath or ridicule, unsure which would be worse.

Aggie stared at him for several endless seconds, during which his heart beat so hard he thought it would burst from his chest. 'Fuck.' She put her head in her hands and stayed that way for some time. Luke watched her, searching in vain for the right words. 'Fuck, fuck, fuck, fuck, fuck,' she said into her hands, and then looking up with red-rimmed eyes, she said it again, with extra emphasis.

'Stop saying that.' Luke needed to sit down or he would pass out. He sat on the floor, the wall supporting his jelly-like spine.

'Fuck you.'

'No, Aggie, fuck you.'

She gasped, putting a hand over her mouth. Luke had not said that word since the house mother had washed his twelve-year-old mouth out with hot soapy water, but he was past feeling shocked at himself. He was past feeling anything but confusion and need.

'Did you just say *fuck you*?' Aggie said in a low, awed voice.

'I'm sorry.'

She started to giggle and he looked up at her sharply, thinking she must be mocking him, but she met his eyes with warmth in her own. She came and sat beside him. The series of movements that resulted in her head being on his shoulder, his arm around her back, her hand on his knee, happened without his consciously deciding that they would.

'God, Luke, why the hell can't I accept the impossibility of this?'

He sighed with the pain of loving such an evil creature and the recognition that Jesus felt this same pain and kept on loving anyway.

His soul split open with grief for his beloved Jesus as he realised what it meant to carry the weight of love. The weight of Aggie's head on his shoulder was nothing compared with the weight of the cross on Christ's back, yet it was almost more than he could bear.

'I have to go.' Aggie's voice was heavy with disappointment. She did not get up, but her body stiffened as though she was preparing to go. Luke burned with wanting to do whatever it was she expected him to do. He wanted to do whatever it was that would make her not go away.

'Please try and understand. I can't be unequally yoked. I've turned it over in my head a million times, but I can't–'

'I'm going.' She lifted her hand from his knee, her head from his shoulder. 'I've had enough Christian shit thrown at me for one day.'

'I don't mean to throw anything at you. Just let me– Let me explain, please?'

She met his eyes, challenging, waiting. He knew what he said next might make her leave forever or it might– What? What was the alternative to leaving forever?

'I think of you as a very dear–' he started, then hearing the insincerity, changed tack. 'We all have our cross to bear, Aggie, and I always thought mine was my loneliness, but it turns out it's you. How I feel about you. Do you see?'

She stared at him, hard. 'Do you care about me, Luke?'

'Oh, Aggie! *Care*? I care so much, it's just that–'

'Every time you talk like this, it hurts me. Every time you talk as if I'm not good enough for you, as if I have some deep, moral flaw that stops you from – I love you, and I know you know that, and when you act as if my love is valueless, it hurts me.'

'No, no. Not valueless. Not that.'

'No a burden. A fucking *cross*. I have to go.'

'No! Look, I want to kiss you, Aggie. Okay? I really do, but– oh!'

Hot breath, dry lips, shock of a tongue forcing his lips apart, surprise at how wet and warm the inside of her mouth felt, kissing back without fear or awkwardness. If he had known it would be like this he would never have resisted for so long – would not have been able to resist for so long. After the initial glorious shock had worn off, he became aware of her hands. One was massaging the back of his head, the other tickling the side of his neck. His own hands had somehow ended up tangled in her incredible curls. The hand on his neck slid to his shoulder and he became aware that she was trying to end the kiss.

'Luke,' she whispered into his open mouth. He silenced her by forcing his tongue back in her mouth, ashamed and excited at the daring of it. Miraculously, she reciprocated, moaning softly, increasing the pressure on the back of his head, squeezing his shoulder hard. Then just as suddenly as it had all started, it stopped.

'Shit.' Aggie was back beside him, her head against the wall, her hands pressed between her knees. Luke noticed that her hair stuck right up at the back of her head where he had been tugging at it. He reached out and smoothed it down, which made her close her eyes and whisper 'shit' again.

'I thought it was nice, although I have nothing to compare it with.'

'It was nice.'

'So when you say shit–'

'I mean it was *really nice*.' She looked at him with narrowed eyes. 'When you say nothing to compare it with, you mean, not much?'

Luke brought her hands up to his mouth and kissed her knuckles. 'I mean nothing. No-one. Never.'

'Shit,' she said, 'So why–'

Luke kissed her again. He didn't know the answer to her question, whatever it was. He didn't care. He was appalled that he had gone without this for so long. If he'd known how lovely it was he would have started kissing her the moment he met her and not stopped all month.

Luke was a really good kisser. So good, that Aggie had trouble stopping, even though she knew she had responsibilities and obligations and work to do. So good, that although he hadn't touched her below the neck, she was more aroused than she'd been in her life. So good, that if she didn't know better, she would swear he was a professional kisser, practising his craft for twelve hours a day.

'I have to go,' she said, for the eleventh or twelfth time.

'Yes.' He drew back. Stared at her, red-faced and glassy eyed. Kissed her again, laughed and wiped his mouth with the back of his hand. 'We better get up.'

They stood, staring at each other. Aggie nodded toward the door. 'Ready to face the world.'

'Yes,' he said, but then grabbed her by the shoulders and kissed her some more. 'Sorry, I can't seem to stop,' he said, pushing her against the wall, then, 'Sorry,' as his tongue invaded her mouth again.

'Are you going to apologise every time you kiss me?'

He kissed her. 'Sorry,' he muttered, barely pausing before kissing her again. 'I really am very, very sorry about this.' His lips, his tongue, his bitter-sweet coffee breath, his hands in her hair, on her neck, on her shoulders, pressing her against the wall.

Aggie was coming apart in his hands. Whatever kept body and mind together was dissolving, so that when she was thinking *Stop I have to go— what is happening to me?* what came out of her mouth was 'I never knew I could want somebody this much.'

'Oh, Aggie!' He moaned and pressed his body hard against her, kissing behind her ear, sliding his hand from her shoulder to her left breast. 'I love you, my Aggie, my beautiful, incredible – oh, you feel so amazing, how can I–'

There was a sharp rap on the door. 'Luke, you in there?'

'Oh!' Luke jumped backwards with his hands held out as though they'd been burnt. He looked from the door to Aggie's breasts to his hands to Aggie's face. 'I didn't mean to–'

The door opened. Belinda and Honey stood staring at them.

Luke shook his head at Aggie. 'I'm so sorry.'

'What did you do?' Belinda said, sounding as though she knew the answer and was already preparing the sermon.

Luke didn't take his eyes off Aggie. She watched the eyes widen, then narrow, then close, as he realised that not only had he felt her breast, but he'd been two seconds away from being caught at it. 'I, ah...' He frowned at Aggie, clearly confused that she was not covering for him. He turned to Belinda and Honey with a smile. 'I swore. We were discussing the people who broke the window and I got so upset that I said something I shouldn't have.'

Relief washed over Belinda's face. She did not need to take him off the pedestal after all. Honey, on the other hand, was looking at Luke as though he had just told them he'd been abducted by little green men who'd performed experimental surgery on his brain. 'You *swore?*' she said, looking from Luke to Aggie to Luke. 'You're apologising to her because you swore?'

Luke nodded, shrugging at Belinda as if to show her that he knew he was just way out of control. Aggie felt like slapping his face. She met Honey's eyes. 'And I'm grateful for the apology. It's not as if I'm defending the people who did it, I think they're total bastards, but saying that they're motherfuckers who should be held down and anally raped with a red-hot crucifix – well, that's going a bit too far.' She turned back to Luke and smiled. 'So thanks for the apology.'

Luke looked as if he was about to throw-up. He smiled tightly, nodded at Belinda and walked very, very quickly out of the room. Aggie tried not to scream.

'Gosh, he must have been so angry!' Belinda shook her head. 'He'll torture himself over this. He'll probably fast for a week.' She turned to Aggie. 'He's very devout. Once he caught some kids from our group calling out insults to a little Muslim girl walking through the park. He went nuts at them. You could hear him yelling from across the street, then afterwards, when I reminded him about James 1:19, he—'

'James 1:19?'

'Sorry, Aggie, I forgot you don't know anything. James 1:19 tells us to be slow to anger. Something dear Luke forgot when he was scolding those boys.'

'Ha!' said Honey. 'Sounds like they deserved it. I would have kicked their arses for picking on a little girl.'

Belinda gave Honey a look which clearly said *Well you would wouldn't you, you baby-killing slut*, then looked at Aggie. 'So anyway, Luke felt so bad about being quick to anger that he didn't talk for a fortnight.'

'Remarkable.'

'That's our Luke.' Belinda beamed. 'So anyway, Honey is feeling a lot better. Unfortunately she is a bit blinded by all that pro-choice propaganda that you – that some people around here disseminate, but it isn't really my place to try and change her mind. Luke says that we aren't to interfere in what you – sorry, what the clinic over the street does, and so even though I really believe that what you – what *they* are—'

'Thanks, Belinda, that's very tolerant of you. Honey, ready?'

'Please.'

Aggie and Honey walked fast, pretending not to hear Belinda calling out to them to stay and have a cup of tea. 'How are you?'

Aggie asked when they were safely across the street.

'Fucked.'

'Sorry you got caught up in all this bullshit. I'm going to organise another appointment for you, and I'm going to pick you up at your house and drive you to the surgery myself, okay?'

'Thanks.' Honey was quiet until they were sitting in the car. Then she turned to Aggie with a sly smile. 'Luke's kinda hot.'

Aggie very carefully checked the position of her rear-view mirror. 'I suppose.'

'Nice guy too. I mean, for one of *them*.'

Aggie turned her attention to the side mirror. 'Sometimes.'

'I suppose he's already taken, though. Probably engaged to that Belinda chick.'

'Ha! She wishes.'

'You've got the hots for him.'

Aggie started the engine. 'Seat-belt please.'

Honey dutifully fastened her belt. 'Come on, Aggie, it's so obvious.'

'You better tell me where I'm going, because I have no idea.'

Honey gave her directions to what was the worst street, in the most violent housing estate, situated on the wrong side of the railway tracks that cut right through the roughest suburb in the district. Aggie didn't even want to *drive* through that area; it was a cause for despair that Honey had to live there. She had a rare feeling of gratitude for her own lot in life. Being born to a self-absorbed lesbian and an ugly, emotionally fragile old man was bad, but at least she'd never had to sleep in a room with iron bars on the windows.

'Give me your number and I'll call to let you know when the appointment is,' Aggie said in a voice bright enough to hide her horror at the house itself. Fibro, tin roof, with chipboard for windows. Not even bars. Chipboard. And grass so overgrown its blades could conceal bodies. The uprooted letterbox lay across the concrete driveway.

'It's nine– oh.' Honey looked out the window. 'The phone isn't working at the moment.'

'No problem. You can pop in and see me after school tomorrow and we'll sort it all out.'

The back of Honey's head moved up and down. Aggie could see in the side mirror that she was crying. Asking what was wrong would only make Honey hate her. What's wrong indeed! Where would she start?

'Is anyone else home right now?'

The blonde plait swung side to side.

'You live with your parents?'

Honey cleared her throat, but when she spoke, her voice was still thick with tears. 'Mum and her husband. Muzza. He's not my father. Thank Christ.'

'You don't like him?'

She snorted. 'He's a junkie. And a pig. Last year he went to jail for a couple of months. God, that was nice.'

Aggie wished her mind did not automatically go down the path of maximum horror, but her training and experience forced her there. 'Does he hurt you? Is that why he went to prison?'

'Nah.'

'He doesn't hurt you?'

'That's not why he got locked up.' Honey sniffed, pressed her forehead to the window, cleared her throat again. 'This is how stupid the man is. He reckoned a supposed friend of his, another dealer, had sold him some dodgy crack. So after he's finished yelling at me and mum about it, he grabs the crack and a steak knife and heads off down the TAB to confront his mate. Of course the manager at the TAB calls the cops, because there are these two stupid junkies swiping at each other with knives. And – duh! – not only are they both arrested for disturbing the peace or whatever, but Muzza – the idiot! – has a pocket full of crack. I've never met anyone so stupid.'

'It must be tough having to see your mum with someone so dumb. You must wonder why she married him.'

The girl shrugged. 'I don't care. She can do what she wants.'

Aggie knew she had pushed too hard. This was not a consultation room and they were not friends. Sometimes you had to give a little.

'You want to know why Luke was apologising to me?'

'Not for swearing?'

'Nope.'

'What then?'

'He grabbed my tits.'

'What?' Honey spun around, her thick plait whipping the window. Her cheeks were wet. 'Just out of the blue?'

'Well, he was kissing me at the time.'

'You!' Honey slapped Aggie's thigh. 'I knew there was something going on there. Sucked in Belinda. The whole time she was lecturing me about morals and her precious Luke was...' Honey gave a short laugh, and then the old haunted look returned to her eyes. 'I've never known a man who would apologise for that. Or for anything.'

'You're only sixteen. You haven't known that many men.'

'You'd be surprised.' Honey said, and Aggie found that she was not surprised at all. The girl was sixteen, bleached blonde, pregnant, living in Hellsville. Her name was *Honey* for christsake! Of course, she had known a lot of men. The girl was straight out of a fucking social welfare training manual. There was nothing about her wiggly walk, smart mouth or sad eyes that Aggie hadn't seen a thousand times. She wished she was not a social worker. She wished she didn't need this pain so much.

She had chosen social work out of loneliness As the shy, ugly daughter of a beauty queen and a financial wizard, Aggie had spent her early school years being tormented for her looks and money. By senior high school her classmates were too mature for teasing, so she was simply ignored. Rather than making her bitter and hateful, this treatment made her almost painfully empathetic. If she saw someone sitting alone in a restaurant her heart would almost break as she imagined their loneliness. Watching kids playing footy in the park she would find herself weeping for the boy who was told to *rack off*, and once she had sat in a bus shelter talking to an elderly man for several hours simply because he asked her to. Hearing *Eleanor Rigby* on the radio made her want to die.

Social work, she thought, would allow her to relieve her own terrible loneliness while she was helping other misfits and rejects to feel better about themselves. She saw herself working in schools and youth centres, dispensing advice on self-esteem and goal setting. She would end the suffering of the lonely and excluded, and in return, those lonely, excluded misfits would love and admire her. They would need her and want her around.

That was her plan on entering university. By the end of her course she had lost her mother to another woman and her father to suicide, been married and divorced and had two abortions. She was no longer lonely and sorry for herself; she was pissed off. She no longer gave a shit about poor little upper middle class princesses who felt victimised because their hair wasn't shiny and the boy they liked didn't ask them to the formal. She wanted to work with the real underprivileged, the invisible and forgotten: drug addicts, alcoholics, prostitutes, the homeless. She would not seek love or even friendship, but would instead dedicate herself to paying attention to those who would otherwise be ignored. If she met like-minded people, then great, but if she didn't – well, that was great too.

Ten years later, Aggie still loved her work, and it wasn't just because the battered and bruised women reminded her she was strong and whole. She loved the shy, careful boys who whispered into their sweaty hands; she loved the brash, cocky blokes, bursting with testosterone but naïve and terrified underneath it all; she loved the bright, colourful girls who were better educated and more confident than Aggie could dream of being but who still wanted someone to tell them they were acceptable. And she loved – *achingly* – the girls like Honey. Parentless, or close enough. Lonely, but defiantly so. Hungry for love but not so much that she'd give up her unknown future just so she could have a little person all her own.

'So I'll see you tomorrow?'

Honey smiled and looked ten years old. 'Can't wait,' she said.

16

For the first time ever, Luke could not pray. He didn't even try. Although his soul cried out for comfort he knew that to pray in the state he was in would be worse than useless – it would be an insult to God. *If I regard iniquity in my heart, the Lord will not hear.* Luke knew that meant him; his heart was as iniquitous as could be.

And to make everything much worse, his penis and testicles were in agony. For fifteen years he had resisted the urge to touch himself, but the pressure in his genitals was such that if he didn't get relief he would have to cut the darn things off. He needed something, anything, to quell the painful, urgent, drive in his loins, so he could concentrate on the duller but deeper ache in his heart. He needed to regain his focus. To stop licking his lips and shivering with the memory of how hers tasted. To stop feeling the surprising softness of her breast in his hand, or the firmness of her thigh against his own.

Oh Lord, why have you forsaken me?

He sought out the only person who could possibly understand. Greg was slouched in a bean bag watching a game show in the rec room, but he turned the volume down and sat up straight when Luke asked him for a word.

'Hey, Luke, listen, man, it was all Belinda's idea. We told her to leave it alone.'

'Leave what alone?'

'The thing about Aggie. Didn't Belinda talk to you?'

The cold hand of fear closed over Luke's hot-with-lust heart as he sat down across from Greg, 'Yes, she spoke to me. I didn't realise she'd spoken to everyone else first. I don't appreciate secret meetings behind my back, Greg. I have never been anything but welcoming to you guys when you want to talk.'

'I know, Luke, really, it wasn't like a secret meeting or anything. Belinda just asked us all if we had noticed that you seemed to be kind of hooked on Aggie, and we all said that just because you hang out a lot doesn't mean you're hooked on her.'

'I've been trying to witness to her. I'm called to save her.'

'That's what Leticia said. Exactly that. And Kenny said that we shouldn't even be talking about it. He said that no good comes of gossiping and guessing. And I, well, like I told you, man, I said just leave it alone: it's none of our business.'

The chill had spread; Luke's mind was horribly clear. He leant forward, keeping his voice low. 'Greg, if you saw that a member of our community was sliding into sin would you think it was none of your business? Would you turn your back and leave them to it?'

'Course I wouldn't, man, but–'

'But I'm different? I'm somehow less human, less prone to weakness and temptation? You think I am above sin, or am I below your concern?'

Greg held up his palms. 'Luke, man, come on. If I saw you losing your way I would totally call you on it, but I haven't seen that. I just seen you making friends with Aggie, who's a really nice lady, and if you–'

'I love her, Greg. I'm half-mad over her.'

'Oh.' Greg dropped his hands to his lap, and then sat looking at them for a while. Luke waited for him to speak. When he did, it was just to say 'Oh' again.

'Greg, what do I do?'

'Oh, man…' He shrugged. 'You should talk to Leticia, she's better at this stuff.'

'But you understand, right? You know about this craziness; you've explained it to me before, but I never understood. Leticia won't understand either; only someone who has suffered this way could know how it feels.'

Greg shook his head, his eyes wide. 'I don't know about love. Not a thing. I just know about the other. The non-love, remember? You told me that, Luke. That lust is the opposite of love. That using someone for your own pleasure is a form of violence, an expression of contempt. I was addicted to the sex, man, but I've never been in love.'

'Right.' Luke put his head in his hands. Lust is the opposite of love. He had said it a thousand times – lust being a great topic among teenagers – but now it seemed laughable. How arrogant he had been in his never-challenged celibacy. He could weep over the lack of compassion he had shown to all those kids struggling with this demon.

'Greg, I think I was wrong, maybe. I think–' Luke looked up. Greg was working a hole into the lino with the toe of his shoe. 'I think that maybe you can love a person and feel lust for them. Maybe the problem is in acting on that lust?'

Greg kept watching his foot grind into the lino.

'What do you think?'

'I don't–' Greg looked up at Luke miserably. 'You gotta pray about this one.'

'Yeah. I am, don't worry.' Luke forced a smile and stood up. 'Can we keep this between us?'

Greg looked relieved. 'Yeah, course.'

Luke headed for the door, but was stopped by Greg's hand on his shoulder. 'Ah, Luke? Just… ah, can I tell you something? It's sorta embarrassing.'

'You know you can tell me anything.'

'It's just… Sometimes my own– my feelings of lust come back and I… I want to pray about it but I feel too…'

'Too agitated?'

Greg nodded, his face turning pink. 'So anyway, I head to the park and I run and I run and I run until the only physical urge I have is for a hot shower and eight hours of sleep. *Then* I pray.' He bit his lip. 'I just wanted to let you know what was going on with me. You know, if you were wondering.'

Luke wanted to hug him, but patted his shoulder instead. 'Good for you,' he said. Then he went for a long, long run.

Afterwards, he forced his exhausted, guilt-ridden, conscience-torn self to attend a counselling session for the parents of a suicide. He had never actually met the parents, because they attended services at the church in Castle Hill, and the child who'd died had never attended youth group, but Pastor Riley had asked Luke to come along because of his expertise on youth issues. It wasn't until he was leaving the grieving family's home that he realised how useless – how cruel, even – it was to have a Youth Pastor talking about youth issues when he himself was the youngest person in the room.

Driving back through the wide, tree-lined avenues of Castle Hill, Luke could not get a grip on the fact that Jonathan Cranbourne, an eighteen-year-old computer science student with a passion for tennis and Coldplay, had shot the back out of his doted-upon head because he believed he could not be with the person he loved. And although Luke was certain that homosexuality was a terrible sin, and even though he was personally repulsed by the thought of two men being intimate with each other, he felt an affinity with the dead boy that was unprecedented in all his years of ministry.

By the time he got back to Koloona Street, it was almost midnight, but he could not imagine sleeping. He hadn't realised until he felt the warm relief flood over him at the sight of her ancient Datsun sitting alone in the lot that he had been hoping Aggie was still at work. Her day had been long and trying, too, he knew. It felt to him like many years since she had hung up on him and months since he had seen the front of her office shatter. But since he had kissed her no time at all had passed and never would. He would be kissing her for the rest of his life even if he never saw her again.

Was it the same for her, he wondered, or was it different for a person who had kissed the lips of many men? Was Aggie forever kissing her ex-husband or the men who followed him to her bed? Did this morning's kiss even mean what Luke thought it meant? Could it?

He drove past the entrance to the NYCC carpark and turned instead into the lot across the street. He parked next to her car in a space marked *Reserved for Staff* and sat for a moment to pray. *Lord, give me strength* he began, and then stopped because what he really meant was *Lord, give me Aggie. Forgive me*, he said, checking his hair in the mirror. *I have to know what it meant.*

Luke rang the night buzzer. There was a scuffling sound from inside, and then her voice came through, low and menacing. 'You're under surveillance by armed security guards who are less than a minute away, and I have a gun pointed at the door right where your head is. Now who are you and what do you want?'

Luke smiled at the intercom. 'You hate guns and have a barely adequate burglar alarm from K-Mart. But you do sound very tough, so I'm a little scared anyway.'

He heard her muttering profanities as she unlocked the three deadlocks he knew were on the inside, and then the door opened and she nodded, but did not smile, as he stepped inside. He helped her relock the door and then reached for her hands, but she snatched them away and held them out in front of her.

'You're pathetic, you know that? Acting like you were about to throw-up just because someone might have caught you kissing me. And what's with waiting until the middle of the night to come and—'

'I just spent six hours praying with a couple whose son killed himself.'

'Oh, Luke.' She dropped the keys and wrapped her arms around his neck. 'One of your kids?'

'No. That's the— I keep thinking that if he'd come to the centre, or if his parents had called me to come and talk to him—' Luke pressed his face into the side of her neck. 'But then, I don't know what I could've said anyway. Thinking that I would have made a difference is just a way to feel better about myself. To feel less useless.'

'We can't know what might have been. Don't torture yourself with it.'

'He was a— he was involved in a relationship with another boy. His parents found out and they—' Luke stopped, feeling Aggie's arms stiffen, her body move almost imperceptibly away. 'I prayed all night with them, Ag, but I was on automatic pilot. I told those people, those poor, heartbroken, decent people, that they were right, that they had done only as God would've had them do, and it's true, I think. I mean, if he had come to me, what could I have told him?'

Aggie stroked his hair, but her voice was icy. 'You would have told him, I'm sure, that you can't help who you love, and that in this violent, war-torn, hate-filled world, love in any and all of its forms is something to be cherished and celebrated.'

'I wouldn't have said that. It sounds good though. It sounds like it should be true— but it just isn't.'

'You break my heart, Luke. If you feel that way about—' Aggie sighed, her body deflating and folding itself into the creases of his own crumpled form.

Traps lay everywhere. To justify the sinful relationship of that poor boy because his own sin was, at heart, so similar, would be to fall into indulgence. To pretend that what Aggie said did not ring painfully true would be to become snared in hypocrisy. To pretend he did not share her passion would be dishonest; to pretend he understood it, even more so. Blaming her for seducing him and corrupting his pure love of Christ would be unforgivably cruel and self-righteous. His heart told him that logic had no place in this, that being with her was all the sense there was. But he knew that the human heart is deceitful above all things, and desperately corrupt.

'I have to get home, Aggie. I shouldn't have even–'

'Yes, you should have.' She kissed his forehead. 'You should always come to me. I always want to see you.'

'I don't understand that. I offend you. I make you sad.'

'True, but I'm tough and I love you.'

Luke knew she meant it. Even when he clumsily insulted her, confused her or angered her, she looked at him with those clear grey eyes and told him she loved him. She did not excuse him his faults, but she loved him anyway. And he had always thought that only God could love unconditionally.

Luke barely registered the shocking blasphemy of this thought, before he was shocking himself further by kissing Aggie with such force that she gasped and stumbled backwards. Daring himself to see how shocking he could actually be, he grabbed her hips and hoisted her on to the edge of the desk, stood between her knees, kissed her deeply while he unbuttoned her shirt, buried his face in her chest, pushed the cold blue satin of her bra out of the way so he could take her right nipple in his mouth, ran his hand along the outside of her thigh, accidentally bit her breast when she grabbed his buttocks, told her he loved her when she slid her hands around to his crotch, told her she was amazing when she stroked him through his trousers, told her he needed her when she unzipped him, moaned *YES* when she asked if he was okay with this, lifted his face and kissed her mouth while she slid her hand under the waistband of his underwear and then when her fingers closed around the top of his painfully hard penis he at last lost his nerve and shouted *NO* but by then it was too late.

'Oh!' Aggie held him tight. He would do himself an injury if he pulled away. Not to mention the mess. Horrifying as it was to be gushing into her hand, it would be much worse to move and have it spurting all over the place. He pressed his face into her shoulder. In a way he wished it would go on and on so he didn't have to face her, but of course, even the few seconds it actually lasted felt like hours and if it had gone on he would possibly have died from shame.

'Oh, sweetie, please don't cry. It's totally fine.' Aggie stroked his hair with one hand while her other held his pulsing disgrace. He hadn't realised that he was crying. He was doubly humiliated, having messed up her shoulder as well as her hand. He knew he should do something – move, apologise, clean himself up, blow his nose – but his limbs were numb and his vision unclear.

'It's okay. Just let me–' Aggie eased her hand out of his underwear. Coward that he was, Luke kept his face hidden, even when he realised that she was groping around behind her with one hand. 'I know there's a box of – aha! Always a box of tissues on a counsellor's desk.' Expertly, she wiped him clean and zipped up his pants, then with both hands, she lifted his head off her shoulder and looked into his face. 'I love you, you know that?'

'Yes.' Luke bent his head and sobbed into her still-bare, so-warm chest and wondered if this was what young Jonathan Cranbourne felt like before he shot himself in the head.

17

Honey went to school even though she was nauseous, her head throbbed and the left side of her face was mottled purple, black and blue. She went to school because the alternative was staying home and that would be just asking for Muzza to get to work on her right side. Besides, if she had missed school every time a parental figure decided she needed punishing, she never would have learnt to write her own name.

From the window of the bus she counted eight posters of herself on telegraph poles. There were probably more but she stopped looking after five minutes, instead resting her head on the seat in front and trying to stay calm. So she would miss classes after all. Maybe just the morning, since Steve would surely come with her and help pull all the posters down. Also, he would understand about the money. He would come up with some simple solution she was too dumb and too panicked to think of. He would not make everything worse.

Steve was waiting for her at the gate. He was short-sighted but refused to wear glasses on account of them looking faggy, and so she was almost level with him before he noticed her face. He squinted, scowled, spat off to the side. 'What happened to you?'

She ignored him, leaning against the fence and lighting a smoke. If he hadn't seen the posters then she still had the advantage of telling him the bad news in her own way. That meant reminding him he was a total bastard first, so he would be more likely to be gentle with her when she told him.

'You not talking to me?'

Honey turned around, leaning her elbows on the fence and blowing smoke into the teachers' car park.

Steve kicked the backpack at his feet. It skittled along the footpath a few centimetres, empty, Honey knew, of everything but smokes and a street car magazine or two. He shuffled along behind the bag until he was by her side. 'Your old man do that?'

'He's not my old man.'

'Right, so why'd you let him beat on you?'

Honey shrugged. Steve put his hands on her waist and kissed the back of her neck. 'I'll get the boys together, fuck him up real bad.'

'Just forget it.'

'He can't get away with beating up on my girl.'

'If I was your girl you would've come over last night.'

'You coulda come to Rex's.'

Honey turned and faced Steve. 'You expect me to come to Rex's when I've just had a fucking abortion?'

'Oh, man!' Steve slapped his forehead, then took hold of Honey's shoulders. 'I forgot, babe. I was so wasted last night. Shit! How'd it go?'

'It didn't.'

His grip on her shoulders tightened. He leant in so close she could see the white down between his eyebrows. His breath was minty as it always was at this time of morning, before the twenty cigarettes, six cans of coke, two serves of hot chips with barbecue sauce, six to twelve beers, three to six cones and one to five bourbons had turned it sour. 'You're still preggers?'

Honey tried to step away but he was too strong. When she moved, his nails dug deeper into her flesh and his face got closer. 'It wasn't my fault, Steve. There was this protester woman and I passed out and–'

'You'll go back today.'

'The thing is–'

'Now. You'll go now.'

'The money's gone. Muzza found it.'

Steve stared at her, his fraudulently sweet face unmoving. Honey did not breathe. She closed her eyes and waited. What difference does it make, she thought, if he hits me or not? If he hits me I'll have more bruises, and if he doesn't I will be indebted to him for his mercy. Hit me or don't. Love me or don't. Leave me or don't. I don't care. I don't care. I don't.

'You know, Honey, that money was very, very difficult to get. Rex nearly got his balls chewed off by a Rottweiler. And I cut myself on that fence, you remember? Blood everywhere. Fucking rusty it was, too. I coulda got tetanus or something.'

She opened her mouth to speak, but his mouth, cold and dry, pressed against her lips. 'Sssh.' He leant his forehead against hers. 'I can see you did your best to hang on to the money. You're lucky he bruised you like that or I might have doubted you.'

'I tried so hard to stop him, Stevo, I swear.'

'I believe you, babe. Some blokes wouldn't. Some blokes would think you were taking advantage. They might think you're pulling a scam on them. Five hundred bucks is a big deal, Honey, a really, big, fucking deal. But I know you're telling the truth and so I'm going to go easy on you.'

'Thank you.'

'But you're on your own now. You sort it out. You sort it out fast, or I'm gone. You understand, Honey? Gone like the fucking wind.'

'Yes.'

'Good girl.' His tongue went in her mouth, his nose smashed

against hers. She kissed him the way he expected her to even though the movement made her jaw ache and her lips sting. 'That's enough, babe, you're giving me a woody.' He stepped away, adjusted his shorts and picked up his backpack. 'I'd come with you but I'm expelled if I miss one more day.'

Honey nodded. He reached out and pinched her unbruised cheek. 'I promise I'll come see you tonight.' He pinched her again, winked and ran through the gate, just as the rollcall buzzer sounded. Honey watched him go, hating him more than she'd ever hated a person. Hating him so much that she almost wanted to have his baby.

When Honey got to the clinic she saw that the window had been replaced, and that the words *Arrange the murder of your children here* had been spray-painted across it. Honey wanted to throw her backpack at the window, or kick it hard with her lace-up boots. She wanted to smash those ugly words into a thousand red shards of glass. She wanted to slam her fists, her head, whatever, into the glass just to show them what she thought of their stupid lying words. But it wouldn't show the fuckers anything; it would just break Aggie's window again.

Just showing through under the red of the final *e* was a sign which told her the clinic did not open until ten on Thursdays. Honey decided to wait in the McDonald's down the road rather than the reserve across the street, because the reserve would put her in religious psycho territory and she really, really wasn't in the mood for that shit. She spent eighty cents of her ten-dollar life savings on an English muffin and sat picking at its edges, drinking the free ice water and hoping that Aggie had an idea of how she could get an abortion for $9.20.

'Honey?'

She looked up and then wished she hadn't. Luke from the Christian centre was walking towards her. His smile lasted half a second before morphing into a horrified grimace 'Honey!' he said again, sliding into the booth across from her. 'What happened?'

'Fell in the shower this morning. Hit the edge of the tub.' She had prepared the lie before school and it came easily.

'Fell?'

'Actually,' she said, leaning forward and lowering her voice, 'I fainted. The pregnancy, you know. Speaking of which, thanks for your help yesterday.'

He frowned deeply. 'I wish I'd been there to help you this morning.'

'Impossible. I'm not allowed to have boys in the shower with me. But I'm flattered really.'

Luke stared at her for a couple of seconds, stood up and walked away. Honey concentrated all her energy on tearing her English muffin into strips of equal width. She had managed three perfect muffin strips when Luke returned carrying a tray.

'Scrambled eggs. Sausage Muffin. Bacon Muffin. Hash browns. Coffee. Juice.' He pushed the tray toward her. 'I got two of everything so dig in.'

'What are you doing?'

He smiled at her over the top of his coffee. 'Buying you breakfast.'

'Why?'

'Because you need to eat.'

Honey pushed the tray away. 'I'm fine, thank you.'

'We both know you're not fine.' He uncovered a plate of scrambled eggs and placed it next to her shredded muffin. 'Your baby needs you to eat.'

'The *foetus* will be gone by the end of the day. No point wasting good food on it.'

A look of genuine pain passed over Luke's face. Honey stood. 'Anyway, I have to go.'

'Aggie won't be in for at least another hour. Why don't you wait here with me and then we can walk down together?'

'You're going to see Aggie?'

Luke nodded at his orange juice.

'You're knocked up too, huh?'

He looked up and smiled, but Honey could tell it was an effort. 'Wouldn't that be a scandal?' The light tone, too, seemed forced. Honey felt sad for him, but wasn't sure why. She sat down and was amazed that such a small thing made his whole demeanour change. He sat straighter and smiled widely. 'Eat up,' he said, in the irritatingly cheerful tone of yesterday.

Honey ignored the food. 'Did you see the graffiti?'

'I did. Incredible.'

'Incredible bastards.'

'I'm certain Aggie agrees with you.'

'You don't?' Honey was ready to bolt if he started lecturing her the way Belinda had yesterday. All that stuff about God saying he knew us before we were in the womb. All that rubbish about how God's laws hold more authority than men's. What about women's?, Honey had said, and Belinda had patted her head and laughed.

'Oh, I agree with you that destruction of property is an inappropriate means of protest, but—' Luke smiled, shrugged. 'I do agree with their sentiments and, honestly, I admire their tenacity. They must have been up all night, just waiting for the opportunity to—' He was smiling. Not really a happy smile, more a weird, creepy, serial-killer smile. Honey thought he looked like he'd been waiting up all night himself. Probably up all night muttering to himself and highlighting Bible passages about the end of days or some shit.

'You look wiped,' Honey said. 'Maybe you should go back and get some sleep before you see Aggie?'

His attention snapped back to her. He smiled in a normal, non-axe-murderer way. 'Actually, Honey, I'm sort of hiding up here.'

'From Belinda?'

'Among others. I usually eat breakfast in the kitchen with my staff, but this morning I felt the need for something stronger than tea and All-Bran.' Luke held up a hand while he ate a Bacon McMuffin. Three huge bites and it was gone. He wiped his mouth on a napkin and smiled. 'Sorry, I'm absolutely ravenous.' He picked up a hash brown and devoured it in two bites. 'Oh, how I miss grease. You know we don't even have oil to cook with? We have low-fat cooking spray.' He sucked his index finger. 'Oh, I love this greasy junky rubbish.'

Honey screwed up her nose. 'That's just because you never get to have it. If you were having it all the time, you'd crave apples and radishes or whatever. Like my boyfriend Steve eats nothing but fried crap, because he can't cook and there isn't anyone else to cook for him, and all he can afford is hot chips with sauce. One time I made him a salad and he just about blew his load he loved it so much.'

Luke smiled into his orange juice. 'Must have been a pretty great salad.'

'Not really it was just – oh, I shouldn't talk like that around you, should I? I should've said, he loved my salad so much he just about turned cartwheels.'

'You should talk to me the way you talk to anyone else. Being a Christian doesn't make me a prude, you know.'

'Really? But yesterday when you swore at Aggie, you were so sorry you had to race off and put on your hair shirt.' Honey's smirk hurt her face, so she stopped.

'You won't ever find me in a hair shirt. I don't believe that God wants us to flog ourselves for our mistakes. He just wants us to be sorry and to do everything in our power to avoid repeating them. He wants us to learn and grow and keep trying harder to be better.' He closed his eyes and it looked to Honey as if he was praying. Either that or he had fallen asleep sitting up. She felt awkward just sitting there, so she slurped loudly on her juice. His eyes snapped open. They were kind of glassy. 'Why do you want to have an abortion?'

His directness startled her. She shovelled a forkful of mushy eggs into her mouth and chewed them slowly while she thought of what to say. She hadn't really considered why. She'd just known from the moment the little blue line materialised on the stick that she had to get rid of the thing. No discussion, no conflicting emotions, no list of pros and cons. Pregnancy confirmation was like finding out she had some awful infection that was fatal if left alone, but completely curable if properly treated at the outset.

'Is someone making you do this, Honey?'

She shook her head, swallowing the eggs with difficulty. It felt like swallowing her own vomit, which it sort of was since it would surely come back up soon enough.

'You sure about that?'

'I've been through this with Aggie already. She's a counsellor, so she'd know if I wasn't telling the truth. Counsellors are trained to know when people are lying.'

Luke smiled. 'Maybe. But I don't need a social work degree – which I have by the way – to figure out that someone has been putting a heck of a lot of pressure on you about something.'

'You're a social worker?'

'No, I'm a pastor who happens to have a degree in social work. Did Steve hit you when he found out you were still pregnant?'

'No.' Ask me again tomorrow, Honey thought. If I don't work out a way to get five hundred bucks… She touched her face, the good, un-beaten side. She wasn't particularly vain, not like her mother who didn't even go to bed without an inch of make-up, but she did have a certain amount of pride in her face, and she liked it much better when it was not smashed up. She had to get the money together or Steve would break her nose, which would mean ugliness *and* pain.

'Because I've seen my fair share of bruises and yours look at least ten hours old. There are several points of impact, too. I just don't believe you fell over four or five times hitting a different part of your face each time.'

'You're a doctor too, huh?'

'You know, you could charge him for doing that to you. Being your boyfriend doesn't give him the right to hurt you.'

'Pay attention, will you? Steve did not hit me. Got it?'

'*Nobody* has the right to lay a finger on you. Your body is your own, Honey, and you should demand that other people respect that.'

'Yeah, yeah, yeah. Nobody has the right to touch me in a way that makes me feel uncomfortable or to hurt me physically in any way. If a stranger or family member touches me in a way I know is wrong I should tell a teacher, my minister or another trusted adult. Got the message when I was like, six, so you can lay off with the lecture.'

Luke pushed the tray to the end of the table and reached across to take Honey's hand. 'Maybe you didn't have a trusted adult to talk to when you were six.'

'And now I do. Saint Luke is going to save me and heal all my childhood wounds.' Honey's sarcasm sounded flat. She considered snatching her hands away. She considered telling him that she knew he touched Aggie's boobs and he wasn't as innocent as he made out, and that she thought he was weird and creepy for buying her breakfast and smiling like he had just killed someone and talking to her about private stuff and holding her hands, and that she would never join his stupid church if that was what he was after, because she thought God was a cruel bastard for making her suffer so much just for being born. She considered telling Luke that he could stop looking at her like that, because she hadn't come here for pity, or sympathy or any of that shit. She had come here to kill time until she could talk to Aggie and work out a way to have someone suck the parasite from her body, even though the abortion money, which had been originally stolen from the Ferris Street wrecking yard, had been stolen from her by a junkie cunt called Muzza who happened also to be her stepfather. She considered saying all this, while Luke held her hands and did not blink.

18

Before she had even pulled into her parking space, Aggie saw the red paint splattered across the newly-replaced clinic window. She had hoped, but not really believed, that yesterday's attack was a one-off, and here, splattered across the glass was confirmation of her fears. She leant against the bonnet of her car, staring at the graffiti, preparing herself mentally for the day ahead. There would be police reports, cleaning, arguments with Mal over security measures. And there would be cancelled appointments, frightened clients and the catastrophising of local reporters hungry for a story with teeth.

And it didn't matter, because somewhere in there, among the turpentine and hard-eyed policemen, somewhere between the stress headache and the unprofessional loss of temper, Luke would appear. He would bring peace – just a little. Happiness – just enough.

The same two young policemen from yesterday filled out the same yellow form, looked at the same piece of pavement, checked the same nearby garbage bins. They wanted to talk to Mal but he wasn't there when he should have been, and Aggie could not reach him on the phone. The cops exchanged glances. One of them asked if there had been any threats made against Mal, while the other began sifting through the papers on top of his desk.

'Like death threats or something? No, not that I– no.' Aggie laughed a little, to show how ridiculous the idea was. The cops did not laugh with her; they exchanged glances again, told her they'd be in touch if they got any leads, then, as they were leaving, the older man tapped the front window with his fingers and said, 'You might want to consider something bullet-proof. Either that or stay out of the way of the window. Just in case.'

She tried Mal again and swore filthily at his answering machine as though pretending she was angry would erase the fear. She couldn't keep still waiting for the graffiti remover to come. She felt like there was a big red dot in the middle of her forehead. Every backfiring car made her freeze, waiting for the heat of the bullet, the paralysis in her spine. Last year, Will had been robbed at gunpoint as he closed up the till at his restaurant down the road. For months afterwards he woke screaming in the night holding in the brains he was sure were spilling out the back of his head. Aggie understood that. By the time the cleaner arrived her shirt was damp with sweat, with imagined blood.

She locked up, asking the cleaner to tell Mal to call her mobile if he turned up before she came back. The bloke knew Mal, from back in the old days when the attached abortion clinic meant almost daily wall and window-scrubbing. He told Aggie he would be sure to pass on her message, and also to tell Mal that he shouldn't leave a lady alone in such a dangerous place. She smiled and waved off his comment, but as she crossed the road she felt exposed in a way she never had before. She would have liked someone beside her, even Mal who was shorter, slower and weaker than she.

Greg was on greeting duty at the centre. He stood when she entered the courtyard, placing his book on the bench beside him and taking both her hands in greeting.

'Aggie, good to see you,' he said. 'I saw what happened. Bummer, huh?'

'Yeah.' She reclaimed her hands. 'Is Luke in?'

'He's in a private counselling session. Some emergency, Belinda said.' Greg gestured to the bench. 'You can wait out here if you want.'

She sat down, hoping Luke's emergency would be over soon, hoping Mal would call. She glanced at the spine of Greg's book: *The Four Loves.*

'Any good?' she asked, to make conversation.

Greg picked up the book and smiled at it. 'Oh, yeah, it's awesome. Have you read any C.S. Lewis? His writings on Christianity?'

'Afraid not.'

'Oh, you'd like this one, really. It says this thing about—' Greg flicked through the book, squinting and furrowing his brow. 'Here: "Love anything and your heart will be wrung and possibly broken. If you want to make sure of keeping it intact you must give it to no one, not even an animal. Wrap it carefully round with hobbies and little luxuries; avoid all entanglements. Lock it up safe in the casket or coffin of your selfishness. But in that casket – safe, dark, motion-less, airless – it will change. It will not be broken; it will become unbreakable, impenetrable, irredeemable." Awesome, huh?'

'Actually, yeah.' Aggie smiled. 'It sounds like something my mother would say.'

'Cool. Is your mum a Christian?'

'Oh, no. She says all religion is a crutch.'

'What your mum doesn't limp?'

'My mother,' Aggie told Greg, 'not only doesn't limp, she doesn't even walk. She leaps, bounds, flies. She treks and hikes.'

'Cool. Maybe you can talk her into leading a hike for some of the kids.'

'Ha. As amusing as that would be, it's quite impossible. Mum's hard to get hold of. She moves around a lot.'

He nodded. So sincere. He was Aggie's age at least, maybe a few years older. His forehead bore a jagged scar and his nose had been broken more than once. His eyes, pale and watery, were those of a much older man. When he smiled, which was often, he reminded her of Kip and she could see in him what Luke could not: the addict, the player.

'You miss your mum?'

'Sometimes. I'm used to not having her around. She's never really been around.'

'And your dad?'

'He's not around either.'

Greg considered her a moment. 'No sisters or brothers?'

She shook her head. Sisters or brothers would have required her parents to have had sex, and her mother had made it quite clear that fucking her husband was a horror she would not put herself through again. Also, she had told Aggie, childbirth was like being torn open from arsehole to peehole to allow the escape of a squealing, stinking piglet which would spend the next three years squealing and stinking and the fifteen after that alternately sulking and chattering.

'Makes sense.' Greg smiled that knowing smile.

'What does?'

'You and Luke. You know he never had a friend outside of church before? Not since I've known him, anyway. I've seen him sit in a pool of vomit, just sit there all night, talking to a drunk until he was sober enough not to hurt himself. One time he sold every personal item he owned – from car to sports jacket – to raise money for Kosovan refugees. Nobody at the church would have known except a whole bunch of Kosovars turned up one day to thank him. Another time he... well, I could tell you a hundred stories, more than that even. But he's never had a friend who was just for him.'

Aggie closed her eyes, feeling the warmth of the winter sun on her bare arms, remembering his fevered skin, the hot surprise of his orgasm, his shuddering grief. Greg gave her too much credit. She was no friend to Luke: she would swallow him whole if he would stand still long enough.

'What about you, Greg? Do you have a friend just for you?'

'Sure.' She heard the smile in his voice. 'I have a couple who I still see. A couple who are happy to see me happy, who don't freak out about me being with Jesus now.'

'Do you have family?'

'I do, but… my mum's okay; she drinks a real lot, and so do my brothers. My dad…' He looked down at his hands, curved his fingers up over his palms to examine his nails. 'Last time I saw him he was begging in Pitt St Mall. I was a couple of months sober, full of forgiveness and all. I went right on over and said "Hey, Dad, it's been a while." And he just looked at me, and I thought, *well, it has been a long time*, so I said, "I'm Greg, Dad." And my Dad said…' Greg clenched his fists. '"Get the hell away from me." And so I did. Then he called me back and asked if I could spare a dollar. I gave him fifty and he said "Thanks, kid." And that was that.'

'That's harsh, Greg. I'm sorry.'

'It's cool. I have my heavenly father now.'

'You sound like Luke.' Aggie jumped at the shriek of her phone. 'Mal? Oh, thank Christ! You okay?'

His voice was high, shaky. 'Yeah. You?'

'Fine. Where are you?'

'Clinic.'

'See you in thirty seconds.' She hung up, already running towards the entrance. 'Duty calls. Thanks for the chat.' She didn't bother to ask Greg to tell Luke she'd come by; she knew he understood her. She knew he would let Luke know she had wanted him.

19

Luke had taken Honey into his office and listened to her cry and rant for an hour or so. He wasn't weird or creepy at all once you got to know him; he was actually really cool. Honey told him about Muzza and her mother, about Steve and Ricky and some other boys who she'd messed around with before. She told him about her dad, the Spanish dancer who had another family in Granada, but who wrote her long, funny letters at least every third month. She told him about how her grandmother secretly hated her for being half-Spanish, and that Steve sometimes called her a spic, even though she looked totally Anglo. She told him how confusing it was sometimes to feel unconnected from part of herself, and Luke understood, because his parents had abandoned him at a railway station when he was a tiny baby, and he didn't know *what* he was. Honey told him he looked a bit Arab and he told her how he'd been called everything from Lebanese to Indian to Aboriginal and he used to hate it, but then he realised the mystery of his racial heritage was a gift from God, allowing him to identify with all races and cultures. He found a sense of belonging through his place in God's forever family.

Then he said: 'Please don't kill that baby, Honey.'

'It's not a baby.' Honey picked up her school bag from his desk. 'It's a bunch of cells. I'm going now. I shouldn't have even come here.

I'm going right across the street and–'

'Honey, please just hear me out. I know you don't have the money to do it today anyway, and if you're so sure that you're doing the right thing then whatever I say will just be water off a duck's back, right? So humour me.'

Honey dropped her bag, crossed her arms and glared. 'Whatever.'

'Thankyou.' He smiled so sweetly that Honey found she could-n't not smile back. It gave her a nice feeling the way he looked so happy every time she agreed to talk to him. It was like she was doing him some big favour, making his day.

Luke scooted his chair across to a bookshelf and grabbed a pale blue book the size and thickness of a fashion magazine. He rolled back over, positioning himself on her side of the desk and opening the book in front of her. 'How pregnant are you?'

'Twelve, thirteen weeks.'

'Right, okay, great.' He flicked through the book and when he found what he was looking for he said 'Great,' again, and pointed at the page. 'See here, at only three weeks, your baby already had a heart, the beginning of a vertebrae, a closed circulatory system totally separate from yours and the beginning of lungs. And see, look at this! Wow! By four weeks, maybe before you knew he was there, his lungs were fully developed, and the heart started to beat on its own.'

Honey didn't say anything. She felt that he must be wrong, because abortion was legal and so the thing in her couldn't be an actual person yet. But the evidence was right in front of her. Scientific cross-sections of wombs and sketches of a tiny little baby with more bits every week.

'Okay, Honey, check this out. A twelve-week-old foetus has everything present that will be found in a fully-developed adult. Isn't that incredible? And look! The little fellow inside you is already wrig-gling his fingers around!' Luke looked up from the book and smiled;

his eyes were shiny. 'I bet you didn't realise your baby was so well developed.'

Honey stared at the picture. *Twelve Weeks* it said. There were the little nostrils, the stumpy fingers, the heart and tiny ribs. She touched her belly; it was as flat as ever. Was it possible all this growing had happened in there without her feeling it? Wouldn't you know if a whole spine was forming inside you? But she had known, hadn't she? That was the sickness, the tiredness, the woolly-headed dumbness. All her vitality being drained by the busy little person making itself a body.

Luke read on. In two weeks, the baby would be able to turn its head, curl its toes and open and close its mouth. A week after that, it would start to grow hair, and around the same time, a doctor would be able to tell her if she was having a son or a daughter.

'A son or a daughter,' Honey echoed, flicking through the remaining pages with rapidly increasing panic. She checked the cover. It said *Your Baby – A week by week guide by Dr. J. Mitchell*. 'This book is real? I mean, it's like a proper medical book?' Luke nodded.

She turned back to the start of the book and went over the stages from conception to today. The kid had done so much already, without any help from her at all. A new panic engulfed her. 'Luke, I haven't been taking care of it. I've been smoking and drinking. Shit, I smoked a heap of pot last week and I haven't been eating hardly at all. What if I hurt it?'

'Oh, Honey.' Luke put his arm around her. 'It'll be fine, I promise. I've known women who have had terrible car crashes, heroin addictions, thrown down staircases, all kinds of stuff and their babies have been fine. Yours will be too, I know it.'

'Steve will kill me when I tell him, and my mum will kick–'

'Honey, calm down.' Luke pressed her head into his neck. He smelt like fried eggs and coffee. He kissed the top of her head. 'I promise you that everything will be okay.'

'I'm so scared.'

He held her tight. 'You're not alone, Honey. I'm with you, in this, all the way. I'll stand by you both.'

On the walk home, Honey pulled down three posters from telegraph poles and six from bus shelters. She wasn't so angry with the people who'd made them anymore; she just didn't want false information spread around. She was too late though. Her mother and Muzza were waiting for her in her bedroom, a poster spread out on her bed. So they knew. It didn't matter now, anyway.

'You wanna explain this?' Her mother was still in her work uniform, a tight white t-shirt with *Nifty Nails* emblazoned in pink across the bust, and tight black pants. In one scarlet-taloned hand she held a can of Diet Pepsi; in the other was a cigarette which dropped ash on to the bedspread as she gestured at the poster. Muzza was in his uniform too: footy shorts and thongs. He didn't bother to speak, didn't bother to hide his delight. He lay back against Honey's pillows, smoking and fondling her mother's thigh.

'It's a mistake.' Honey went to her wardrobe and pulled down her sports bag from the top shelf. 'Now get out of my room.'

'This what that cash was for?'

'Yeah.' The smell of chlorine assaulted her as she opened the bag. She hadn't used the bag since the day three months ago when she'd won the 1500m at the district swimming carnival. She was supposed to go on to the regionals, but Steve said that all the girls at regional were ugly dykes, so she'd pretended to be sick when the day came. Honey had seen the picture of the winner in the local paper; she had shoulders like a wrestler and short spiky hair. Honey was bitterly jealous of the ugly dyke and had vowed never to listen to Steve again, but of course she had listened to him every day since. No more.

She began to pull her clothes off hangers and stuff them into the bag, every muscle tensed and ready for the blows that would surely come. She could hear her mother slurping her Pepsi, and both of them sucking back on their cigarettes.

'You goin' somewhere?' her mother said.

'Yeah.' She had never felt so lucky to have such a limited wardrobe. Clothes packed, she threw in her shoes: black heels, white sandals, sneakers. She was definitely running out of time, but she was determined to not leave a single thing for Muzza to hock or her mother to use. She carried the almost-full bag to her dresser.

'I'm getting sick of this, Honey. You come and go at all hours of the day and night. You hide money from us, get yourself knocked up, your ugly mug is stuck up all over the streets. You better tell me what the fuck is going on, and you better tell me fast.'

Into the bag went bras and undies, three lipsticks, deodorant stick, blush, foundation, powder, hair clips, scrunchies, tweezers, cleanser, moisturiser, nail polish, razor, pimple gel, sunscreen. There was no room for her collection of Cosmopolitan magazines, but she managed to squeeze her photo album and address book in.

Honey was on her knees, zipping the sports bag, when the first blow struck the back of her head. It wasn't even hard enough to knock her over. He was just warming up. She picked up the bag, stood and faced him. He was smiling. She looked past him and addressed her mother. 'I'm moving out.'

Her mother laughed. 'Oh, yeah? You gonna go live in that fucking caravan with Steve and his old man, heh? That'll be nice. You gonna bring your little sprog up in a fucking caravan park, Honey? Good luck to ya.'

Honey took a step to the side. Muzza stepped across with her. She met his eyes. 'I don't wanna be here, and you don't want me here. So get out of my way.'

'Leonie?' he said, without moving.

'Let her go, Muz. She'll come back when she remembers that Steve is a bigger cunt than you.'

Muzza smiled and stepped to the side, waving her past, theatrically. Then as she stepped through the doorway, he grabbed her by the neck and slammed her head into the door frame. 'Leave her, Muzza,' her mother said, in the same bored tone she always used. 'Fuck you,' he said, the way he always did. Honey did what she always did: closed her eyes, pressed her lips together and prayed he'd get bored before he did too much damage. But she had an extra thought this time: *Please don't let him hurt the baby.*

Muzza released her neck and pushed her out into the front hallway. 'Fuck off then, you dumb slut.' Honey stared at him for a few seconds, barely believing that she was free. 'Well? What are you waiting for? Fuck off!' Honey turned and fled, feeling blissfully light despite the bag containing her entire life thumping against her legs as she ran.

20

God surprised, always. Just as Luke was certain his sin was too enormous to allow him to continue as a minister of God, Honey and her precious baby appeared, needing Luke to do what he had always done. Needing him to forget his personal torment and become once more, Jesus' hands and voice on earth. The baby's life was safe, and although the girl had hard times ahead of her, she had been spared the eternal torment which is the fate of unrepentant murders. Luke's calling had not been revoked; God worked through him, still.

This was not to say he had been let off the hook. Although his mind was eased in regards to knowing God's will for his future in the ministry, the enormity of what he had done – of what it meant! – had him in anguish. The honest truth, which could not be hidden from God, was that last night, in the midst of his shame, he had felt bliss. His despair at the thought of never again experiencing such ecstasy manifested itself as a gnawing pain in his stomach and a tightness in his chest. He asked himself what it meant to deny a drive that was more intense than hunger, more insistent than thirst, stronger even than his calling to the ministry. What did it mean to deprive himself of an experience that made him feel more connected to God's creation than any other?

There was a knock on his door and Belinda entered. He was

about to ask her, yet again, why she bothered knocking when she never waited for a reply, when he noticed that Honey was standing behind her. The sight of them brought back the memory of yesterday, when their arrival had interrupted his first passionate encounter with Aggie. He felt the weight of her breast in his hand, like an amputee feels his legs. He wondered if her phantom flesh would haunt him forever. It was surprising how substantial absence could be.

'Hello, Honey.' He pressed his empty hands together. 'It's nice to see you back so soon.'

'You'll be sick of the sight of me,' she said, stepping into the room, a bulging bag in each hand. 'What's this, three times in two days?'

Luke's heart felt like it would burst with love. God was indeed great! Three times, Honey had appeared before him, just as the angel of the Lord appeared before Balaam three times and caused his donkey to change direction. As Balaam had been saved from stubbornly taking the wrong path, so too had Luke been gifted with an unlikely angel of his own.

'I was hoping,' Honey said, 'that you might help me find a place to stay? Somewhere safe for me and the baby?'

Luke almost wept. 'You'll stay here.'

'Oh, no, I couldn't. I just thought you might know of, like, a shelter or something, for until I can get a job?'

'*Come to me, all you who are weary and burdened, and I will give you rest. Take my yoke upon you and learn from me, for I am gentle and humble in heart, and you will find rest for your souls. For my yoke is easy and my burden is light.*'

'Huh?'

'Let me take care of you, Honey. Let us all take care of you, in His name.'

'In His name,' Belinda echoed.

'You're serious?'

Luke nodded, taking her bag.

'I don't know why you're being so nice to me, but thank you.' Honey's voice broke a little at the end.

'Thank *you*, Honey,' Luke said 'And thank our saviour Jesus Christ.'

'Amen,' said Belinda.

Honey shrugged and smiled. 'Amen.'

21

al was waiting in the office, pacing in front of the freshly replaced and scrubbed window; his eyes and nose were red. He didn't answer Aggie's enquiry about what had happened, just thrust a sheet of paper into her hand. Her heart skipped a beat as she took it in. It was like the poster that crazy bitch had presented to Honey yesterday, except the photo was of Malcolm and the text read '*Do you know this man? Maybe you've passed him in the hallway or on the street. But did you know he makes his living slaughtering babies and peddling pornography at the Parramatta Free Sexual Health Clinic on Koloona Street??? Help us obtain JUSTICE FOR THE UNBORN. Do not let Malcolm Addison of 7/19 Rosebud Place live in peace while thousands of babies are destroyed at his hands.*'

'Every telegraph pole in the street, every wall and door of my building. We stopped answering the phone at about seven this morning. The police want the answering machine tapes, because of the death threats. We had a police escort out of the building.'

Aggie stared at the poster. It was a terrible photo of Malcolm, taken yesterday during the stoush outside. His face was screwed up tightly, except for his mouth which was open in rage. So even then, when Honey was fainting and Luke was arguing and Malcolm was yelling, the fuckers were lurking around with cameras. They were probably *always* lurking around, waiting to take their next shot. Aggie thought of the clients she had seen yesterday afternoon: a thirteen-year-old needing a pregnancy test, a thirty-seven-year-old father of three addicted to prostitutes, one teenager and one twenty-something needing abortion referrals, and the usual stream of kids picking up free condoms, lube and dental dams. How many of them would wake up tomorrow and see their faces beaming back at them from a bus shelter or telegraph pole?

'How's Will?'

Malcolm pressed his lips together, shrugged and looked over Aggie's head. 'He was pretty freaked out. It's not his choice, you know, to be part of... not everyone wants to be a martyr. He's going to stay with friends for a while. He, uh, he needs some space from—from all this.'

'And you?'

He shrugged again, looking lost and lonely and afraid. All of which were strange expressions on an overly large, bad-tempered fifty-year-old bloke.

'Mal,' Aggie said, taking his hand and squeezing it, 'we can't let these fuckers get the best of us. We'll step up security, maybe get a guard to stand outside looking scary, but apart from that, business as usual, right? We're not going to let them win.'

Malcolm sighed. 'I knew you'd say that.'

'You don't agree?'

'Sure, just— it would be a lot easier to shut up shop, go back into substance abuse or homeless advocacy.'

'It would be easier. That's why there aren't many of us left doing this. Everyone's doing the easy thing. But this is worth doing, Mal. Look at that young girl yesterday, Honey. She was so lost and confused. Where would she go if not here? Who would help her?'

Malcolm smiled tiredly. 'You're channelling your mother now, Ag. But I get it – you're right. We'll fight on. How'd it go with that poor kid anyway?'

'I got her home safely. She's coming in this afternoon to sort things out.'

'I was afraid we'd never see her again after handing her to the fundies. I thought they might have stashed her away in some brain-washing chamber and refused to release her until her soul was saved.'

'Ah, well, they tried to, but I fought dirty and won her back.' Aggie felt the heat spreading through her chest, up her throat onto her face.

'Good, good.' Malcolm nodded, staring over her head at the back wall.

'I said, I fought dirty.'

'I said good.'

Aggie slapped Malcolm's thigh. 'Mal! Pay attention! I'm saying *things got dirty*. Me, Luke, a month's worth of simmering passion.'

Mal raised his eyebrows. 'Go on.'

Aggie told him everything that had happened yesterday. She hesitated slightly before divulging the full details of the encounter on her desk, but decided that Malcolm could do with some smut on a day like today.

'Aggie!' Malcolm jumped to his feet. 'Here, on this desk?'

'Right about where you were sitting actually.'

'Ugh! Excuse me while I go and bathe in disinfectant.'

'Mal, seriously, I'm so rapt in this guy I can't think straight. I know it won't be easy, but—'

The phone rang. It could be Luke or a psycho. It could be love or death threats. Her hand shook as she lifted the receiver.

'It's me,' Luke said before she'd gotten out a word.

'Hi, you.' Her insides were instantly squishy at the sound of his voice. 'Busy morning, huh?'

'Yes. Ah, can I see you?'

'Of course. I thought tonight we could—'

'No. Now.'

'I don't really have time right now. Those protesters who—'

'It won't take long.'

The squishiness in her gut turned to nausea. 'What won't take long?'

Luke took a loud, ominous breath. 'Can you just come over here?'

'No, tell me now. What?'

Silence.

'Luke? Sweetheart, please I—'

'I can't see you any more. Not at all.'

Aggie closed her eyes. 'What?'

'I'm sorry.'

'Luke, please—'

'God bless you, Aggie.'

God bless you, Aggie. It couldn't be goodbye. Impossible. They were in love. He had admitted as much. He had given himself to her in a way no man ever had before. It couldn't be the end. They had barely started. What did he mean he couldn't see her any more? That was nonsense. They would spend long hours kissing until their faces ached and talking until they went hoarse. Of course, they would see each other! Probably they would even live together. That's what people did when they loved each other. He was freaked out, was all. He was flipping out. When she got the feeling back in her legs, she would go over there and make him see sense. Make him see *her.* And if that snotty, stuck-up, husband-hungry Belinda tried to stop her, Aggie would punch her so hard she wouldn't wake up for a week. Then she would take Luke home with her and she would talk to him. She would show him pictures: mass graves in Bosnia, Cambodia, Rwanda; piles of clean-shaven skeletal corpses at Auschwitz and Dachau; the ripped apart bodies of black men destroyed by white, and gay men killed by straight. She would make Luke look at stuff like that, stuff that made her chest hurt just to think about, and he would see that there wasn't any – couldn't be any – God. She would make him see that the love they felt for each other was the closest to sacred a person could get. She would take up the cross for him. He could drive nails through her and she would forgive him anything.

'Aggie, damn it. Get over here.'

Aggie managed to bring Malcolm into focus. He was very pale and breathing hard. 'Look,' he said.

Aggie looked out the window she had spent yesterday getting replaced and today cleaning. A white van was parked in front of the clinic and on its side was a billboard-sized poster of a dismembered foetus. On the footpath between the van and the clinic stood a man with a megaphone, a girl of about fifteen holding a stack of pamphlets and two women holding placards of babies' skulls on sticks.

Aggie looked straight past them to the figure watching from across the road. Orange shirt, blue jeans, brown hand massaging smooth forehead and brushing aside dark curls. Aggie lifted a hand; he turned and went inside, closing the door behind him.

'Right,' Aggie took a deep breath, squared her shoulders. 'Right.' She inhaled deeply. 'Right then.'

Mal put his hand on her shoulder. 'Are you okay?'

She nodded, zooming in on the man with the megaphone. The minute he opened his mouth, Aggie would be all over him. It looked as if he was getting ready to start, tucking a handkerchief into his pocket, checking some little detail with one of the women, nodding and passing the information on to the young girl. Aggie couldn't wait. The fuckers had really picked the best possible day for it.

'Citizens of Parramatta, be warned,' boomed the man.

'Mal, call the police. Tell them there's a fight.'

'What are—?'

'Call them now.'

22

Luke had just got off the phone from Pastor Riley when Greg came and told him that the protest across the street had been on the Six o'clock News. A man had been treated at the scene for a bloody nose and split lip. An unnamed female employee of the clinic had been arrested over the assault.

Greg cracked his knuckles. 'Does that mean Aggie?'

'I assume so.'

'Gosh. Have you talked to her?'

'No.' Luke pressed his fingernails into the tops of his thighs.

'They haven't locked her up, surely? '

Luke had been thinking the same thing. He shrugged.

'I don't reckon they would.' Greg cracked his knuckles again. 'I broke a bloke's nose in a pub brawl once, and they never put me in a cell. They just took prints and got me to sign something and told me to get lost. I expect that's what they'll do with Aggie.'

Luke did not acknowledge the relief that washed over him. He continued gouging holes into his own legs. 'Yes,' he said.

'So, ah…' Greg rocked back and forth on his heels.

'Yes?'

'Are you, um… are you going to see if she's okay?'

'I'm sure she's fine.'

'But–'

'Greg, sit down a minute.'

Greg frowned and bit his lip. He sat across from Luke and cracked his knuckles three times in quick succession. 'What's up?'

'I just talked to Pastor Riley. He's given us the go-ahead to use the Caring for Our Community fund to support Honey through her pregnancy. Sixteen is the age of legal emancipation so we don't need parental permission, but we do need to get some kind of contract drawn up, saying she's under no obligation except to abide by the rules and principles of the NCYC for so long as she is staying here, and outlining what we agree to be financially responsible for. I want you to work with Kenny on this. Get it to me by twelve tomorrow so I can run it by legal and have the whole arrangement finalised by tomorrow afternoon. Okay?'

Greg stared.

'Problem, Greg?'

'Nah, nah.' He shook his head. 'No problem. Consider it done.'

'Thank you.'

Greg stood slowly. 'Anything else?'

'That's it – thanks.'

'Right.' Greg nodded and headed for the door. When he got there, he turned, screwed up his face and cracked his knuckles. 'Ah, Luke?'

Luke pretended to be already absorbed in something on his desk. 'Mmm?'

'Do you think Aggie–?'

'Agatha Grey is no longer welcome here. Tell the others. No phone calls, no visits.'

'But–'

'Get to work on that contract, please.'

Greg left the room. Luke was pleased with how he had handled it all. His self-control was exemplary. Everything was back to normal.

Everything would be okay.

He went to the window and looking out at his favourite oak tree, he prayed: *Dear Lord, Thank you for giving me the strength to turn away from the one who caused me to sin against you. Thank you for sending Honey and her precious child and allowing me the honour and privilege of introducing two more souls to your glorious Kingdom. I thank you for all you have given me in my life, and because I know you are great and good and endlessly generous, I dare to ask you for still more.*

I ask that you lift the blindness which your enemy has inflicted upon Aggie. I ask that you create in her a hunger for your Word. I ask that you send your strongest labourers to her, so that she receives the Gospel from those who are not at risk of being drawn into sin, and are not at risk of contributing further to her sinfulness. And I pray, dear Lord, that you provide her with the armour to repel all attacks on her by your enemies and by those here on earth who would harm her. I ask you to protect her from those who would end her life before she has given it to you. I ask you to keep her safe until her eternal life is ensured. Dear Lord, I pray these things, knowing that you have a plan greater than I can conceive, and trusting that you will, in your way, in your time, ensure the salvation of Aggie Grey and therefore her place in your Kingdom. Amen.

Luke explained to Honey that she would have to study the bible at least two hours a day, take part in all age- and gender-appropriate NCYC activities and contribute to the household chores along with the live-in staff. When she felt ready, she would dedicate her soul to the Lord Jesus Christ in a private ceremony, and give her testimony in front of the Christian Revolution Church in the city.

'What if I never feel ready?'

'I believe you will. God has brought you here for a reason; I don't think he'll let you leave again without opening your heart to him fully.'

Honey nodded, as if that made sense. She figured she'd be doing that a lot around here, but that was a small price to pay. Free room and board, fully paid pre-natal care, the option to train as a Junior Pastor after the baby was born. It was a sweet deal and if the price was having to pretend to be a Christian, it was worth it.

'And, Honey,' Luke went on, 'it is very important that you don't have any contact with the father of your baby, at least until after the birth. I'm going to see about getting approval to home school you. How does that sound?'

'Fine with me. Steve'll probably hold me down and kick me in the stomach if he knows I'm still knocked up. I think it's better he doesn't know I'm here. Or my mum. I don't want her to know either.'

Luke smiled at that. 'I don't have any problem with that at all. Completely removing yourself from the people and situations which led you to where you are today is the only way you'll be able to move forward. This is your home now, and we are your family. All of us. From now on, no-one is going to beat you or assault you or seduce you. No-one is going to manipulate you into doing something you don't want. You're safe, and so is your little one. Okay?'

Honey nodded again. She did not feel at home and she did not see how a bunch of people she didn't know could be considered her family, but she did believe him about the rest of it. She didn't have to worry about anything now that she had Luke to take care of her. She and her baby would be safe here, with him.

The answering machine message light was blinking when Aggie got home from the cop shop just after midnight. The promise of it paralysed her. She showered and washed her hair and dressed in clean pyjamas and made a cup of tea and two slices of vegemite toast and ate them and washed the plate and cup, all the while seeing the flashing red light in her mind. She went to the machine, staring at it as though it could possibly give her a clue. If it wasn't him…

Her hand shot out and slammed down the play button, before her mind could turn over the implications for the thousandth time. The crackling of a bad connection filled the silent house. She thought of Luke's mobile phone – orange, with yellow sunbursts and a *Jesus Loves Me* ring tone – and imagined his face scrunching up with concern as he realised she was not at home.

'Aggie, darling girl, it's Carrie. I called you at the office and Malcolm told me there'd been some terribly dramatic scene involving dead babies and megaphones and swinging fists and ending in you being carted off in chains. Malcolm said you were fabulous and I believe him and he said I was not to worry about you and so I won't. Rosa and I just got into the country. We're in Alice Springs, which is why I was calling in the first place, because we're heading into the interior and Goddess only knows when we'll emerge. Anyway darling, stay strong and I'll call you when I return to civilisation.'

The machine beeped. The light had stopped flickering. It was dark and silent and cold. 'Love you, Mum,' Aggie whispered. 'Love you, Dad.' She pressed her head to the wall. 'Love you, Luke.' She went to bed.

PART TWO

23

Honey changed everything. Where before meal times had been nothing but staff meetings with food added, now they were opportunities to listen to Honey talk about whatever it was that happened to be annoying her or entertaining her at that particular moment. At Monday breakfast she had them all in hysterics with her recounting of stupid things her stepfather had done; Thursday lunch she had Leticia and Luke in tears when she casually announced that she had never actually sat down at a table to eat a meal before she lived here. On Saturday night she had turned the radio to some pop station and danced around the table, infecting them with her vivacity until all except Luke put down their cutlery and joined her, turning the kitchen into a nightclub. Luke watched, happy, so very, very happy that the Lord had sent them this miracle. He watched and thought *Thank you* – but he also thought *I miss her so much*.

Luke rewrote the staff roster so someone was always available to supervise Honey's schoolwork, and he asked Leticia to talk to Honey about her personal needs so they could come up with a pregnancy care plan.

'She and I read some pregnancy books together, worked out what she'd need. I've made an appointment with an obstetrician and booked her into pre-natal classes, but that's all I can do, Luke.' Leticia handed him a sheet of paper with a bunch of dates and addresses. 'She

wants you to go with her to the doctor and the classes and everything.'

'Really? That's odd. I thought she'd want a woman with her.'
Luke showed his surprise, but not his gratification.

Leticia shrugged. 'You saved her. You're her hero.'

'Nonsense. It's just that she knows me the best,' Luke said, but
when he went to the girl to double-check that he was the one she
wanted with her at the doctor she set him straight.

'You promised you'd take care of me.'

'And I will, I just assumed a woman would be—'

Honey's eyes filled with tears. 'I knew you didn't really want me
here. I'm just another good deed for you to impress God with then
pass on to someone else to take care of.'

Luke was alarmed at her quick tears, her sensitivity. Hormones,
he thought, stroking her hair and reassuring her that, of course, he
wanted her here, and of course he would go to the doctor with her.
He would have to read up on all this: the mood swings, neediness.
He looked forward to it; it was something else to be busy with, something else to stop him thinking about *her*.

Honey sat at the window of her room pretending to read her student
bible, but really watching the back entrance of the main building. The
routine was the same every day. Luke was always first up, striding
across the lawn whistling or singing in that goofy way that made you
forget he was totally hot. Then Kenny would jog out of his apartment
and head off down the slope, out of Honey's sight, returning to his
room exactly forty-seven minutes later, then re-emerging, shaking his
wet hair, nine minutes after that. Belinda usually went in to breakfast
not long after Kenny left for his run, and Leticia soon after he
returned. Greg was always last. His cabin was right next to Honey's

and he always tapped on her glass and smiled when he passed. Most days he still looked half-asleep, his hair all ruffled and sleep crusting up the corners of his eyes.

Once they were all inside, Honey put on her shoes and coat, slipped a cigarette and lighter into her pocket and crept out of her cabin. Then she ducked around the back, leant against the wall and lit up. It was blissful. She knew it wasn't good for the kid, but… oh, it was nice to stand out in the crisp early morning air and suck that soothing smoke down into her lungs. Anyway, she hardly smoked at all. Just this one before breakfast and another before bed. How much harm could two little cigarettes a day do? Honey's mother had smoked the whole time she was pregnant and Honey had turned out okay.

She finished her cigarette, squatting down to grind it out into the concrete at the base of the wall, and then buried the butt under the bark of the border garden. She remembered how a couple of years ago when her mother and Muzza had first got together, she'd been sent to stay at her grandma's in Auburn for two weeks so the happy couple could have some 'grown-up time'. Honey used to smoke behind the house and throw the cigarette butts into her grandma's orchid garden. One morning, grandma went to water her orchids, saw the butts and blamed it on the black kid next door. Honey, sick to death of her grandma's Hansonist rants, pointed out that the butts were stained with red lipstick. Grandma screwed up her face, marched next door and accused the poor kid of being a cigarette-flicking-orchid-killing-black-bastard-transvestite. After that, Honey made sure to bury the butts carefully.

She stood again, ready to face her morning bowl of All-Bran with calcium-enriched milk, and looked right into the sleepy eyes of Greg.

'I thought you stopped smoking.'

'I did.' Honey met his raised eyebrows with a smile and a guilty show of hands. 'Well, almost totally. Don't tell Luke?'

Greg bit his lip. 'Honey, you're asking me to lie.'

'No, not a lie. Just don't volunteer the information. For his sake.'

'For Luke's sake?'

'Yeah. You know what he's like about this baby. He worries so much.'

Greg lowered his head and mumbled something into his turtle-neck.

'What?'

He looked up and cleared his throat. 'He's not the only one who worries.' He cleared his throat again. His cheeks had gone red. '*I* worry about you, Honey.'

Honey felt rotten. Greg was such a sweetie. Since the day she'd moved in he couldn't do enough for her, always making her cups of tea and offering to help her with her schoolwork or with her Bible study. She hadn't appreciated him, really; she had just sort of thought he did those things because Luke told him to, but maybe he did them because he was a good bloke.

'Um, thanks, for, you know, worrying and being nice and stuff.'

Greg turned redder and mumbled into his sweater again.

'Okay, so, ah, we better go in, heh?'

'Yeah, um…' Greg bit his lip and rocked back onto his heels.

'Look, if you feel you have to tell–'

'Nah, it's not that. Just, ah, I actually came out here looking for you. I wanted to…' He swallowed three times, hard. 'I can hear you crying at night.'

'Oh.'

'Not that I listen in– just that our cabins are so close, if the window's open…' He patted her shoulder. 'What's wrong?'

'Apart from being alone and pregnant at sixteen, you mean?'

Greg frowned. 'You're not alone.'

'Yeah, I know. I have you and Luke and everyone. I just meant… I'm alone with the baby. At night, it's just me and the kid.'

'And Jesus.'

'Oh, yeah, of course.' Honey smiled reassuringly. Greg was very old – at least thirty – but he seemed kind of childlike. She felt that he needed her to believe in God even more than Luke did. At least with Luke you could ask questions or tell him he was full of it, and he would come right back at you with answers or explanations or questions of his own. But if she told Greg that she doubted more than she believed, and that no matter how hard she studied the special Bible or how sincerely she prayed, she did not hear God speaking to her, she felt it would really hurt him.

'Honey, if you, ah–' He cleared his throat three times. 'If you need someone to talk to, I mean, apart from Jesus, I, ah, I'd be happy to listen.'

'Thanks, really.' She squeezed his arm to show she meant it. 'Let's go eat, hey?'

In the kitchen, Luke was telling everybody about an idea he had to start a support group for pregnant teenagers. Honey already knew all about it because he'd got the idea after he went with her to the obstetrician the day before.

The receptionist had been all snooty to Honey, shaking her head and muttering under her breath when she read Honey's age off the form. Then in the waiting room, two women about Luke's age had a really loud conversation about how disgraceful it was that teenage girls got themselves into trouble and expected taxpayers to support them. Luke told them that he, not the government, was supporting Honey, but that made it worse. 'The Arabs like them young so they're easier to control,' one informed the other.

Doctor Lovell was actually quite nice, but he didn't seem to believe that Luke was not the father. When Luke insisted on leaving the room during the internal examination, the doctor laughed and told him they wouldn't be there if Luke had been so shy in the first place. For a second Honey thought she might see the legendary suppressed anger that Belinda had told her about, but Luke took several deep breaths, patted Honey on the head and walked out of the room.

Honey was glad he had left. An internal examination was not something you wanted an audience for. The doctor told Honey to relax. She closed her eyes and remembered all the hands that had touched her where the doctor was touching her; she started with Steve and worked backwards to her first stepfather. That had been the only time she'd felt actual pain; after that, it was all like this, lying back and waiting for it to be over. Then when he was finished, she smiled and said she was fine, so that was just like all the other times too.

Luke came back in for the ultrasound. The sonographer asked him if they wanted to know the sex of the baby. Honey said 'yes' and at exactly the same time, Luke said 'no' and they all laughed. 'Dad says no,' Dr Lovell said, and that made Luke turn really red. 'No, I'm sorry. It's up to Honey. It's her baby.' Dr Lovell shook his head at the sonographer and frowned, as if he was annoyed at Luke for saying that. 'Tell me, please,' Honey insisted, and the doctor shrugged and said she was going to have a son.

A son. That was bad. A little boy who would grow to look like Steve and act like Steve. A boy. She felt like crying. She looked at Luke and saw that his face was practically split in two by his smile. 'Oh, Honey! A little boy! How wonderful! A lovely little boy.' Honey smiled at him, because she couldn't bear to disappoint him, but also, because seeing him standing there, all excited and happy, made her think that maybe her boy wouldn't turn out to be a shit after all. If he had Luke around to take care of him, to be like a role model, maybe he would turn out okay.

In the car on the way home, Luke apologised for the receptionist and the women in the waiting room and the doctor. He told her he had never considered how tough this sort of thing was for girls in Honey's situation. He wanted to start a group for pregnant teenagers to come and discuss the problems and issues they faced, and to build strategies to deal with discrimination and prejudice. They could invite experts – doctors, midwives, financial planners – to come and speak. As babies were born, a group for new mothers would be created, while the old group would, sadly, continue to take in new girls.

Honey thought it was a great idea, but it seemed Luke's colleagues were not so keen. Belinda was worried about the message they'd be sending to the youth of the community by being seen to encourage teen pregnancy. Kenny and Leticia objected to the centre running groups without explicit worship or Bible study aims. Greg was worried that controversy caused by the program would cause parents to withdraw their teenagers from the centre.

'Come on, guys!' Luke pushed his half-eaten cereal away, his face glowing. 'I thought we were revolutionaries? I thought our mission was to be as radical as Jesus, to dedicate ourselves to the needy and ignorant, to the sinners. Or am I wrong? Is our mission to sit around telling good Christians what they already know?'

For a few moments no-one spoke. Honey was embarrassed at how loud her chewing sounded, so she stopped and just held the All-Bran in her cheek. Belinda was the first to break the silence. 'Have you discussed this with Pastor Riley?'

'Not yet. I was hoping to have the whole team involved in the proposal.'

'I don't think the elders will approve.'

Luke tapped his fingers on the table, his enthusiasm visibly waning with every unsupportive moment. Honey felt bad for him; he was nothing but nice all the time and it was just rotten that people wanted to bring him down. She swallowed her bran and sipped some juice to wash the cardboard taste from her mouth.

'You're all hypocrites,' she said. Everyone turned and looked at her. Luke smiled and nodded encouragingly, so she went on. 'You don't want girls to have abortions, but you don't want to help them with being pregnant either.'

'She's got a point,' Greg said. 'We're great at fighting abortion—'

'Or we used to be,' Belinda muttered.

Luke gave her a stern look and then nodded at Greg. 'Go on.'

'Well, we're not providing an alternative, are we?'

'True enough,' Leticia said. 'But pregnancy support isn't neces-sarily the answer. Abortion is the cure for pregnancy to these girls, right? So shouldn't we work on prevention?'

'We can do both.' Luke was coming alive again. 'What about that talk Honey gave the senior girls-group a few weeks back? I don't think anything could have got the abstinence message through to them as much as that witnessing.'

'Yeah.' Kenny was nodding. 'Like talking to girls who are suf-fering the consequences of pre-marital sex will show the other kids that God has darn good reasons for forbidding it.'

'Right,' Leticia was smiling now. 'And at the same time, the preg-nant girls will be learning from the rest of the kids how awesome it is to be a Christian. So it's like education all around, isn't it?'

'Plus,' Luke said, 'we don't want to stigmatise girls like Honey. Social disapproval is a powerful disincentive; it will only drive young women back to the abortionists. Girls who publicly confess their sin and admit they need to change, that they need God, girls like Honey...' He reached across and patted her hand. 'Heroines. That's what girls like this are. We should treat them as such.'

Belinda made a clicking sound with her tongue and teeth. 'I don't know, Luke. Is social disapproval such a bad thing? Like you said, stigma is a fantastic reinforcer, better than any law.'

'Come on, Bel, a caring church should help girls who make mistakes and then take the heroic path of choosing life. I'm not suggesting we dole out money to teenage mothers with no strings attached. I'm talking about ministry to those most in need of it. A hospital for sinners, remember? Remember?'

'Yes. Yes, of course I do, Luke,' Belinda said, reaching across the table and patting his arm. 'Okay, yes, let's do it!'

There were cheers all around, and excited chatter about how they would go about getting elder approval and when they would start. Honey finished her breakfast and took her plate and cup to the sink. Today was Saturday, but when you're home schooling that doesn't really matter. She had to write an essay about *Pride and Prejudice* by Monday, and she hadn't even started the book yet, so her weekend was pretty much guaranteed to be shit. Not that any of her weekends were much fun. Friday night was football and sausages; Saturday was games and trivia; and Sunday was morning service at Castle Hill followed by a long boring roast lunch with everyone talking about how the morning's service inspired them, then afternoon Bible study with Luke or Greg, then an evening service in the city, and then eating the leftovers from lunch with whoever didn't have dinner plans, which was usually all of them.

'I'll be in my room.' Honey headed outside. At the door to her cabin, Luke stopped her.

'One second.' He put an arm around her shoulder. 'You were great in there. You really got everyone inspired.'

'I thought it was a good idea.'

'It is. And I hope you'll play a key role in getting it established.'

'Sure.' She nodded toward her room. 'I have to go study.'

Luke withdrew his arm from her shoulder. 'One other thing. I saw you hiding out here before breakfast this morning.'

Honey felt her face going hot. Luke looked really worried. She mentally swore to never smoke again. For good measure, and just in case he was listening, she repeated the promise to God. For Luke though, she couldn't seem to come up with any words. He had been so nice to her for no reason at all and she was a rotten, rotten person for lying to him.

'Now don't get me wrong,' Luke said. 'Greg is an awesome bloke, and I personally recommended him to this ministry. It's just that I don't think it's a good idea for you guys to be meeting in secret like that.'

Honey thought fast. He hadn't seen her smoking, which was good. But he thought she was behind the building to be alone with Greg, which was bad. Greg could really get in a lot of trouble. Luke always said when she had a moral dilemma she should try and think what Jesus would do, but that didn't really work, because Jesus would never have been smoking behind the building in the first place. Instead she thought about what Greg would do. Greg would cover for her − *had* covered for her − even though it would get him into trouble.

'I was smoking.'

He blinked. 'What?'

'I went out for a smoke and Greg saw me and told me off.'

'Oh, thank goodness.' Luke laughed. 'Not the smoking. That is very bad and if I catch you with a cigarette in your mouth I'll make you eat the darn thing. But − oh! Greg was just giving you a telling-off?'

Honey nodded.

'Great. Wonderful.' Luke laughed again. He really did seem to be very happy. 'Okay, well, I'll be in my office. Let me know if you need a hand with your study.'

Honey watched him go. He was practically skipping. Sometimes she really did feel she was in topsy-turvy land here. Sticks into snakes, walking on water, talking donkeys, living for three days in the belly of a whale or in a burning furnace, causing the sun to stand still, turning water into wine, creating humans from dirt, a great flood covering the whole planet and all the animals of the world gathered two by two into a big boat. Sometimes she felt like calling the authorities and telling them that there was a whole big bunch of crazy people who needed locking up. But sometimes, like when Belinda gave her another baby blanket she'd made, or when Greg spent three hours explaining trigonometry to her, or when Luke filled out her hospital papers and put himself as Next of Kin and Emergency Contact, she thought crazy was good, and she hoped they'd all stay this way forever and never be touched by the whole world of mean, hard reality that was just outside these walls.

24

In the month after being dumped, Aggie worked even longer hours than usual, because Mal and Will decided to work out their problems far away from it all in Morocco. Aggie pointed out to Mal that it really wasn't the best time to be taking a holiday, what with the pickets and death threats and all, but he was an ugly man in love with a beautiful one, and there was no reasoning with him.

Aggie didn't mind the long hours so much, since work was the only thing that could distract her from the desperate pain of missing Luke. Distract was perhaps too strong a word, *dull* might be more accurate, or *muffle*. It didn't help that he was just across the road and at least once a day she saw him, or at least his car as it pulled into the underground carpark. For the first week she tried to attract his attention by waving or calling his name, but his steadfast refusal to even nod in her direction hurt too badly, and so she forced herself to go about her day as if he wasn't there at all.

So with no-one to tell her not to, Aggie worked sixteen hours every day and drank herself to sleep every night. Often, she woke up in the early hours of the morning, sweaty and confused. Lying awake, heart beating too fast, she would try and remember the dream that had woken her. Sometimes clear, strong, too-real flashes of Luke's lips and eyes and hands. Sometimes snatches of conversation, declarations and promises. Mostly she could not remember the dreams, and just felt disoriented and sad. She started to sleep with the television on, so when she inevitably woke in the night, she would not feel so alone. It didn't work. She always felt alone.

Four weeks after Aggie had spent the evening in a cell at Parramatta Police Station, the Justice for the Unborn protesters returned. The man she had punched appeared to be fully recovered and was supported by four women and one other man. They set up their ghoulish display at eight in the morning and continued broadcasting their hate until two or three in the afternoon. This was repeated daily and the police, ever-cheerful and useless, simply warned the protesters to stay off the clinic's property and told Aggie that was all they could do.

After a week of this, there was an overnight attack on the clinic. Someone painted the word BUTCHERS in two-metre high red letters across the front window. The side wall was branded with BABIES SLAUGHTERED HERE. It took Aggie almost two hours to clean the window and then another three hours to repaint the wall. She could have hired someone to do it, but the budget was tight and besides, hard labour was a wonderful way to release stress. Also, there was the barely-admitted hope that Luke would come and talk to her, that he would not be so cold as to watch her silently from across the street. At one point he walked right by her, but did not so much as glance in her direction. It was all she could manage not to throw her paint tin at his head.

Having lost a day to the cleanup, Aggie was still in her office catching up on paperwork at eleven that night, when the new message icon popped up in the corner of the screen. *You have 1 new message from: SBKeating@StJohnHospital.gov.au.* Simon Blaine Keating, the doctor of love. The e-mail had come through her private address, not the clinic's enquiry box, which was odd since she knew she had not given Simon the address. And why was he writing to her anyway? It had been well over a year since she'd seen him.

She was not enlightened by the message which read: *Aggie, call me ASAP. Am v. worried. S.*

Aggie was too curious not to call and too creeped-out to be nervous about speaking to him. She dialled the number at the bottom of the e-mail; he picked up on the first ring.

'Simon, it's–'

'Aggie! Damn it!'

She laughed. 'That's a nice greeting after all this time.'

'You're still at the office?'

Aggie was struck by his tone. The only time she had ever heard Simon so brusque was when a patient was in immediate danger. 'Yes. What's–'

'I'll be there in twenty minutes. Stay.' He hung up, leaving Aggie with the bizarre sensation of feeling annoyed, exhausted, excited and afraid all at once. She double-checked all the locks and waited. The last time she'd seen Simon was over a year ago at the birthday party of a mutual friend, just before Matthew left her for the final time. Simon had tried to kiss Aggie in the kitchen and was genuinely confused when she turned him down. He said she wasn't so hot that she could afford to be turning men down. Aggie had not spoken to him since.

By the time Simon arrived, twenty-seven minutes after his e-mail, there were twenty-two messages in her private box. Each one had the subject line: STOP STATE SUBSIDISED MURDER!!!!!!!!!!

'What's going on?' she asked him, as she re-locked the door.

Simon took off his coat, threw it over her chair and sat down in front of her computer. Without so much as a glance at her to see if she minded, he began flicking through her messages, swearing under his breath and shaking his head. After a few seconds he looked up and gave her his doctor-with-bad-news-trying-to-soften-the-blow-smile. 'You're the target of an e-mail bombing campaign. The alert I received came from a group calling themselves Justice for the Unborn. It appears to have been sent to everyone with a government health e-mail account. It accuses you of referring non-critical termination cases to the public health system, thereby directing health services that should be used saving lives, into ending lives. It urges all health care professionals to write to you demanding that you desist in forcing them to use their expertise, not to mention state resources, to terminate pregnancy in perfectly healthy women.'

'I suppose it didn't mention that I also refer women wanting to continue their pregnancies to government hospital obstetricians and public health clinics? I'll have to change my e-mail address, I suppose. Bugger.'

'You're very calm about this.'

Aggie stared at him. The bastard actually appeared worried. 'Simon, I spent the day removing hate graffiti from the building, I get at least five abusive calls a day, there are malicious posters of my clients all over town and last week I received a letter telling me that God demands an eye for an eye and I should watch my back. I just can't afford to get stressed out by a bunch of e-mails.'

Simon shook his head and smiled. 'Aggie Grey, you're a hell of a woman. More balls than brains.'

'Fuck off, Simon.'

He laughed, clasping his hands behind his head and swinging his feet up onto her desk. 'You still seeing that feisty young lawyer?'

'No. You still seeing that, oh, what was her name? That shrew with the big hair?'

'We just celebrated our twentieth wedding anniversary with a week in Tahiti.'

Aggie snorted. 'It's cheating to count the time you were living with me. Just about every couple would get to twenty years if they were allowed to live apart for a couple of years in the middle.'

'It's true that my time with you gave me a greater appreciation for my wife.'

Aggie picked up a herpes pamphlet from the shelf beside her and threw it at his head. He caught it easily, threw it back at her, laughing when it hit her right in the face. She laughed with him, then felt foolish and quickly put the pamphlet away. 'Well, this has been fun, Simon, but it's late and I'm tired.'

'Seriously, Aggie.' He took his feet off the desk, and leant forward, looking and sounding like the solemn doctor once more. 'I think this mob is dangerous. That bloke who tried to blow up that Melbourne clinic a while back was associated with a group very much like this one. These people are not afraid to resort to violence to get their point across.' He smiled kindly. 'I know things got a bit ugly between us at the end, Aggie, but I do have a soft spot for you and I'd hate to lose you to a bunch of religious right loonies.'

Aggie rolled her eyes, dislodging and dissolving the forming tears. 'I appreciate the heads-up on the e-mail thing, but you don't need to worry. I'm really fine.'

Simon stood up and pulled on his coat. 'You're a fantastic girl, Aggie. I wish things had been different.'

'Yeah, well.'

'You know…' He bit his lip, tilting his head to the side. 'If you're not seeing anyone…'

She turned her back on him and shuffled the papers on her desk. She certainly felt as if she was seeing someone. She felt very much in love and loved. But that was just stupid, because the man she felt so entwined with had not spoken to her for five weeks and could not even be bothered saying hello when he passed her in the street.

But Simon was a creep, a sleazebag, a very bad idea. 'Good night, Simon.'

'Fiona is at a conference in Canberra for the week.'

Aggie stood and brushed past him without looking up, because if she looked at him she would be taken with how attractive he was and she might forget that it was being taken in by his attractiveness that had ruined her life for two years. She sat in front of the computer and began deleting the toxic e-mails. She took in random words of hate and abuse as each message flashed at her before disappearing. *Bitch. Butcher. Murder. Abuse. Die. Evil. Ugly. Blood. Stop. Hate. God. You.* It occurred to her she should save the messages for evidence – of what, she didn't know.

He cleared his throat. '*Are* you seeing anyone?'

Deserve what you get, she read and deleted. *Healing. Sick. Termination.* Delete. *Destroy. Life. God. Loves. You.* Delete. *Consider. Trauma. Death. Killer.* Delete.

'I just thought… if we're both alone and… well, seeing you again has rekindled all these feelings. You remember how we used to swim? Every morning we'd have those brilliant long swims in your pool and afterwards we'd shower together. I never swim any more. How about you?'

Aggie deleted the last message. In the morning there would be many more, and from the look of the ones she'd received so far they were not just from government health employees; many of them appeared to be from religious domains and domestic accounts. She would call tech support and have them change her address first thing. And she'd ask them how the bastards could have found out her personal address in the first place. Then she'd have to call the police and make a complaint even though she knew they'd tell her there was nothing they could do about it. Then she'd type up yet another incident report for Malcolm to read when he returned from his love-in, see some fucked up kids and stare out the window hoping for a glimpse of Luke.

She wondered how much longer she could go on living like this. Always looking over her shoulder, wondering if she was in the crosshairs of a high-power rifle scope. Always looking out the window, her eyes scanning the street for a masked man with a shotgun or Luke with a smile. Waiting for death or redemption.

'What do you say, Aggie? Let's go for a swim. For old times' sake.'

She shut down the computer. Grabbed her handbag, jacket, keys. Checked all the windows and doors, set the alarm to activate in ninety seconds. She undid all the internal locks, opened the door wide and gestured Simon through, without looking at him. Then she deadlocked the door and started walking for her car. Simon trotted along beside her.

When she got to the carpark she took one last look across the road. All the interior lights were out. She turned to Simon, who was leaning on the bonnet of his Pajero, watching her. 'I'm in love,' she said.

'That's nice.'

'No, it's really not.'

'Oh, what's the story?'

'I don't want to talk to about it.'

Simon rolled his eyes and sighed in that awful, derisive way that Aggie had almost forgotten. 'You're the one who brought it up.'

'Only because…' Aggie took a deep breath. 'I thought you should know that if we do this, it will just be sex. You mean nothing at all to me, Simon.'

'I don't mind.' He grabbed her arm and pulled her to him. His hand closed on her arse and squeezed. She remembered how much

Simon loved her arse, how he would grasp it in both hands, press his face to it and become Mellors, 'Aye, it's the finest woman's arse there is,' he would say, and she would laugh and let him do as he pleased, because he was charming and clever and beautiful and she was none of those things.

But that was then. Now she would let him do as he pleased because he wanted her, and when she touched him he would not quiver and make a mess and cry and say *God Bless You*. She would take Simon home and his creative experiments would remind her that she was not, as certain people thought, the most sexually depraved person in the world, but was, in fact, inexperienced and naïve and easily shaken. She would take Simon into her home and she would let him fuck her however the hell he wanted to, for as long as he wanted to, and it would not make her happy, but she would content herself with knowing that if Luke knew what she was doing he would be appalled and jealous and just possibly, he would be as utterly miserable as she.

25

Honey's salvation had been Luke's too. At the depth of his despair over his feelings for Aggie God had sent him Honey, reminding him of his true calling in life and providing him with the ultimate distraction. The transformation of Honey was nothing short of a miracle and Luke's faith had never been stronger than in the month he spent establishing her within the church. Of course he thought about Aggie. A lot. But Honey's conversion was a sign from God that Luke was on the right path, and it would be deplorably ungrateful of him to wilfully step off that path after such a sign.

Throughout his separation from Aggie, Luke convinced himself that not seeing her was the right thing for both of them. He continued to pray that God would see fit to save her, and reasoned that although each day apart was painful for him, Aggie would be clearer of mind and more likely to find God without her feelings for Luke confusing the issue. A faith declared under the influence of human passion could never be as pure and strong as a faith discovered through personal conviction. He had to give her up, so that one day, God willing, she would be his wife with a relationship to God all her own.

Of course he wished he could still see her, talk to her, hear her laugh, but that would be playing into Satan's hands. Luke had learnt that sexual desire was more powerful than he had believed possible. He saw now that he was arrogant to have ever thought he could resist the temptations of the flesh when greater men had failed. How had he dared to think he was stronger than Samson, godlier that David and wiser than Solomon? Just because he had never had a problem with lust in the past, he had assumed he was immune to it, and now he had been humbled when he found that his faith and devotion were no protection at all against his wilful flesh. His chastity depended on physical separation from his temptress.

One morning as he was drinking his tea, he gazed out the window and was confronted with the sight of Aggie, slumped against the bonnet of her car, with her head in her hands. Fresh graffiti covered her window and walls. He spilt his tea in his rush to get up. Enough was enough: she needed him. But then as he ran on to the street, she stood, squared her shoulders, nodded at the wall as though accepting a challenge and marched inside the clinic. Luke gritted his teeth. Aggie did not need him. She was resilient and capable, and aside from salvation, there was nothing or no-one she needed. It was Luke who had needed to rush to her side, to feel he had a role in her life, as her saviour, her protector, her man. It was vanity. Selfishness. He had been saved from indulging it just in time.

He was still thinking about his near-capitulation to his passion several days later. The way he had instinctively leapt to his feet to run to Aggie at the first sign of trouble was disturbing, as was the very real stomach ache he got whenever he thought about the danger she was in every day. It was a mystery why God would not relieve him of his painful interest in her, even though he had done all he could to remove himself from temptation. Wasn't God supposed to help those who help themselves? Luke trusted the Lord as ever, but he wondered if he was being dense. He had repented truly; he had removed himself from temptation; he had wholeheartedly recommitted himself to his ministry and his mission. Yet his feelings for Aggie grew. His passion festered. *What else?* Luke implored, pacing his office praying with his whole body and spirit. *What else do you want me to do, Lord? What is it you want me to learn? I am your loyal servant, but I am lost and do not know where you want me to go.*

There was a knock on the door. It swung open immediately, and in the half-second before the intruder was revealed, Luke resolved to buy a lock. If people around here did not have the natural courtesy to wait to be invited in, he would just have to force it on them.

'May I disturb you a moment, Luke?' Pastor Riley stood in the doorway, leaning forward with one foot slightly off the ground, ready to charge ahead.

'Of course, come in.' Luke was surprised to see his superior, since the older man, in his own words, *despised* Parramatta. In fact, the last time he'd seen Pastor Riley had been the night they'd counselled the Cranbournes together. That night had been the last time with Aggie too.

Pastor Riley closed the door behind him, ignored Luke's invitation to sit across from him in the visitor's chair, and instead crossed the room to sit on the low bookshelf by the window, forcing Luke to swivel in his chair and sit unprotected by his desk.

'We seem to have a problem,' Pastor Riley said.

'Oh?'

'Have you heard of a group called Justice for the Unborn?'

Luke thought immediately of Aggie. 'I don't think so.'

Pastor Riley sighed and removed his glasses. Taking a handkerchief from his top pocket he began to rub the lenses. 'I received a telephone call this morning, asking me some odd questions and directing me to a certain internet site.' He blew on his glasses, then returned to rubbing them. 'The site is dedicated to outing abortionists and their supporters.' He replaced his glasses and looked through them at Luke. 'You're listed.'

'Ah, well that would be because of Honey. I told you there was a scene with the protestor who took her photo. The woman seemed to think that it was un-Christian of me to want to help a teenager rather than harass her.'

'Yes, I remember. How is the child settling in?'

'Wonderfully. She really is an extraordinary girl.'

'I'm sure.' Pastor Riley nodded, removing his glasses and rubbing his eyes, before replacing them. 'This isn't about Honey. Tell me, Luke, this woman, Agatha Grey, do you know her well?'

'Yes.'

'How well?'

Luke considered the question. He had no intention of lying; after all, God knew the worst of his sins already. But equally, he had no desire to divulge his most intimate feelings to a man whom he saw once a month at best.

'You seem to be having some difficulty with the question. Let me rephrase.' He cleared his throat. 'Is this woman your lover?'

Heat flashed through Luke's body. 'My–' He found himself unable to repeat the accusation, even to deny it. 'Is that what they are suggesting?'

'Are you having an affair with her, Luke?'

'No!' Luke unbuttoned his cardigan and wrenched it off. 'We were close friends, but I realised the relationship was inappropriate and I ended it.'

Pastor Riley nodded slowly. 'You were photographed embracing her outside her office at four in the morning. A strange thing to do if you are not intimately involved with a person.'

'Aggie and I never–' Luke heard the rage in his voice and stopped to regain control of himself. He took several deep, slow breaths and continued, in a calmer tone. 'We were never lovers.'

'I'm told Miss Grey visited you here at the centre.'

'She helped with meetings a couple of times.'

Pastor Riley stood and glared down at Luke. 'You allowed an abortionist, an avowed atheist, a feminist, to participate in your youth ministry? You provided her with access to these children?'

'She wasn't here to influence them in any way. She was here–'

'Yes?'

'For me. She was here to see me.'

'Do you think the parents of these young people would approve of you conducting your romances in front of their children?'

Luke stood and met Pastor Riley's glare. 'I'm losing patience with this conversation. My friendship with Aggie Grey was formed in the spirit of fellowship and with the hope of witnessing; when my personal feelings deepened I severed the connection. I have nothing to apologise for or be ashamed of. If you have a particular grievance, I wish you would state it.'

The older man lowered his gaze. 'I have no particular grievance. What I have is enormous concern for you and for this ministry.' He removed his glasses and squinted at Luke. 'You have a bright future ahead of you, Luke. I would hate to see it jeopardised because of a woman.'

'As would I. Anything else?'

Pastor Riley sighed. He put his glasses on and went to the door, pausing and turning back to face Luke as he opened it. 'I'll have to discuss this situation with the elders, Luke.'

'There *is* no situation.' Luke gripped the back of his chair with both hands. If the stupid old git didn't get out, he didn't know *what* he would do.

'The elders will decide that. I'll be in touch.'

The door closed and without thinking, Luke picked up the chair and threw it at the door. It slammed into the frame and clattered noisily to the floor. The door re-opened, scraping the upturned chair along the slate. Pastor Riley frowned at the chair, then at Luke. 'Your uncontrolled anger and hostility have been noted, Pastor Butler.'

The door closed again. Luke counted to one hundred. Picked up the chair, carried it back to his desk and sat on it. He stared at the door while he counted to one hundred again. Then he stood, picked up the chair and hurled it, harder than the first time. It made an ungodly racket as it impacted with the door and bounced back, knocking the edge of his desk before landing. 'My anger is perfectly controlled,' Luke said to the chair, as he picked it up, held it over his head for the count of fifty and then slammed it into the floor until a leg broke off. 'Perfectly under control, thank you very much.'

The Website for Justice for the Unborn was home to the most sickening collection of photographs Luke had ever had the misfortune to view. Under the heading AUSTRALIA'S HOLOCAUST VICTIMS were photos – *please God let them be fake* – of dead babies. Bloodied corpses, some with umbilical cords attached, some with half-formed limbs, some with black muck covering their misshapen bodies. Luke stopped scrolling when he got to the picture of a slimy head with black staring eyes, held aloft on a stick by a protestor wearing a *Justice for the Unborn* t-shirt.

He clicked on the link that read MEET THE SCUM RESPONSIBLE, and an alphabetised list of 'offenders' appeared. Luke recognised the third name: Malcolm Addison was apparently a despicable homosexual who started a sexual health clinic in order to recruit young boys into his deviant lifestyle. There was a photo of Mal with his face contorted in anger. Luke could see by the date in the corner that it had been taken that terrible, wonderful day. The day he had met Honey, the day he had kissed Aggie in this very room, the day he had counselled the Cranbournes that they were right to condemn their lovely gay son, the day he had let himself go so shamefully in Aggie's office.

Luke felt as though something inside him was splitting open. How could the simple series of numbers *10:47 11/08/05* barely visible against the grainy background of a photo of an ugly, angry man fill him with such longing and melancholy? It was unendurable. How could a man live his life when something as meaningless as a cluster of numerals made him feel as though his heart was leaking liquid metal, hot and heavy?

Luke picked up the broken chair leg from the floor and returned to his desk. He pressed the jagged edge of the leg into his left palm, holding it there until tears ran from his eyes. When he removed it, there were three long splinters lodged in his palm and blood seeped through the lines there. He was not usually one for self-flagellation, but the best way to fight the self-pitying urge to disobey the Lord was to remind oneself of the suffering Jesus endured so that sinful humans could have everlasting life. Sometimes knowing this intellectually and spiritually was not enough. Sometimes, like right now, it was necessary to have a stinging, bleeding reminder of the debt owed to Christ. Luke slammed his hand into the desk, forcing the splinters hard into his flesh. He did not cry out; this was but the tiniest fraction of the pain Jesus suffered on the cross, and if Luke were to deliberately sin against the Lord he would be showing Jesus that he did not care one whit for that terrible agony, that unimaginable sacrifice.

His left hand buried now between his thighs, the pressure working to increase the pain of the splinters but also stem the flow of blood, Luke returned to his exploration of the Website. He scrolled past the photo of Mal, past several names he did not recognise and then there it was, marked by a blue bubble declaring NEW LISTING! *Twenty-nine-year-old Luke Butler calls himself Pastor, but we refuse to bestow the honour of this title upon him. Mr Butler confronted one of our agents outside the Parramatta Free Sexual Health Clinic and accused her of being un-Christian! This from a man who spends his evenings locked inside abortion advocate Agatha Grey's (see separate listing) office, emerging just before daybreak for a shameless display of intimacy. We have very little information about Mr Butler as his employer, the Christian Revolution, will not co-operate in our investigation, nor will his colleagues at the Northwestern Christian Youth Centre, and we have been unable to identify any of Mr Butler's family or friends outside of the TCR or NCYC. If you have any information about this false-Christian abortion supporter please contact Justice for the Unborn.*

The photo below the text was just as Pastor Riley had described it: Luke's white Camry parked alongside Aggie's orange Datsun, the sign above the clinic door clearly visible. In the corner of the photo the time and date were recorded as 04:11 12/08/05. And in the foreground were a couple embracing in a manner that looked passionate, but that Luke remembered as bruisingly tender. She was telling him everything was fine, he was lovely, what had happened inside was wonderful. He was apologising, explaining, thanking her for her compassion, begging her forgiveness. Prising himself away from her had been the second most difficult thing he'd ever done in his life. The most difficult had been telling her he wouldn't see her again.

The throbbing in his hand drove him on. He scrolled down until he found *Agatha Grey*, and below her name, a photograph of Aggie with her arm over the shoulder of a tall blonde wearing a leopard print leotard. The caption read: *Abortion advocate Agatha Grey poses with her mother, lesbian activist Carrie Grey, at the 1999 Gay and Lesbian Mardi Gras.*

Luke touched the picture and smiled. So this was the famous

Carrie Grey; she was every bit as stunning as Aggie had promised. Shorter than Aggie, with a smaller waist, bigger breasts, smoother hair, clearer skin. She looked maybe five years older than Aggie, and a thousand times more glamorous. But Luke was not smiling at Carrie Grey's remarkable legs or knock-'em-dead smile; he was smiling at Aggie, who wore baggy brown trousers, black lace-up boots, an oversized *PFLAG* t-shirt and a ridiculous pink tiara atop her shaggy head. He knew she must have felt plain and awkward alongside her sensational mother, that at the time of the photo being taken she would have been twenty-three, divorced, lonely, trying so hard to be supportive of the woman who had neglected and then abandoned her. She must have been conflicted and pained, and yet there she was, embracing her difficult, embarrassing mother, grinning gamely at the camera and being so very *Aggie* that Luke felt he would collapse under the weight of the love he felt.

He read the text with rapidly-growing disgust. *Man-hating feminist Agatha Grey is the manager of the Baby Killing referral service owned by known homosexual Malcolm Addison (see separate listing). Ms Grey is the daughter of lesbian rights advocate Carrie Grey and Sydney financier Roland Grey who committed suicide when faced with the prospect of having to live alone with his daughter.*

There was more, but Luke found himself unable to read on. He pressed his palm to his mouth and sucked on the tiny wounds, trying to draw the splinters out. It hurt and the taste of his own blood turned his stomach, but it gave him a break from the evil text on the screen. In a minute, when he had cleaned up his hand, he would force himself to read the rest so he knew what Pastor Riley and the elders would use as the basis of their accusations. For now, he sucked at his hand and waited for his pulse to slow.

There was a rap on the door, simultaneous with its opening.

'Why knock?' Luke grumbled, then seeing it was Greg, who was usually the only person who *did* wait to be invited in, forced a smile. 'Yes?'

Greg was biting his thumbnail; his face was very pale. 'On the news just now. A man was–' Greg stopped and stepped into the room. He was staring at the floor. 'What happened to the chair?'

'It broke. What's the news? What happened?'

Greg looked from the chair to Luke and back again. 'If it's not a good time, I can–'

'It's a fine time. Tell me what's happened.'

'A man's been shot. In Adelaide. Killed, Luke. Shot dead. Someone just shot him while he was walking to his car. Broad daylight. Just shot him dead.'

Luke was chilled not so much by the news, which was tragic but commonplace, but by the intensely personal, even *guilty* tone. His mind was spinning as he tried to determine who Greg knew in Adelaide. Not family. They were all in Wollongong. Maybe an ex-lover? A friend?

'Greg, sit down a minute. Calm down.' Luke stood and went to take Greg's arm and lead him to the chair.

'No, Luke, man, no!' Greg shook his head, his eyes wild. 'You don't understand. He was a counsellor at a– clinic, a pregnancy crisis centre. A note was sent to all the papers saying it's justice for all the babies he's condemned to–'

'Oh.' Luke stumbled backwards until he felt the edge of his chair against the back of his legs. He sat down heavily. 'Oh, dear God. Justice. Oh, God, have mercy on us all.'

'I know, man, I know. I was thinking we should do something? Send, I don't know, condolences or something? Belinda said we should prepare a statement. She says because we've opposed Aggie – ah, the clinic across the street before, maybe the papers will ask us to comment.'

Luke stared at the computer screen. Swallowing the vomit that was bubbling up in his throat, he closed the foul Website and opened a new document. He began to type.

'Luke?'

'Give me a minute.' Luke's gut was churning but his mind was clearer than it had been in a long while. The words flowed so easily he knew God was guiding his hand. He read over what he'd typed:

Today, a man in the midst of a sinful life was shot in cold blood. Killing [victim] didn't stop abortion. It didn't save one single life. All this killer has done is rob a man of the chance to repent and be reconciled with God. The person or persons responsible cannot call themselves pro-life, as being pro-life means loving all life, not just the lives we personally approve of. Nor can the perpetrators of this evil call themselves Christians, since they have disobeyed God's commandment not to murder and ignored the words of our saviour Jesus Christ who implored us to love our enemies.

The Northwestern Christian Youth Centre calls on all true Christians to speak out against this horrific murder even while they continue peacefully to protest the legalised killing of unborn children. Remember, they'll know we are Christians by our love, not by our guns.

Luke hit *print* and opened the file containing last month's financial reports. He couldn't touch the Caring for our Community fund, since it was earmarked for Honey, but there was just over eight thousand dollars in the public relations account. He took the cheque book from his top drawer and wrote a cheque for the full amount. Then he switched back to the computer and started a new page.

The staff and congregation of the Northwestern Christian Youth Centre wish to express their deepest sympathies for the family and friends of [victim]. We hope his family will accept our prayers along with this small contribution to assist them in rebuilding their lives after this tragedy.

In His Name.

Luke waited until the page was printed and then handed both

pages to Greg, along with the signed cheque. 'Find out the man's name and his family's names. This first statement is for the media; get Belinda to read it to anyone who calls. The second should be rewritten onto a card and sent with the cheque to the family. The cheque's signed; you just need to fill in the recipient details. If it turns out he had no family then the cheque should go to the clinic where he worked.'

'We can't give money to a—'

'We can and we will. But I don't think it will come to that. How many people you know have no family at all?'

Greg's hands were shaking. 'Just, uh, just you.'

Luke patted him on the back, pushing him towards the door. 'Right. Even in an orphanage, I was the only one with no-one at all. This poor man will have a family somewhere. Find them and send them the cheque, okay?'

'Luke, I really think we—'

'Oh, I have to go out tonight. Not sure when I'll be back. Help Belinda with the VIBE group, for me will you? Ta.' Luke nudged Greg over the threshold and shut the door. He went to his desk and picked up the phone, dialling the number he knew by heart.

The first thing he said when he heard her voice was: 'Oh.' Then he said, 'If I come over, will you talk to me?'

'Okay.' It was practically a whisper.

'Ten minutes.'

26

Aggie answered the door before he had a chance to ring the bell. She was swamped by a shapeless black dress, but her hair had been slicked off her face with a blue headband and she had applied a deep plum lipstick which made her lips look thin and mean.

'Come in,' she said, her eyes roaming from his face to his chest, legs and stomach and back to his face.

'Wait.' Luke remained in the doorway, locking his hands together to stop from grabbing her. 'Hear what I have to say first, then decide if you want to invite me in.'

She smiled, revealing a slick of lipstick onher front teeth. 'Sounds dire.'

'Oh, no. It's just…' Luke had it all planned out, but he hadn't counted on her having lipstick on her teeth. That she had rushed to apply the awful stuff, imagining that he would somehow prefer her painted than bare – oh! She was unaware that what was most love-able about her was her raw humanity; she masked herself in worldliness and sophistication, but he saw through it. He saw through to her inherent purity and was awed by it.

'Come on, spit it out, the suspense is killing me.'

Oh! That there! Her tone was jokey, detached, but she meant what she said. She spoke the truth because she was unable to do otherwise, but she had learnt not to be too honest about being truthful. So it was sarcasm that wasn't really. A casual remark that was deeply sincere.

Luke knew he had to speak. He looked away from her mouth, focusing instead on the curls disobediently poking out from under her headband. 'I have concluded that friendship between us is an impossibility due to the fact that I have romantic feelings towards you, also feelings of a physical nature and, well, I am in love with you.'

'Oh, Luke—'

'But as you know,' he continued, looking away from the curls that begged to be smoothed down and talking instead to the wall behind her, 'I believe that physical intimacy should be reserved for people married before God, and that same belief system dictates that I cannot marry outside my faith.'

She sighed. 'I understand.'

'No, you don't. I haven't finished.' Luke looked back into her face, which was all squished up as if she'd taken a bite of something unexpectedly sour. 'I believe these things with all my heart, and still I want to be with you. It doesn't make any sense, I know, but there you have it. So nothing is sorted out, the time apart has increased my confusion and multiplied my doubts, but I've come here tonight to ask if you think you can love me anyway. I mean, knowing that I am so conflicted and selfish and wrong-headed and that anytime I could—'

'Get inside,' she laughed, already sliding her hands under his shirt as she kicked the door closed behind them. 'You don't want the whole neighbourhood to see your fall from grace.'

Kissing Aggie was so much better than he'd remembered it, and he'd remembered it as being wonderful. He wondered, as he had the first time he'd kissed her, why he'd wasted so much of his life *not* kissing her. Pressed up against her front door, her tongue in his mouth, her fingertips on his belly and his hands in her hair, he could not think of a single reason not to kiss her.

Her hands slid lower, and he kissed her harder than ever, sick with fear and crazed with need as she unbuttoned his jeans. When she took hold of his erection he nearly exploded, and she must have sensed this, as she released him immediately, moving her hands to his hips and working his jeans down. That was almost as bad, her hands on his buttocks while his insistent penis drove itself into her thigh. Luke knew the time was horribly near.

'Stop, I'm going to—'

'Hang on, sweetie.' She wrenched his jeans and shorts down hard so he was naked from hip to mid thigh. Naked and burning and about to make a big mess of her again.

'Aggie, I can't wait any—'

'I know.' She grabbed hold of his bare hips and forced him downwards until he was lying flat on the hardwood floor, the top of his head pressed into the door frame, his jeans tight around his thighs, and Aggie astride him in her big, ugly dress.

'You okay?' she said, in a voice that didn't even sound like hers.

Luke nodded, although he wasn't really. He was terrified of her hands, which were hidden under her skirt, moving fast at something, but barely touching him. But touching him enough to make him sure that he was going to lose control.

'I love you,' she said, lifting her hips, taking hold of his penis and then — oh — and then he was inside her body. He looked at her in astonishment, and she looked right back at him, her eyes wide and bright. She smiled, red-faced and wild-haired and he hated to close his eyes but found he couldn't help it as the inevitable happened. And when he opened his eyes again she was smiling still and rubbing the outside of his thighs with firm soothing strokes.

'I didn't–' He closed his eyes again, hardly able to believe that he had just had sexual intercourse. That he had done it, without doing anything. That he had done it and it was over.

'Didn't what, sweetie?'

Luke kept his eyes and mouth closed, trying not to cry. He didn't expect it to be like this. He had known they would make love; he was not fool enough to think he could come to her and confess his feelings and not have one thing lead to another. But one thing *hadn't* led to another. There was kissing and there was arousal and then there was a squelchy heat and it was done.

He had never allowed himself to fully imagine what making love to her would be like, but he had expected there would be a bed, and soft lighting, and surely there would be nakedness. He had had an idea that afterwards there would be a streak of blood staining the crisp white sheets. He understood now, in the aftershock of the dreadful reality, that this was a ridiculous fantasy to have, but still, he was certain it wasn't unreasonable to expect at least to know he was actually *doing it* when he did it.

'I just didn't expect–' He choked on the words and could not go on.

'I thought it better to get it over with quickly. I thought you'd be too nervous if we drew it out too long.' She leant forward and kissed his forehead giving his now lifeless penis the opportunity to slip out of her. It was thoroughly, totally over.

'Are you going to leave now?'

'I don't know. I don't know what to do now.'

She climbed off him, helped him with his shorts and jeans, then sat cross-legged by his side and stroked his face. The absurdity of losing his innocence fully-clothed in an entrance hall without having known he was doing so struck him anew and he covered his face with his arms.

'How about getting off this floor and letting me wash all that dust out of your hair?'

Luke caught his breath, wiped a hand across his face. 'There's dust in my hair?'

'A little. Mostly it's an excuse to get you naked in the shower with me.'

And then he realised he was a complete idiot, and that the fast, impersonal undercover release had been just that — a release of his tension and fear, and that it wasn't over, but was just beginning, and that he hadn't missed out on her, but had not even started to have her, see her, touch her, know her. It was all just beginning.

Luke woke up in Aggie's enormous bed. Her pale, freckled arm was flung over his chest, her knee stabbed his thigh and saliva dribbled from her open mouth onto his shoulder. 'Aggie,' he whispered, tickling the soft skin of her forearm, smiling as she pulled her arm away and rolled over. He unthinkingly sent up a small prayer of thanks for the pleasure, the luxury, of examining her up close while she slept.

Last night, under the fluorescent bathroom light, the skin she had revealed to him had been blotchy pink, red and white; then when she was laid out on the lounge room floor, illuminated by a single candle she was pure gold. Later, in her bedroom, with the moonlight streaming through the windows, she had been all shadowy shades of blue and grey. Now, in the dawn's light her skin was as translucent as the finest bone china, but speckled with pale brown and gold freckles. It reminded him of the shell from some exotic bird's egg.

He was concerned with how visible her ribs were and how prominent her spine. She was impossibly small and fragile. Impossibly, because Luke knew from standing and walking beside her that he was smaller than she was. It was conceivable that her height was a trick of footwear, but that didn't explain why her hands had always been larger than his, her shoulders broader, her calves thick and muscular, yet here she was beside him, waiflike and in need of his suddenly superior strength. He traced her spinal cord, feeling uneasy at how far each little notch, each vertebrae protruded. He tried to think of a way to ensure no harm ever came to these unprotected little bones.

'Tickles,' she mumbled, swatting at him blindly.

'Ah, you're finally awake.' Luke pressed himself to her, thinking how incredible it was that she did not seem to mind his misbehaving organ prodding her lower back and more incredible still that he felt no agony of embarrassment.

'It's barely six. Go back to sleep.'

'I can't possibly sleep when the sun is shining, the birds are singing and the most wonderful woman in the world is by my side.'

'You're a dag, Luke. And I am tired and sore, so shut up and go back to—'

'You're sore? I hurt you?' He was sickened by his self-involvement. Of course he'd hurt her! He had been clumsy, heavy-handed and ignorant of basic female anatomy. He had spent the entire night in an orgy of self-satisfaction, oblivious to the pain she must have been experiencing.

'No, it's just...' She took his arms and pulled them tighter around her middle. 'You wore me out a bit. All that pent up desire. You're not exhausted?'

'I've never felt better.'

'Typical. It's always the woman who suffers for illicit love.'

'What about Peter Abelard?'

'Who?'

'Peter Abelard, my uncultured, uneducated heathen princess, was a brilliant French monk in the twelfth century. He had been celibate all his life, but then, in his forties, he fell passionately in love with a young student named Heloïse. When the girl became pregnant, her uncle had Peter castrated and exiled to a monastery. Heloïse entered a convent, studied hard and ended up greatly respected throughout France, while her lover was physically, spiritually and socially ruined.'

Aggie was quiet for several seconds and then she burst out laughing. 'Okay,' she said, slapping Luke's arm, 'so women always come off second best except that one time in mediaeval France.'

Luke had told her the story hoping to entertain her and was pleased that it had, but he found that telling the familiar tale had discomfited him. He had always admired Abelard, whose scriptural interpretations, once considered scandalously heretical, were now recognised as brilliant and important. The inspiration Luke drew from his early life had never been tarnished by the monk's eventual fate. But although he had studied Abelard in depth, written of him for college essays and drawn from his teachings in sermons, Luke had never, until this moment, understood him.

'I suppose you have come off second best,' he told Aggie. 'I mean, I'm this inexperienced, clumsy, hopeless lump and you're this... sexual superstar.'

'Spare me!'

'No, really. I had no idea what I was doing last night. I was a fumbling fool.'

'I liked being on the receiving end of your fumbling. You're a really, really good fumbler. A natural.'

He knew she was just saying that to make him feel better, because he had been shockingly inept. His whole adult life he had avoided sex and everything related to it. If he was reading a novel that had an unexpected sex scene he would close it at once and throw it in the garbage. Likewise, he had walked out of films when the PG rating proved to be false. He talked about sex only to emphasise the importance of *not* doing it, and he listened to others speak of it only to hear testimonies about STDs, unwanted pregnancies, extra-marital affairs, prostitution and despair.

His understanding of the act itself was, he now knew, embarrassingly juvenile. Year 9 health class and pre-pubescent late night mumblings in the dormitory were his only education in the mechanics, and the dreamy pleasure of kissing combined with the humiliating relief of orgasm into a hand gave him his only clue as to what it might *feel* like. So he was woefully unprepared for the myriad of sensations and emotions she had led him through last night.

'Well, I'm pleased,' Luke said, 'that you enjoyed my fumblings, because I feel the urge to fumble some more.'

Aggie groaned, and rolled onto her back. 'You're not going to let me go back to sleep, are you?'

Luke answered by covering her breasts with his hands. Oh, what breasts! He had spent half the night squeezing, kissing, pulling, pinching, sucking and nuzzling them, and here this morning they were brand new again. The sunlight showed him pale blue veins radiating out from her nipples, and three tiny freckles on the underside of the left. Oh, wonderful, surprising breasts! He worshipped them with mouth and hands and eyes until Aggie indicated — with claws in his hair — that she was no longer interested in sleeping.

He kissed his way over her ribs, down to her soft pale belly, paying loving attention to her belly button and then each jutting hip bone. She was fully with him now, stroking his hair and face, whispering *oh Luke oh love*. He pressed his face to the thing he could not bring himself to call by any of the names he had heard used, scientific or slang. He was just so glad he had not known about this secret part of her during the last few months or he would never have been able to remain chaste for so long. To think all those days and nights they had spent together talking and longing and arguing, and under her jeans she was hiding this wet, pulsating, terribly welcoming *thing*.

With Aggie's ever-quickening breath as encouragement, Luke explored it fully, thinking, as he had about every other part of her, that it looked so different in daylight. Moving to lie flat on his stomach between her legs he began to make sense of the design in a way he had surely not done in the dark of night, with his own urgent need rushing him to push past all this interesting stuff and get right inside. Now, with his selfish genitals pressing harmlessly into the mattress, Luke prodded and stroked and licked and sucked until he figured out which actions on which bits caused her to pull his hair the hardest. It took a while – much longer than it had taken her to bring him to ecstasy with her mouth – but eventually she said *that that that don't dare stop doing that exactly that oh oh THAT* and then he felt a million little muscles pulsing around his fingers and her pubic bone smashed into his nose.

He moved up, resting his head on her belly, while he caught his breath and felt her catch hers. His jaw ached and his tongue was numb. His hand and half his face were soaked with her. And his desire for her was stronger than it had ever been.

'Jesus,' she said, after a little while. 'You sure you haven't done that before?'

'Barely knew it could be done. I had no idea women were so complicated down there. All those colours and textures and that dear little–'

'Okay, I don't need a description.'

'It's just so beautiful. And I never guessed. To think you have a part that is perfectly designed so as to allow me to actually enter your body and to bring us both pleasure with all those nerve endings and soft folds of skin and oh–' Luke kissed her stomach all over, while his hands tried again to gain entrance to her body. She giggled and wriggled, kept her legs clamped shut and eventually succeeded in throwing him off her altogether.

'You're so sweet and strange,' Aggie said, settling again on to her side and drawing his arms around her waist. 'I still can't believe you're here. Don't ever stay away for so long again, please?'

'No. I couldn't. It felt like forever.'

'Thirty-nine days, and every one of them felt like a week.'

Luke stared at the back of her head. Thirty-nine days. He had not kept track, but he counted back quickly and discovered she was correct. On the twelfth of August the photo had been taken outside the clinic; yesterday was the nineteenth of September. For thirty-nine days he had survived in the desert, starved and thirsting but strong in his faith and his love of God. Could he have resisted temptation one day longer? Would it have made any difference if he had realised he was suffering as Christ had suffered, lonely and despairing of finding his direction? Luke thought not. Even now he felt glad that nothing had stopped him from coming here. What if he had never known *this*?

He tightened his arms around her. 'I love you, Agatha.'

'I love you too, but if you call me that again I'll murder you.'

'You don't like Agatha?'

She groaned, pushing back into him with her hips. 'I hate it. My mother's revenge on me for being born.'

'I think it suits you. *Agathos* is Greek. It means good.'

'How do you know this stuff?'

'I happened to come across the word when I was working on some scriptural translations. Of course, when I say "happened to come across" I actually mean, I looked up your name in every text I own and when I found it I sat in my room and re-read the entry until my vision blurred.' Luke felt tears springing up at the memory of his wretchedness, and how unnecessary all that suffering had been when all along he could have been here, where he belonged. 'I found you in a Latin text too. Do you know about Saint Agatha?'

'There's a saint?'

'A third-century martyr from Sicily. She spurned the advances of a Roman official who then tortured her, cut off her breasts and killed her.'

'How gruesome.' Aggie twisted her upper body so she was looking at him. 'Was there a Saint Luke?'

'Of course.'

'Of course.' She lay down so her back was to him again. 'What did he do?'

'You heard of the Gospels, Ag?'

'He wrote them?'

'One of them. The most beautiful of them, in my opinion. Luke was a doctor and exceptionally compassionate for the time. He wrote of the Good Samaritan, the penitent thief, the healing of the lepers. His Jesus is the sinners' friend, a minister to outcasts and slaves. Luke's is the gospel of the underdog.'

'Was he married?'

'No.'

'But he sounds so nice. Was he gay or something?'

'Don't be ridiculous. He just happened to agree with Paul that a man should only marry if he is tempted to immorality by staying single.'

'Who's Paul?'

'You are astonishingly ignorant. Paul is only the most significant figure in Christianity outside Jesus himself.'

'And it was his fault that poor Luke was celibate? Sounds like he wanted him all to himself, if you ask me.'

Luke closed his eyes and pressed his face to Aggie's hair. She had no idea what it was she mocked, that right at this moment, Luke was suffering just as Paul had promised he would. Paul advised that a man aflame with lust should marry; he warned that a man who has given himself to a woman can no longer concentrate on the affairs of the Lord; that a man, once joined to a woman, will no longer own his own body. If you are free from a wife, Paul wrote, do not seek to be married, but if you cannot control yourself with your betrothed, if your passions are strong, marry her.

Marry her. Do not be unevenly yoked. It is better to be married than to be aflame. Do not seek a wife. Luke knew giving into his lust was a sin, but beyond that... He would have to think about all this some more. Later.

'Luke wasn't celibate because of Paul,' he said, pressing himself against her. 'He just never found the right woman.'

27

He woke to find her gone. A horrible panic overcame him, his heart beating hard and fast. He sat and took deep gulping breaths of stale, musty air. The bedroom had been well-used and not aired out. It stank of sex and sweat. He swung his legs over the side of the bed, but it was too high and his feet did not touch the ground. He sat there, legs swinging, doubled over, trying to calm the storm in his chest.

He gazed at the floor in front of him. Bare, empty of the discarded towels and barely-worn underwear which had littered it yesterday and also the pale pink sheet that he had ripped from the bed some time in the night when it became tangled in his feet. Had it even been last night? He felt he might have slept for a very long time. He was unsure about anything except the drumming in his chest which told him something was horribly wrong.

'Aggie?' he called, sliding off the bed and looking around for something to cover himself. 'Ag? Where are you?'

She appeared in the doorway, dressed in blue jeans and a yellow shirt. She was wearing brown boots and her hair had been gathered back behind a headband. 'Hi, sleepyhead.'

'You're going out?'

'Duty calls, I'm afraid.'

'You can't go to work!'

'Just for a little while. Mal got back yesterday but he was jetlagged as hell. He promised he'd be in by twelve.'

Luke looked at the clock over the bed. It was only eight-thirty. He had slept barely an hour, so why did he feel so disoriented and out of whack? Why was he sure he would lose his mind if she left the room? He was finding it hard to breathe again. He leant on the bed-post, wondering what on earth was happening to him.

'Will you be here when I get back?'

Luke nodded. Where did she think he'd be?

Aggie came across to him, oblivious to the trouble he was having. She kissed him, slow and deep and pressed herself into him. 'Stay like this for me, all sleepy and naked and warm. I'll be as fast as I possibly can. Okay, baby?'

He nodded again, unable to speak. She kissed him on the forehead and was gone.

Luke climbed back into her bed, pressing his face into her pillow and inhaling deeply. It was no good; he could not smell her. The sour stench of his own body was everywhere. He got up again and ripped the coversheet from the bed. Stiff patches of dried fluid scraped past his fingers and made him gag. *Oh, Lord, what have I done?* He stripped the pillows of their cases and then climbed on the bed so he could reach the windows over it. He drew back the heavy velvet curtains and threw open the windows. The warm, fresh breeze instantly refreshed him.

The laundry was on the ground floor, out the back near the kitchen. He found that Aggie had put the dirty things from the bedroom floor in the basket, so he added them to the machine with the linen and doused the lot with detergent. It was only after he had set the machine to SuperWash and was leaning against it heaving with fear at God only knew what, that he realised he was stark naked.

Having problems to solve was good. It kept him from thinking about whatever it was that was lurking in his chest, waiting to eat him from the inside out. So clothes – yes, right.

He set off to find them, retracing the route of last night's multi-roomed love-making. Twice he scared the heck out of himself when he passed by mirrors. The second time it happened, he lingered after the initial shock of reflection and examined his body with a mixture of pride and disgust. Pride because he had worked hard at taking care of the body the Lord gave him and it showed – he looked strong and lean. Disgust because he had abused the body God had given him in the worst possible way. He had performed acts of – oh! And there was that hammering in his chest again, accompanied now by a roaring in his ears. He ran from the mirror, gasping for air, thinking only *clothes*. The panic was merely because he didn't have any clothes on; the feeling he had forgotten something incredibly important was from the same source. Clothes were the problem and finding them the solution. *Clothes clothes clothes clothes, where are those darn clothes?*

Underwear and socks were on the bathroom floor, wet. His jeans were in the hallway between the bathroom and living room, and his belt and shoes were in the entrance hall. The shirt was a real mystery and searching for it kept him occupied for almost an hour before he remembered that Aggie had worn it while she made toasted cheese sandwiches late last night. Driven wild by the sight of her pale buttocks peeking out from beneath the hem, Luke had pinned her to the kitchen bench and done something which he had, in the past, campaigned to have made illegal.

That wasn't the point (*oh God, oh God, oh God!*). The point was the shirt. It was in the kitchen, and that was the important thing. He found it on the floor, a smear of (*dear Lord oh, oh, what have I done? What am I doing?*) something sticky on the hem. Well, that was the next problem wasn't it? He had all his clothes but he couldn't very well wear them in the crumpled, wet, sticky condition they were in.

(*And how they got that way, oh, God, my Father in Heaven? I never knew I was capable of such things. Who put this in me if not you?*)

Luke put his clothes in the washing machine, placing the clean load in a wicker basket he found on the window ledge. He would have to cover himself before he could hang out the washing, which meant finding something of Aggie's to wear. This was so amusing that he laughed out loud, and finding that laughing helped to ease, or perhaps only disguise the panicky churning of his stomach and hammering of his heart, he resolved to keep laughing until he was dressed and could focus again on the washing.

He went through her closet, laughing so hard he was occasionally forced to sit down on the bed and hold his stomach. Her jeans and trousers were ludicrously long and her shirts all pulled across his back or bulged across his chest. There were several dresses and skirts but wearing those would not have been funny; it would have been depraved and whatever he'd done last night and this morning, he was not a pervert. In fact, the whole enterprise of searching her closets was ridiculous. What was wrong with him to get such enjoyment out of trying on a girl's shorts? It was obscene.

Furious now, he stalked out of her bedroom and stormed through the house opening and closing doors until he found the linen cupboard. He grabbed a candy pink towel and wrapped it around his hips, and then chose a set of pale blue and green striped bed linen and took it back to the bedroom. As he fluffed and placed the final pillow, he glanced at the clock and saw it was eleven-twenty.

They would be missing him by now, leaving messages on the phone he had turned off and left in the glove box of his car, discussing possible meetings he had failed to mention or outings they had forgotten he had told them about. They would not have called head office yet, though Kenny would have wanted to. Belinda would be calming everyone and telling them that dear Luke had never given them reason for concern before and they should trust that there was a very good explanation for it all. Honey would be rolling her eyes and wondering why the heck everyone got so stressed out about a bloke missing breakfast.

Better not to think about all that right now, because thinking about it made him feel as if he was going to have a heart attack. Better to concentrate on getting all this work done before Aggie returned. The second load of washing would be done and the first was still waiting to be hung out. His nakedness was at least partially covered and so what if some noisy neighbour peered over the fence and saw him in his towel. Nothing so shocking about a man in a towel, is there?

He was just pegging up the last item, a particularly ugly pair of underpants which she had worn for only a few minutes last night before Luke had voiced his displeasure both at the hideous green parrot print and the fact that she was covered, when he heard her laughter ringing out. He turned and saw her leaning over the balcony, her face a picture of joy. 'I must have died and gone to Heaven,' she called out. 'There's a gorgeous half-naked man doing my housework.'

'Send him over here when he's done,' came a voice from over the fence.

Aggie laughed and ran down the stairs to meet Luke halfway. He crushed her against the railing, kissing her mouth and burying his hands in her hair. He hadn't realised how very frightened he'd felt without her until he felt the relief of her return flood through him. She kept laughing through his kisses, and after a little while, he was laughing too, the anxiety and despair of the last three hours forgotten.

28

ggie's morning had been execrable. A television news van had beaten her to the clinic and she got caught off guard with a question about yesterday's shooting. She answered as best she could on a moment's notice, saying it showed the disgusting depths that anti-choice protestors would go to, but now she worried that she had sounded harsh and unfeeling. She should have expressed her sympathy for the dead man's family and said her thoughts were with her colleagues at the Adelaide clinic. This was all true, and she had expressed it in a series of ghastly phone calls yesterday afternoon, but she wished she'd remembered to say it on television too.

The usual gang of protesters was telling the reporter about how they condemned yesterday's attack, of course, but people need to remember that these clinics are places of extreme violence, and if you live by the sword you have to accept the possibility of dying by it. Aggie considered turning the hose on the lot of them, but the thought of being hauled off to the cop shop again while Luke was waiting for her at home restrained her. She went inside and drew the newly-purchased curtains over the front window.

Then when she fired up her computer she found a fresh stream of hate-filled e-mails waiting for her. Their message was to the point: *Abortion War Death Toll. Abortionists – 1, Innocent babies – 1 million.*

Let's even the score. There was also an e-mail from Simon. *Ag,* it read, *V. worried about you in light of Adelaide incident. Hospital admin has doubled security – suggest you do same. Simon. P.S. Monday's meeting was a great success. Request follow-up at your earliest convenience. xxx*

Aggie smiled as she replied: *Dr Keating, No need to worry. The police and media are everywhere. Agree that Monday was a success but must regretfully decline your request due to recently arranged merger with more favourable party. Rgds, A.*

The reply came back within minutes: *Congrats. Would be obliged if you kept me in mind for future vacancies. Casual or contract work preferred. Simon. P.S – I'm serious about security. Terrorists love an audience + copycats are a concern. Be careful! xxx*

Aggie was warmed by Simon's attention. She felt that sleeping with him had not been so very stupid, after all. It had been a fun night, no-one had been hurt and she had re-established contact with a knowledgeable insider in the public hospital system. Also, she had realised that he did actually care about her and that his cheating on and leaving her had not actually indicated otherwise. He was just a sleazebag and she had been silly to take it so personally.

The incoming stream of quasi-death threats quickly chilled the warm glow Simon's e-mails had given her. The noise from outside was getting louder, too. 'Do not be afraid to go out on the streets and into public places like the first apostles, who preached in the cities and villages,' came the megaphone-distorted voice. 'This is no time to be ashamed of the Gospel. It is the time to preach it from the rooftops.'

Aggie went to the door and opened it just enough to put her head around. She could see that the dented tin megaphone of days past had been replaced with an enormous red shiny thing plugged into some kind of amplifier. The noise was fantastic. 'The Gospel must not be kept hidden because of fear or indifference,' the man hollered. 'It was never meant to be hidden away in private. It has to be put on a stand so that people may see its light and give praise to our heavenly Father.'

'Fuckers.' She slammed the door. There was no chance of any clients coming in while that racket was going on, not to mention the presence of the television van. She couldn't stand the thought of her beautiful boy alone in her big house while she sat in this purgatory deleting hate-mail from her computer.

The phone rang and she braced herself to give the stock answer about sympathy to the family if it was a reporter, and grabbed a pen to quickly note the number on caller ID if the call was abusive.

'Well, hi Aggie,' came the chirpy voice.

Aggie knew instantly who it was, but was so surprised she needed time to compose herself. 'Who is this?'

'Oh, sorry. It's Belinda.'

Aggie was silent, trying to remember if Luke had said anything about what he'd told the others. They hadn't really talked about anything except how happy they both were to be finally together.

'Belinda Swan. From across the street.'

'Oh, right. Hi.'

'Pressure's really on over there, huh? Greg said he saw a Channel 10 van.'

'Yeah. I'm actually pretty flat out, Belinda, so…?'

'Right, sorry. Ah…' Belinda made a little clicking sound. 'This might seem an odd thing to ask, but you haven't seen Luke, have you?'

Aggie barely missed a beat. 'No.'

Belinda sighed. 'Haven't heard from him today at all?'

'What's this about?'

'Oh, nothing, nothing. He just seems to have forgotten to turn his mobile on or something and we can't track him down. Never mind, I'm sure he'll turn up sooner or later.' Belinda gave an affected little laugh. 'Sorry to bother you.'

'No bother.' Aggie hung up, wondering how to feel about this bit of information. Had Luke really taken off without telling anyone, or was poor Belinda just really out of the loop?

The voice from outside was getting louder, more strident. 'But the fearful, and unbelieving,' it roared, 'and the abominable, and murderers, and whoremongers, and sorcerers, and idolaters, and all liars, shall have their part in the lake which burneth with fire and brimstone, which is the second death.'

Aggie dialled Mal and told him she was locking up and getting out. When he got there he could decide for himself whether it was worth opening for the afternoon.

'But, Aggie—'

'But nothing. I can't sit here and listen to any more fire and brimstone. I've had this shit all month. I'm taking a couple of days off, starting right now.'

'That's fine, but I haven't even seen you yet. I want to catch up.'

She wanted that too, but not as much as she wanted to get back to Luke. 'Later,' she told him. 'When things settle down.'

Back at home she made waffles with maple syrup and fresh fruit with whipped cream. Luke made the coffee and then stood behind her kissing the back of her neck while she finished preparing the food. She told him about her morning, but left out the phone call from Belinda. She would ask him about that later; right now she wanted to enjoy his pink-towelled, shockingly horny presence without the need for serious discussion about the responsibilities he might or might not have skipped out on to be here.

'So what did you do all morning?' she asked, when they were seated at the table. 'Apart from the washing.'

Luke shrugged and mumbled something that sounded like 'nothing', through a mouthful of waffle. He was really packing away the food, shovelling it in as though he hadn't eaten in a week. In the past she had only ever seen him pick at the edges of his plate, barely eating enough to sustain a child, but here he was eating like a sumo wrestler.

'Hungry?'

He nodded, pouring syrup over another waffle with one hand, while the other spooned a strawberry drowning in cream into his mouth. 'I don't think I've ever been so hungry in my life. I hope you got more food than this.' He indicated the one remaining waffle and two rockmelon slices.

'I think you've had quite enough.'

'No, not at all. Come on, Ag, what else you got for me?'

Aggie stood up. 'More fruit?' she offered, undoing the top button of her shirt. Luke shook his head, smiling broadly. 'Toast?' She undid the second and third buttons. 'Cereal?' Aggie backed towards the kitchen, undoing her buttons as she walked. Luke stood up. 'Or I could make you some scrambled eggs, I guess.' Her shirt was all the way open. Luke was wiping his mouth with the back of his hand. 'I'd hate for you to be hungry.'

'I'm full,' he said, coming towards her.

'But a minute ago you were—'

He kissed her, his hands already working at the back of her bra. 'Full,' he said.

'Now we've dirtied these nice clean sheets,' Aggie said, wriggling over to avoid the brand new wet patch.

Luke's blissed-out smile disappeared. He looked at Aggie with concern. 'Should we be using something?'

'Plastic sheets?'

Impatience flashed in his eyes. 'I'm serious.'

She kept forgetting he hadn't been doing this for years like normal people. She was so used to being the less experienced partner. 'Sorry.' She reached across and stroked his chest. 'It's safe. I'm on the pill.'

He was quiet for a long while. It occurred to Aggie that he might still be worried about her alleged promiscuity. 'Oh, I'm clean, if that's what's bothering you. Matthew and I got tested when—'

'Stop!' Luke pressed his lips together, his eyes tightly shut. 'I don't need to know. You told me it's safe, and I believe you. I can't...' He opened his eyes and looked at her. She had never seen a person look so hurt; it took her breath away. 'I can't think about you being with other men. To think of anyone... It's like a nightmare.'

She rolled towards him, not caring about the wetness under her thigh. She put her head on his chest and was shocked to feel a great sob rip through him. His hand was on her head, stroking her hair but also holding her to him. There were no words that would make this better, so she just lay with him and let him stroke her hair until the heaving of his chest stopped.

'What would you do,' he asked after a long while, 'if you discovered your pills had failed?'

'What?'

'Would you keep the baby?'

'Depends.'

'On?'

Aggie pulled herself up so she could see his face. He was lovely with his big, sleepy eyes and messy hair. It was astounding how happy she felt just from looking at him. 'We don't need to talk about this, Luke. I'm not going to get pregnant.'

'But if you did.'

'I would do whatever you wanted.'

'I would want you to have the baby.'

'Right.' She moved away from him, lying on her side so he couldn't see her face.

'You wouldn't want it, would you?'

'Since it's never going to happen we don't need to worry about it, do we?'

'I just need to know. Would you want an abortion?'

'Yes.'

He made a noise like she'd winded him. She was sorry for that but could not lie about something so fundamental. She'd told him about her past abortions and he had taken it well – but that was before they were lovers. Now he was taking it personally, imagining himself as Matthew, discovering too late that his lover had aborted his child. Aggie realised the whole relationship was going to be like this, him obsessing over her past sins, trying to force her belatedly to repent.

'You never want children?'

'I'm sorry, but I don't.'

'Don't be sorry. I don't particularly want children either.'

Aggie turned over and stared at him.

'I just want us to be clear on this. If you did fall pregnant, obviously I wouldn't want it killed and I couldn't bear to give it away, but– I don't think I'll ever be a father. I know it's not up to me, really. If God wants me to– well, anyway, I just can't even imagine. I have no idea what parents and children are to each other.'

'I know.'

'You do know, don't you?' He was radiant as he pulled her closer. 'We're so alike, Ag, it blows me away to think how alike we are.'

'Except for–'

'Yes. Except for that.'

'Belinda called me this morning.'

His body tensed, but his expression was calm and interested.

'Oh?'

'She wanted to know if I'd seen you.'

'Oh.'

'I lied.'

He relaxed. 'Thank you.'

Aggie kissed him for a little while. She had to know what he was planning on doing, but she was afraid of pushing. She had a dread of finding out that this was a lost weekend, that the experience would be forever cherished but never repeated. She ended the kiss with difficulty; he had been clinging to her even harder than he usually did.

'So no-one knows where you are?'

'Not a soul.'

'Won't they be worried?'

'Probably.' He leant in to kiss her but she moved her face to the side.

'When are you going back?'

Luke sighed and flopped dramatically onto his back. 'Sunday, I guess. I'm supposed to be doing the service at the city church, unfortunately.'

'Why didn't you tell them? What's wrong?'

'I'm in some trouble. There have been... rumours and...' Luke sighed and covered his face. 'I wish I didn't have to go back. I wish I could just stay here forever. I swear, Ag, if it wasn't for Honey I think I'd–'

'What?' Aggie sat up. 'Honey?' Aggie remembered the swinging blonde plait and tough-girl laugh. She remembered the boarded up windows and disconnected phone. The girl had never returned to the clinic and Aggie assumed she had made her own way to the doctor.

'Oh!' Luke laughed. 'I forgot to tell you about Honey! She's with us now.'

Aggie was out of bed and pulling on her underpants in a flash.

'You are fucking kidding me.'

Luke sat up. 'Ag, you've got to hear this. It's really a miracle.'

'I'm listening.' She pulled a t-shirt over her head.

Luke told her how he had come across Honey in the McDonald's, battered and broken. He told her about how she had miraculously decided not to abort her child, and how she had miraculously consented to move into the NCYC for the duration of her pregnancy. By the time he was finished talking she was dressed. She looked into his face, amazed at how comfortable he seemed. More than comfortable – proud!

'It makes me sick that you would take advantage of a pregnant girl from a violent home. And to encourage a girl with no money, no support network, barely able to take care of herself, to have a child is disgusting. You are disgusting.'

'Aggie, sit down a minute.'

'No, I won't. You're repulsive.' She ran from the room, tears coursing down her face. He was a monster. What he'd done was virtually kidnapping – and if it wasn't illegal it was certainly immoral. God, that poor child! Aggie tried to remember how far gone she had been: was it ten weeks or twelve? Either way she would be too far gone now to have a simple D&C. Her only option would be a full surgical procedure, which was a hell of a lot harder to arrange, not to mention physically traumatic. Damn him!

She let her tears run free as she cleared the remains of brunch from the table. She made as much noise as possible, throwing plates hard into the sink and slamming the cupboard doors.

'I don't understand why you're so upset.' Luke leant on the kitchen bench, watching her fill the sink with water. He had wrapped the pink towel around his waist again, which made Aggie furious because how *dare* he look so delicious?

'I'm upset,' Aggie said, throwing a coffee cup into the sink and splashing herself with hot, soapy water in the process, 'because you're an unethical, immoral, slimy, lying, selfish bastard.'

'But you love me anyway, right?'

'Fuck you.'

'Now listen, Aggie, you and I disagree on some fundamental issues and Honey and her child happen to be one of them. I don't–'

'She's not an *issue*, Luke! She's a kid.'

'Stop washing up. Come and talk to me properly.'

Aggie sighed and wiped her hands, but did not go to him, choosing instead to cross her arms over her chest and lean on the edge of the sink. 'I really don't see what you can say to make this better. You've ruined a young girl's life.'

'No, I've saved the life of an innocent baby, and also saved the mother from a lifetime of guilt and an eternity of suffering. I am absolutely thrilled by how the situation has turned out and there's nothing you can say that will change my mind about it. So you might as well stop sulking.'

He crossed back to the table and sat down. Aggie watched as he foraged through the fruit bowl, discarding apples, oranges and pears, before finally selecting a peach which he pressed to his nose, inhaling deeply. He gave a contented sigh and took a bite, closing his eyes as he chewed. Aggie was melting. Here was this astonishing man – a man of depth, a man of learning, a man of compassion and strength – sitting at her kitchen table on a Friday afternoon, sucking the flesh of a peach in the most obscene way. He looked at her from under droopy lids, suggesting with his eyes that he knew exactly what he was doing to that innocent piece of fruit and that if she would only forgive him he would do the same to her. How could religious differences matter? How could anything?

'Luke…' She began but could not finish; she was stupid with lust. He had finished the peach and was licking his fingers. She went to him, letting him put his sticky, dishonest hands all over her.

'Maybe,' Luke said, his mouth sliding across her collarbone, 'maybe it would be best if we didn't talk about my work or your work or–'

'Anything at all,' Aggie said and they both laughed, but it sounded forced and hysterical. Aggie realised with a shock that he was as morally confused as she. The peculiar mix of self-hatred and self-righteousness she had been nursing melted into a deep, deep sadness. There would be no happy ending here, but that made it all feel so much more valuable somehow, the way that life itself seemed infinitely more precious once you understood it would end.

29

L uke was woken on Sunday by dawn's harsh white light. He watched Aggie sleep, counted the freckles on her arms, the lines around her mouth. He was physically exhausted, emotionally confused and spiritually bereft. He was terrified he would never be able to leave her side and terrified at the idea of being apart from her. And every time he touched her or even thought about touching her, his penis got so hard he thought it was going to burst out of its considerably chafed skin.

If he did not drag himself out of this bed, today, this morning, *now*, the damage would be too great to repair. In three hours approximately one hundred Christians would fiddle with their hair and yank their ties, anxiously watching the empty pulpit and rectory door for signs of their wayward Pastor; in four hours the gossip-mongers would have him hospitalised or dead in a gutter or tied up in a basement. Already Belinda and the others would be frantically searching for him, thinking, quite rightly, that almost nothing in the world would keep him away from his ministry. What that minutely possible something might be, they would be racking their brains to figure out. Pastor Riley would guess at something approximating the truth, which was revolting to think about, because that man could never understand the intense goodness of what had occurred in this house over the weekend.

'I have to go, Ag.'

She moaned and reached for his arm, pulling it tight to her side.

'I'm sorry. I have responsibilities. The sooner I face the music, the better.'

She opened one eye. 'You're expecting trouble?'

'Certainly.'

She opened the other eye. 'Because you took off?'

'And because of where I took off to.'

Aggie crinkled her brow. 'You'll be in trouble for staying at your girlfriend's house?'

Luke stroked her precious face. 'My girlfriend. I like that.'

She would not be softened. 'But they won't allow it, right? They'll make you choose. You'll go back there and they'll make you choose between your job and your whore.'

'Ag, please, don't–'

'And as long as you're with them, that's all I'll be. Your whore. Your fucking cross. I'll always be the thing that's dragging you down, the thing to be ashamed of, to regret.' She sat up, pulling the sheet up over her breasts. 'How do you think I feel, knowing that this week-end represents the lowest point in your life for you? You can hardly wait to get out of here so you can start putting me in your wicked past.'

'If you think that, then you don't know me at all.'

'Oh, I'm sorry, did I underestimate you? You're going to take me to church with you and introduce me around? You planning a romantic proposal sometime soon?'

Heloïse would not marry Peter Abelard. She knew that a belated wedding would not confer respectability on their passion, nor would it negate their sinfulness. She saw marriage as a sham, something which would bestow her with a meaningless title and cause her to commit what she saw as the greater sin of dishonesty. *God is my witness that if Augustus, emperor of the whole world, thought fit to honour me with marriage and conferred all the earth upon me to possess for ever, it would be dearer and more honourable to me to be called not his empress but your whore.*

But Aggie was not Heloïse. She didn't understand that having wilfully entered into sin, he could not ever mock God by pretending this union was sanctified by Him. Worse would be the dishonesty between the two of them. To pretend that making a marriage vow was the ultimate commitment when Luke had already sacrificed eternity for her. But to her, eternity was a construct, a fantasy. So too then, was his sacrifice. She would never understand.

'I promise you, Aggie, I will never, ever disown this. But I can't just walk away from my life and not look back.' Luke got up quickly, thinking of pulling off a bandaid. He stood leaning on the bedpost for a moment, dizzy with the blood rushing to his head, and then dressed in his freshly-washed but unironed clothes while she watched him and wept. He would have to sneak into his room to change clothes before anyone saw him looking so sloppy. Although surely everyone would be able to tell just by looking at him that he was a man who knew what carnality was, and so he supposed no-one would even notice the crushed clothing.

'Are you ever coming back?'

'Of course, I'm coming back,' he told her, sitting on a chair in the corner to lace his shoes. 'I just don't know under what circumstances. I have to assess the situation.'

'Please, Luke, I can't stand the thought of you back in that place. Just stay here with me. Please?'

He wondered when he had become the kind of man who could make love to a woman and then leave her to sob as if her heart was breaking. There was an old Jewish proverb he liked to quote to the kids: *The thief who finds no opportunity to steal considers himself an honest man.*

Perhaps he had always been a weak and selfish man; perhaps he had just never before met the right woman.

30

They were waiting in his bedroom: Pastor Riley, Pastor Graham and Mrs Berlotti from the Board of Elders, Kenny, Greg, Leticia and Belinda. Luke remained in the doorway. 'This door was locked,' he said, addressing Pastor Riley.

'Kenny was kind enough to unlock it for us.'

Luke turned to Kenny, who shrugged and looked at his feet. 'Right. Why?'

'We were worried, Luke,' said Belinda, who was sitting on his bed, her feet tucked up under her. She did not look particularly worried. Beside her, Leticia stared at the bedspread. She looked as though she had been crying, and Luke felt the first twinge of remorse. Leticia's fear of abandonment hadn't crossed his mind. Nor had he considered Greg's tendency to imagine catastrophe. Luke quickly looked across to Greg; he had his back to the room, his forehead resting on the window frame.

'I'm very sorry,' Luke said, forcing himself to step fully into the room. 'I have no excuse. I've been thoughtless and irresponsible, and I hope you can all forgive me.'

'What exactly are you asking us to forgive you for, Pastor Butler?' said Pastor Graham in an incredulous tone. 'For all we know you have been just this morning released from hospital and it is we who should be asking forgiveness from you.'

Luke nodded at Pastor Graham. 'I'm sorry I wasn't clear.' He glanced around the room, locking eyes with each of them in turn, except for Greg, who was still facing the window. 'I had some personal business to attend to. I am sorry that I did not inform my colleagues of my intention to take leave, and I am sorry that I did not contact the Church to advise of my absence. I am deeply sorry for any distress or inconvenience my absence has caused.'

There was a brief silence, followed by Pastor Riley clearing his throat. Luke looked at him questioningly. Pastor Riley rubbed his glasses. 'And the nature of this personal business?'

'Well, that's personal. That's why it's called personal business. Because of its personal nature.'

Leticia giggled and Belinda shot her an annoyed look. 'I am not amused by this, Luke,' said Pastor Riley. Pastor Graham nodded his agreement. 'For a Christian Revolution minister there is no such thing as personal business.'

'Then I also apologise for having personal business. I will endeavour to avoid having any in the future. '

The Pastors and Mrs Berlotti exchanged dark glances. 'Your attitude strikes me as rather flippant,' Pastor Riley said. 'Perhaps you don't understand the gravity of the situation.'

Luke was so tired. He wanted to crawl back into Aggie's bed and sleep all day. Except, if he was in her bed he would not be able to sleep; that was why he was so tired right now. What he really wanted was for everyone to get out of his room so he could go catch up on the sleep he had missed for the last two nights. Then he wanted to check on Honey. And *then* he wanted to go back to Aggie's bed.

'Pastor Butler.' Mrs Berlotti addressed him for the first time. Her voice was tiny, but Luke knew from his year working at head office that the voice was as misleading as her grandmotherly appearance.

The woman was a pit bull, as her next sentence confirmed. 'The elders have ordered your immediate suspension pending a full investigation into the allegations against you.'

Leticia began to cry. Belinda tut-tutted and patted her shoulder. Luke closed his eyes and counted to ten. Mrs Berlotti continued. 'Kenny Driscoll will act as Senior Pastor in the interim. You will continue to be paid during the investigation and your residential arrangements will be unchanged. You will, of course, be expected to co-operate fully with the investigation. If the allegations are found to be true—'

Luke reached ten and opened his eyes. 'What are the allegations?'

Mrs Berlotti narrowed her eyes. 'If the allegations are found to be true then the elders will decide on disciplinary action. You should be aware that the maximum penalty is expulsion.'

'I'm aware. What are the allegations?'

Pastor Riley stood, noisily scraping the chair against the tiles. 'Belinda, could you please take Leticia out of here?'

Belinda sat up very straight. 'I don't see why—'

'Greg and Kenny are leaving too. And I don't need to remind any of you that insubordination is not looked upon favourably by the elders.'

Wordlessly, but with much sighing and heavy placing of feet, the Junior Pastors left. As they filed past Luke, only Greg met his eyes. He smiled for a split second, then was gone.

It was alleged, Mrs Berlotti informed him, that he had been sexually intimate with a person to whom he was not married. It was alleged that when his superior asked him about this relationship, he had lied. It was alleged that he had conducted this affair on Christian Revolution property, during Christian Revolution functions. It was alleged he had supported the activities of the Parramatta Sexual Health Clinic, specifically, that clinic's abortion referral program. It was alleged he had neglected his duties as Senior Pastor of North-western Christian Youth Centre by taking a leave of absence without permission or notice.

'Will I have an opportunity to respond officially?' Luke asked when she was finished.

'Of course. The Board will formally interview you on Monday, and conduct further interviews as necessary.'

'Fine.' Luke sat on the bed. *Oh*, he was so very tired. 'See you all on Monday then.'

31

Honey was thinking about running away. She knew this was a stupid thing to be thinking, because she'd never had it as good as she had it here. Three meals a day, hot water that never ran out, always someone to talk to when you were freaked out or lonely, always someone to help with your homework.

But she was finding that being taken care of was kind of like being dead. She just lay on her bed all the time now, staring at the ceiling or at the insides of her eyelids. She thought about the baby a lot, and sometimes allowed herself to feel a bit excited about having a soft, clean little person who would love her and need her, but then she freaked out again because the poor little guy would be screwed from the minute he was born. Honey didn't have the first clue how to be a mother. All the books Luke had given her talked about feeding and sleeping and bathing and crying, but she still didn't know what you were supposed to do if you looked at your baby and didn't love it. She was so afraid she would not love it.

And what if she did love it – loved it as much as the books said she'd love it – but it came out wrong anyway? What if it was retarded or blind or deaf? In birth, the cord could get wrapped around its tiny neck and it would turn blue and die before it even left her body. And say it survived the birth, and she loved it, and she brought it back here and figured out the bathing and the feeding and everything and then it got sick or something. She was so afraid of that, of loving it.

Now Luke was gone. Okay, so it had only been a couple of days, but it was so unlike him. Honey stared at the ceiling and wished she could believe that her prayers were being heard, her requests considered. What she wanted was for Luke to come back and sit on the end of her bed and rub her achy feet and tell her she wasn't alone. She used to get annoyed at the way he was always in her face, lecturing about taking her pre-natal vitamin, and walking around the grounds an hour each day, and making sure to eat enough fibre. But when he was suddenly gone, for no reason, with no warning and no explanation, Honey realised that if it wasn't for Luke's nagging she would probably just lie and look at the ceiling until she died. The baby would die too, of course.

She had started smoking again. Quitting had been easier than she'd thought, but after a few days the smells started getting to her. Sweat and toothpaste and perfume and hairspray. Face cream and shampoo and detergent. Food was the worst: garlic and coffee and tuna. Even the lawn smelled too strong, too green, too grassy, and so she started smoking again. Those raw, real smells faded away. If Luke came back she swore to God she would stop smoking for good. She would learn to live with the smelly world, truly.

There was a knock on the door. Her heart leapt with the thought that he might have come back, but she suppressed her excitement. No point getting all hopeful then being disappointed again. She yelled for the person who wasn't Luke to come in. She stayed where she was, just to prove that she didn't expect it to be Luke. If she'd expected it to be him, she would have got up, ready to hug him and tell him she was sorry to be such a pain and please never to leave again.

'Ah, Honey?'

Honey turned her head towards the door. She knew it. She knew it wouldn't be him. 'Greg, hey, what's up?'

Greg stood awkwardly in the doorway. He didn't come right in and sit down and start talking like Luke would have done.

'Ah, can I talk to you a sec?'

Honey nodded. 'Come and sit down.'

Greg rubbed his chin a few times, rocked back on his heels, coughed and finally, closed the door behind him and came to sit, not on the end of the bed as Luke would have, but far away on the desk chair.

'Luke's back.'

The muscles in her thighs twitched with how much she wanted to leap out of bed and sprint to Luke's room. 'Oh?' she said.

'Yeah, he, um– he's in some trouble with the elders.'

'Is he?' Honey sounded like she didn't care.

'But you don't need to worry, okay?'

Honey pulled herself up on to her elbows and looked at Greg. His eyes were very wide. Honey had never seen him look so awake. 'Why would I worry?'

Greg twisted his hands in front of him. He cleared his throat three times. 'You'll always be taken care of. Even if Luke…'

She felt so sick. Her heart was racing. 'Even if Luke what?'

'Even if he has to leave, you don't have to worry, because I'll take care of you.'

Honey lay back down and closed her eyes. Luke was the only one who understood. He had known her when she was going to kill her baby and he still cared about her. He knew she'd done all those bad things with boys, knew she'd stolen money from her grandma and clothes from K-Mart. He knew about her being half-Spanish. He knew she was terrified of having a baby by herself, and that she could only do it if he was there holding her hand. Luke had sworn he was her family now – and she didn't want this kid if it wasn't going to have a family. Luke *knew* all this. He couldn't, couldn't, *could not* leave.

'Okay, so I'll leave you alone,' Greg said. Honey heard the chair scraping back, then his footsteps.

'Wait,' she said. 'Can you come and sit with me a minute?'

Honey heard his hesitation. The sound of his heels rocking, the throat clearing and coughing, two steps forward, pause, rock, cough. She lay still, her eyes closed, her hands over the belly that was growing out of her control. Greg rocked and coughed a few more times, and then Honey felt the mattress shift as he sat beside her.

'I wonder where he was,' Greg said, fast, faux-casual. 'Not that it's any of our business, you know, but I just wonder what could make him take off like that?'

'I wish I could take off.'

'Honey?'

'I want to go to Spain. My dad's there, you know. In Granada.'

Greg exhaled loudly. 'I didn't know that. Have you ever been?'

'I've never been anywhere.'

'You should go. Granada is incredible. You can visit the church where Christopher Columbus prayed before he set out and discovered America. It's really beautiful, even if it is Catholic.'

'I think my dad is Catholic.'

'Well, maybe he'll take you to the church. Then after that he could show you the old castle. Then you can both go to the village square and eat tapas.'

Honey turned and looked at Greg's hand on his thigh, right near her head. 'He has this whole other family. I don't think he'd have time for all that.'

Greg's long white fingers tapped against his thigh. 'So you could go yourself anyway, right? I went on my own, all over Europe. Man, that was a fun time. Except…' His hand formed a fist for a second, then relaxed and recommenced tapping. 'I wasn't saved then. I had fun, but it wasn't right, you know? If I went back now, I'd do things differently. I bet I'd have an even better time now.'

'When were you saved?'

'It'll be five years in December. I think I'd be dead if Luke hadn't found me. Or sleeping under a bridge or something.'

Honey smiled at him, although he couldn't see her. 'We have that much in common then.'

His hand stopped moving. 'We have more than that in common, Honey. We're converts. It's hard for the others to understand why that makes a difference, but it does. Belinda and the others were all born Christians; they haven't lived in the world without knowing Jesus. They don't know how hard it can be to forget all that, to change.'

'Do you find it hard?'

'Sometimes.' Greg was quiet. His hand clenched and unclenched. 'I would be dead if it wasn't for Luke saving me. I always have to remember that.'

'Luke says only Jesus changes hearts.'

'Right. Jesus changed my heart. Luke showed me the way to Jesus.'

Honey reached out and took the restless hand. It froze, then fought for a split second, then relaxed and closed around her hand. Honey lay still, looking at the strange fingers wrapped around her hand. She sort of wished he would move, stroke her hair, maybe slide down on the bed so he was beside her. She wasn't sure whether she wanted him to kiss her. When Luke held her hand she never thought about kissing.

'I miss Luke. I don't know what I'll do if he goes away forever.'

Greg released her hand. 'We'll be okay, Honey. I promise.' He began to stroke her hair.

32

Luke woke sweating, reaching for the woman who should be sweating beside him. Opening his eyes he saw the bleak timber panelling of his bedroom wall and felt the desolation of missing her. Three nights in her bed and the habits of twenty-nin years were erased. It felt all wrong to be alone, clothed, well-rested.

It was two o'clock on Sunday afternoon, and he had no sermon to read over, no meetings to arrange, no teenagers to counsel or parents to advise. He stripped off his sweat-soaked clothes and stepped into the shower. That was all wrong too. How had he managed all these years without Aggie to wash his back? How come he had never noticed how big the shower recess was, how obviously designed to accommodate two bodies, a woman and a man, with interlocking parts?

So there would be an investigation. They would ask him: Do you support the aims of the Parramatta Free Sexual Health Clinic? He would say no. They would ask him: Do you believe in the sanctity of life, specifically, do you believe that the killing of unborn children is evil? He would say yes and yes. Then they would ask: What is your relationship with Agatha Grey? And he would tell them: *She is mine. If you saw the way we fit together, you would have no doubt that the woman was designed especially for me. No document of church or state could make us any more married than we are. She is mine. Like Paul, I care not if I am judged by you or by any human court; indeed, I do not even judge myself. My conscience is clear, but that does not make me innocent. It is the Lord who judges me.* Or probably he would stand stony-faced and say *we are lovers* and they would not understand why that wasn't a bad thing, and they would expel him.

He combed his hair, thinking of how she would muss it up. He dressed quickly in running shorts and a t-shirt. He had no official duties. He had no official reason to dress well. And Aggie would say *you look nice in shorts.* Then she might pull them off him with her teeth. His penis throbbed to life, reaching towards her phantom mouth.

He would call her first. Tell her what had happened. She would forgive him for walking away like that this morning. She would tell him to come over. This is exactly what she wanted. *All to myself* she'd say, and he wouldn't argue. He'd lose himself in her, and forget all this controversy, all this politicking and judging.

She did not answer her phone. He tried nineteen times, then threw the phone onto the floor in disgust before he hit twenty. She must have gone out. Sometimes she walked to clear her head. Sometimes when she was upset, she got drunk. But surely not at two-thirty on a Sunday afternoon. But Aggie didn't care about Sunday. She thought it was a good day to sleep in, have a swim, wash her car, drink some wine in the sun. She didn't know about the gaping emptiness of not having a sermon to give or a service to attend.

He would wait ten minutes and then try her again. If she didn't answer, he would go over anyway. He would wait on her veranda all afternoon, all night, if he had to. When she got home, he would not ask where she'd been. He would follow her inside and lock the door. He knew each minute in her company destroyed him a little more. He knew he was hurting her, disrespecting her, using her, dooming her. He knew that Jesus wept for them both. But he would follow her inside and he would pretend nothing else mattered and after a while, nothing else would.

Luke tried to phone her again. Still no answer. He had to grip the edge of the table to stop from ripping the phone out of the wall. His ten minutes wasn't up, but he had to get out of this room before he lost his mind. He decided to do something constructive. Since the investigators would no doubt gather their information from every grubby little place they could find it, he had better know what was out there. The grotty Justice for the Unborn Website was the obvious starting point. Luke decided to download everything they had on Aggie and himself, and *then* he would go to her house and wait for her to come home.

The main building was quiet. Sunday was traditional worship only. Everyone was expected to go to at least one service, but the rest of the day was free for rest and relaxation. They would all be visiting their families or napping under a tree by the river. Luke felt a pang at missing his services, but he was pleased to have the place to himself. He got to his office unseen.

While he waited for the computer to fire up, Luke went through his desk drawers and removed the few personal items he kept in there: half a roll of peppermint Lifesavers, a travel pack of tissues, a hair comb, the white leather-bound Bible he had been issued after completing his missionary year. Then he went to the wall by the window and took down the framed ordination certificate and photograph.

Up until this weekend, the most momentous occasion of Luke's life had been his ordination. He had worn a white linen robe belted at the waist with a strip of brown leather, and sat on a hard wooden chair he had made himself. The elders had knelt before him and washed his face, hands and feet. *You are the body of Christ*, they recited. *Jesus has no hands on earth except your hands, and no mouth on earth except your mouth. Being His body, you must express Jesus through all that you are.*

This weekend, Aggie too had knelt before him and said *My God you have a beautiful cock.* She had closed her eyes and called out to the heavens *Jesus Christ, I love the way you fuck me.* She had washed him all over saying *Oh God, your body is divine.* It was a baptism of sorts. Satan must have been laughing his tail off.

The dead babies on the Justice for the Unborn website made Luke think about Honey. Seeing her should have been the first thing he'd done, but he didn't know what to tell her. She wouldn't accept his personal business line. She would demand to know where he was, and although she was just a child she had *been there, done that* and she would know if he fudged the details. *Slept over* she would scoff, *oh, right, Mr Sin-free, I suppose you slept in the spare room with your flannelette pyjamas on.*

The thought that Honey had done the things he and Aggie had done made him dizzy. How could any man look at poor, sweet Honey with her big brown eyes like a terrified deer, and feel anything but protective? The father of the baby was not the only one to have done those things to her. Luke had known this all along, but now the knowledge made his hands begin to shake. He imagined Honey lying beneath him, naked, her scrawny legs pressed together, her arms crossed over her chest so as not to reveal her little girl breasts, her doe eyes looking up at him. He wanted to cover her with a blanket and bring her good food to eat. But men had looked at Honey like that and found her enticing. Men had driven into her body the way Luke drove into Aggie. Grown men had opened up Honey and dumped their disgusting stuff inside her. She had let them. Maybe even asked them to.

Luke thought he might throw up. He put his head on the desk and concentrated on breathing until the sensation passed. Resolving to keep his mind free of all but the task at hand, he turned back to the computer.

There she was: Agatha Grey, all crazy curls and gangly limbs. He skimmed the breathless description of her personal life. There was nothing he didn't know already – mother's desertion, father's suicide, broken marriage, friendship with homosexual activist Malcolm Addison. Further down the page there was the photo of Luke and Aggie embracing in the carpark, with a hyper-linked caption advising readers to *check out the disgraceful double life of Pastor Butler of the Christian Revolution – when he's not making out with abortionists he's preaching to your children*. This was an accurate description and yet it said nothing at all about him. Only God and Aggie truly knew him, because only God and Aggie knew him wordlessly.

He scrolled down. There was another photo almost identical in composition to the first. Two cars, side by side in the staff parking area of the clinic. A man and a woman embracing passionately. A date and time stamp in the corner. But the car next to Aggie's was some kind of four-wheel drive, and the hand tangled up in her hair was not Luke's. The photo had been taken less than a week ago. Luke read the text over and over. *Aggie Grey demonstrates her high moral standards by publicly making out with married father of two Dr Simon Keating. We wonder if Pastor Butler knows how quickly he has been replaced!*

33

When Mal opened the door to Aggie on Sunday morning, she was already crying.

'Pastor Butler?' he asked, ushering her in.

Aggie nodded and allowed herself to be pushed into an enormous armchair and fed hot tea and chocolate biscuits. Will was so kind to her, rubbing her shoulders and handing her tissues, that she cried all the more.

'I'm so happy you guys sorted everything out. You give me faith.'

Will leant down and whispered in her ear. 'We got married.'

'Aggie doesn't want to hear about that right now, darl.'

'Of course I do. Tell me!'

'We were on the balcony of our hotel, drinking tequila and watching the sun set over the desert, and Mal turns to me and says, "It's about time we got married, don't you think?" and I said – well, I didn't say anything, I just squealed in an alarmingly camp way, and then we went out and bought rings and found a crazy old priest who married us in his garden and then had his wife serve us mint tea.'

'They were ninety years old,' Mal said. 'I don't think they realised we were both men. It's not legal, of course.'

'Oh, bugger legal. It's incredibly romantic. I'm thrilled. You'll have to let me throw you a wedding party. You can do it all again in my garden.'

Will kissed her cheek. 'You're the best fag-hag-in-law a boy could ask for. I want you to be the mother-influence of our unborn children.'

'Enough with the Queer as Folk audition. What's that little shit done to you, Ag?'

Aggie told them about the three-day fuckfest, the revelation about Honey, the desperation she had felt about letting him go, and the fear that he would never come back. She started crying again and could not stop. She could not recall a time when she had felt so miserable. Luke existed on an entirely different moral plane from her. How could she love him? He had virtually kidnapped a pregnant teenager, for fucksake!

'You're not seeing him again,' Mal said when she had finished talking.

'I love him.'

'You're. Not. Seeing. Him. Again.' Mal emphasised each word with a fist to the coffee table. 'Ever.'

Will covered Mal's fist with his hand. 'She loves him.'

'Even more reason to put a stop to it now. It'll only get harder, and he's not going to change. He's going to keep doing evil shit, and you're going to keep getting hurt. Your mother would go nuts, Aggie.'

'Fuck her. Where's she when I need her?'

'She's off being true to herself. Like you should be.'

Aggie covered her face with her hands. Mal was wrong. She had never felt more truly herself than when she was with Luke. There was no place for the mind, just passion, love, joy. The real Aggie, the strong, powerful, fully-alive Aggie, existed only in his presence. Without him, she was a shadow, all thought, no heart.

'We had sex. That means something.'

Mal threw his hands up. 'Oh, give me a break.'

'No, she's right,' Will said. 'The boy is a hottie; if he was a virgin then you can bet it wasn't through lack of offers. Pathetic or not, Mal, the kid gave Ag what to him was the most precious thing he had. Tell me that doesn't mean something.'

'It means he's a fucking fruit-loop. Anyone who gives that much importance to sex is seriously warped.'

He was right, of course. Having spent his life repressing his sexuality, Luke had no idea how to express it in a reasonable, healthy way. He didn't seem to realise that people have limits. He had hurt Aggie badly with his explorations and invasions. He had also made her come harder and for longer than she thought possible. He had burst into a song about the miracles of rainbows while she sucked his dick and he had woken her in the night by licking her arsehole. He said and did the most obscene things without the slightest embarrassment. When he had lost his virginity he had lost every inhibition, and the more she thought about it the more she realised what a very big deal it was.

If Aggie's head was spinning, how much worse off would he be? A life-long vow broken, devastatingly intense intimacy, and then *boom* he's back in church, surrounded by people who cannot possibly know what he has experienced. It was too much, too fast. He needed to be debriefed. He needed to take stock, with her, his partner in crime. God, she'd been selfish, worrying about herself when he was probably off losing his mind.

'I'd better go home. He's probably called.' Aggie stood, ignoring Mal's expression. 'I'll see you later.' She ran out before he could tell her why she shouldn't.

34

By the time Luke had cleaned up all the pieces of the computer monitor and washed and bandaged up his hands, it was after four. He dialled Aggie's number, and this time she answered straight away. Hearing her husky voice was just too much; Luke hung up without speaking and then smashed the receiver into the desk until it was nothing but a bunch of wires with a few bits of black plastic hanging off here and there. The cut in his right palm split open and so he had to wash and wrap it again.

It was time to come clean with Honey. He would tell her about Aggie, not in detail of course, just a sketch. He would apologise for letting her down and beg her forgiveness. He hoped she would e-mail him from time to time to tell him how she was getting on. He dearly hoped she would permit him to visit her in hospital after her son was born. If not, well, he hardly deserved any better.

The door of Honey's cabin was not properly closed; a sliver of light showed from inside. He knocked and waited. There was no response. He pushed it open a fraction more, wary of invading her privacy but concerned she had perhaps fallen asleep and left her room unlocked.

Stepping inside, Luke saw that Honey was indeed sleeping soundly. What he had not anticipated was the fact that she was not alone. Beside her, his chest acting as a pillow for her head was Greg.

Pain whipped Luke's chest and stomach. Greg gave a little moan as he opened his eyes.

'Luke…' Greg reached for him with one hand, then abruptly stopped and turned his attention to the sleeping girl. 'Honey!' He half-sat, easing her off him by holding her shoulders. 'Wake up, Honey, you have to–'

'Luke?' Honey blinked at him. She sat up straight, rubbed her face, blinked again. 'What happened to you?'

Luke's words got stuck in his throat. He coughed and held his aching guts. Greg came towards him, put his arm around his back and led him to Honey's bed. He feared sitting there, feared he would smell sex and lose his mind, but he had neither words nor strength, so he sat and allowed Honey to pick up both his arms.

'What happened to you?'

Luke couldn't bear to look at her. He turned to Greg, who was hovering over them, rubbing his chin and making small panicky noises.

'How could you?' he managed to say.

'Luke, man, don't freak out. Everything's cool here. We just fell asleep.'

'Don't freak out.' Luke laughed, pulling his bandaged hands away from Honey. 'Why would I freak out? It's just fornication, right? Just sex. Everybody's doing it with everybody. Doesn't mean anything. Jump from one bed to another within a week. Easy come, easy go, nothing to it.'

'I think something's wrong,' Honey said. 'Maybe we should call someone.'

'Luke?' Greg crouched in front of him. 'You look tired, man. I'll walk you to your room, heh?'

Luke laughed. He couldn't seem to stop.

'I don't know what happened to you this weekend, but I know

you're strong enough to handle it. We'll go to your room, and we'll pray together. Like old times, right? Remember, Luke, when I was lost and you'd sit and pray with me for hours, all night sometimes? You said God never gives us something we can't handle, and I believe that. So whatever's wrong, we'll go talk to Jesus and with His help, we'll sort it out.'

'He and I are not on speaking terms at the moment.' Luke laughed and laughed. 'He's in a bit of a sulk with me, I think.'

'What? Greg, what's he saying? I can't understand. I think something's really wrong,' said Honey.

The laughter had morphed into something else. Cackling, Luke thought, or maybe this was hooting. Whatever it was called it sounded dreadful. If only he could stop.

'He needs help, Greg. He's lost it.'

Luke turned on Honey, the laughter dying in his throat. 'I *have* lost it. How did you know? Can you tell by looking, Honey? Is there some kind of radar that tells you when a man is fallen? Is that how you knew Greg would hop into bed with you?'

'That's it.' Greg grabbed Luke's arm and pulled him to his feet. He was very strong; Luke didn't bother struggling. 'I'm sure you don't know what you're saying, but if you keep saying it, I'm going to lose my temper with you.'

'I know what I'm saying. I'm saying that you are a hypocrite. That you pretend to be saved and as soon as you find a girl willing to spread her legs for you—'

Greg's fist slammed into Luke's nose. Luke stumbled backwards, hit the back of his knees on the bed and stumbled forwards again, right into the path of Greg's follow-up punch. Behind him, Honey was crying and saying *Greg, no*. Luke thought of how she should have thought to say that before she'd lain down for him. Maybe he said it out loud, because the next two punches were faster and angrier than the first. The first had just been a polite request to shut up; now he was really getting it.

Luke touched his face; it felt squishy and wet. He laughed, cackled, howled, choked on blood and mucus and rage. He swung out weakly, feeling a small shiver of satisfaction as his knuckles made contact with Greg's cheekbone. The satisfaction was quickly overtaken by pain as the wound on his hand reopened, and at the same instant, Greg's knee collided with his stomach. He swung out again, blindly, clumsily. He hit something, but the something moved on impact and he fell forward. Opening his eyes, he saw the floorboards flying towards him.

35

Honey was in the kitchen making up an ice pack when she heard banging on the front doors. They kept them locked on Sundays because there were no groups or meetings on, but somebody obviously did not know this. Honey swore under her breath, hurriedly finished packing the ice into a tea towel and then jogged out to tell whoever the hell it was that God was not in the house.

'Honey, hi,' Aggie said. 'I heard you'd moved in. How are you?'

Honey stared. Aggie looked even worse than usual; her face was red and puffy, and her hair was all over the place. She had black bags under her eyes and her lips were all chapped and flaky.

'Okay if I come in?'

Honey bit her lip. Just after Honey had moved in, Luke had told her that he and Aggie were no longer friends because *what can darkness and light have in common?* He'd told everybody that if Aggie called or came around they were to say he was out and take a message.

'Um, we're kind of closed on Sundays.'

'Yeah, I know. I just want to see Luke. Is he in?'

Honey looked down at the ice pack in her hand. She liked Aggie and did not want to lie, but Luke would not want her to see him the way he was right now, if at all. And Aggie looked kind of worked up about something so it probably wasn't the best time to – oh!

'He's been with you!' Honey said, seeing Aggie how she really was: tired from being up all night, with chapped lips and beard rash from kissing. 'What did you do to him?'

Tears leaked from Aggie's eyes. 'Is he okay?'

'You better come through.'

'Shit! Oh, Luke!' Aggie ran into the room and threw herself to the ground, lifting Luke's head onto her lap and stroking his bloody face. 'Oh, baby, what happened to you?'

Luke was barely conscious. He gurgled, rolled his eyes right around then closed them.

'You did this?' Aggie demanded of Greg who sat on Honey's bed, his head in his hands.

'He was out of control. I had to.'

'You had to knock him unconscious? You had to break his nose?'

Honey sat beside Greg and took his hand. 'Leave him alone. It wasn't his fault.'

'Sweetie? Luke, baby, can you hear me?' Aggie patted his cheek. 'I can't believe what you did to him. Jesus, Greg, it's *Luke*.'

'I can't believe what *you* did to him,' Honey said.

Aggie stopped patting Luke's face. She stared hard at Honey. 'What does that mean?'

'You screwed him.'

Aggie opened her mouth. Closed it. Made a dismissive sound through her teeth and returned her attention to Luke. 'Come on, Luke, baby, I'll take you home.'

'He is home,' Greg said.

Aggie ignored him. 'I'll get you all cleaned up. Give you a nice bath, tuck you up in bed. Heh, sweetie? Sound good?'

Luke coughed. A clump of bloody phlegm landed on Aggie's

arm. Honey thought she'd be sick if someone sprogged on her, but Aggie just wiped it on her jeans and then used her shirt sleeve to clean around Luke's mouth. Luke gurgled and coughed and his eyes fluttered open.

'Aggie?'

'I'm here, baby. How's your nose?'

'It's—' Luke raised his head from Aggie's lap and winced. 'Where's Greg?'

Greg cleared his throat. 'Luke?'

Luke pushed Aggie's hands away and sat up, cradling his head. 'You're fired.'

'Hey!' Honey stamped her foot. 'You can't fire him! You're not even the boss anymore. Kenny's the boss.'

'Leave it, Honey.' Greg patted her hand.

'They fired you?' Aggie asked.

'Just suspended, until an enquiry can be held,' Greg said.

'The allegations are true. I'm fucked.'

'Luke!'

'Well, I am. Fucked because I got fucked, right?' He laughed the crazy laugh from before.

'You better get him out of here,' Honey said to Aggie. 'Before someone sees him.'

Aggie nodded. 'Let me take you home, baby.'

'His home is *here*.' Greg stood up.

'Yeah, well, I don't trust you to take care of him, funnily enough.'

'And I should trust you? This is all your fault.'

Aggie leapt to her feet. She towered over Greg. 'Is it?'

Greg, to his credit, did not back down. He looked her right in the eye, even though that meant he had to crane his neck. 'You should know better.'

Aggie nodded slowly. 'Yes, I suppose I should.' She turned and looked down at Luke. 'Sweetie, do you want to come with me now?'

Luke didn't answer. Aggie put her hands under his arms and dragged him to his feet. 'I don't think I'm welcome here,' Aggie said, as she led Luke out. 'But I'd appreciate it if one of you would come across and see me tomorrow. Help me work out what to do with him.'

'Sure,' Honey said. Greg was back on the bed, hiding his face. She stood in the doorway watching until Aggie and Luke had disappeared out of the side gate. Then she locked the door, went to the bathroom, washed her face, brushed her teeth and fixed her hair. When she came out, Greg was crying.

'Stop crying.'

He looked at her through wet fingers. 'Sorry. Not very manly, is it?'

Honey held out her hand. 'Let's clean you up.'

She led him to the bathroom, and he sat on the toilet and let her wash his face and hands with her special daisy cloth. There was a bit of blood on the knuckles of his right hand, and when he saw it he started to cry again, but Honey held up her finger like a stern school-teacher and he pressed his lips together and got himself under control.

'Okay, so here's what I'm thinking.' Honey rinsed the face cloth under the hot water tap. 'Luke has gone crazy because he did the thing he said he'd never do. He didn't know how much it would change everything. The whole world and everyone in it looks different, and he feels as though he's just seeing everything properly for the first time. He doesn't like what he sees. He wants to go back to not knowing, but he can't; that's his punishment. He has to see the world as it really is forever now.' She squeezed out the cloth and hung it over the tap. 'What do you think?' She turned to Greg.

'I think you're really smart. How'd you figure that out?'

'It's Biblical. Eating the fruit of knowledge, and all that. Jeez, you'd think I was the bloody pastor.'

Honey took Greg's hands, pulling him off the toilet and leading him back to her bedroom. They lay together on the bed, right back where they had been before Luke interrupted them. It felt like the right place to be.

'Since you're so clever,' Greg said, 'maybe you can tell me why I got so angry?'

'Oh, that's easy. You got angry because your illusions were shattered. He was your role model and you saw that he could fuck up just as badly as the rest of us. You freaked.'

'You're very good at this.'

Honey realised he hadn't stuttered or cleared his throat the whole conversation. This must be what he used to be like, how he got all those people to sleep with him. She smiled into his chest. 'So what you'll probably do next is act out in some way.'

'Really. And how am I going to do that?'

'You're going to revert to the behaviour he helped you stop.'

Greg lifted her head with one arm, and rolled on to his side. He looked into her eyes. 'You're wrong about that.'

'I don't think so.'

'I'm going to go to my room, and sleep off this pain in my hand. Then I'm going to go and talk to—'

Honey planted a kiss on his lips. He gasped and covered his mouth with his hand. Lightning-quick she leant in and kissed his right ear, then darted back to his lips just as he moved his hand away. He gave a little moan of protest but then showed he didn't mean it by taking her face between his hands and kissing her hard. It was only when she started unbuttoning his shirt that he pulled away and said 'No!'

Honey felt very warm. Greg did not kiss like a Christian. Not that she had ever kissed a Christian before, but she knew from the meetings that Christians were not supposed to kiss in a way that could lead to arousal, which would definitely mean long, deep, wet kisses on beds, with hands flying all over the place. She lunged for him again. This time she got his shirt all the way off before he pushed her away.

'Stop, please.' He moved to the far edge of the bed, grabbing the pillow and placing it on his lap. 'Just give me a second.' He was breathing hard. His eyes were closed and Honey could tell by the way his lips moved in silent prayer that he was trying to gain control of himself. Once he'd done that, he would leave.

Honey quickly lifted her dress over her head and removed her bra. She hoped her distended belly and large breasts would not repulse him. 'Greg?'

He opened his eyes, moaned and closed them again. 'Put your clothes back on.'

'I thought you liked me.'

'I do, Honey. I like you a whole lot, which is why I'm not gonna do this to you. So be a good girl and cover up.'

Honey threw her dress over her head. 'Covered. Open your eyes, please.'

He did. He smiled and touched her cheek. 'You're beautiful, but I'm not going to take advantage of you.'

'You wouldn't be, I swear.'

'It's not happening, Honey.'

Honey lunged for his crotch, grabbing the pillow away before he could stop her. He went to get up but Honey straddled him, pushing him onto his back and opening his fly. 'I want you to fuck me.'

Greg took hold of Honey's hands, holding them up over his stomach so she couldn't touch him. 'Don't talk like that. I don't like it, and it won't make me change my mind. I'm not stupid, Honey.

You're hurt and you're scared, but this isn't going to fix anything. It'll just make things worse.'

'Stop playing hard to get.'

'I *am* hard to get, and you should be too. Our bodies belong to Jesus Christ and shouldn't be used for–'

'My body belongs to me.' Honey pulled her hands free. She lifted her dress over her head, ignoring his cries of protest. 'Look at me, Greg, please. At least look at me when you say you don't want me.'

He opened his eyes and stared at her face. Honey sat very still, willing him to want her. After a long painful moment of doubt, he moved his gaze to her body. She watched as his eyes flickered all over her, the wrinkles around them becoming more pronounced with each passing second. He never let his eyes rest: they darted from breast to hip to stomach to breast to throat to face. He blinked rapidly and licked his lips. 'So lovely,' he murmured, putting his hands on her stomach. 'You are so precious, Honey. I wish you realised how very, very special you are. Your baby is very lucky to have you.'

Honey felt sick with shame. She ripped his hands off her stomach and rolled off him, landing face down on the bed beside him. She sobbed hard into the mattress, remembering when men used to beg her to let them touch her breasts. It wasn't that long ago, yet it was forever in the past. Her body was not her own, but it was not God's either. Her body was an incubator. Then it would be a delivery system. Then a feed trough. Her body was not for men's pleasure but for a child's survival. Honey cried harder than she had in her life. She didn't know how she could possibly go on.

She wanted to be clean and girlish and odourless. She wanted to wear tight white shorts and midriff tops and giggle and poke out her tongue at the middle-aged men who leered as she passed. She wanted to hang with her friends in the senior girls' bathroom, smoking and bitching about some stupid slut who had got herself pregnant. She wanted to be sixteen, then seventeen, then out of school and working in a café wearing a short black skirt and a white shirt buttoned low until she'd saved enough to fly to Spain and meet her daddy while she was still girl enough for him to love her.

She felt Greg moving beside her. After a moment she felt the breeze of a sheet being pulled over her and then the sheet itself as it floated on to her bare skin. She rolled on to her side and looked at him. He wasn't even good looking. His hair was like something from the 1970s and he had those stupid sleepy hound dog eyes. And he was old enough to be her father, practically. Really, he was disgusting. And he did not want her.

He finished buttoning his shirt and looked down at her with a sad, pitying kind of face. It made her feel so sick of herself, his sympathy.

'I have to go. Service is in twenty minutes. You'll be okay?'

'Sure. I'm sorry.'

'Don't be. It's been a tough day.' He finished getting dressed and then bent to kiss her lightly on the lips. 'I'll tell the others you're sick. They'll understand.'

'Thanks.' Honey closed her eyes and kept them there until she heard him leaving. She got up and dressed and waited until she was sure everyone would have gone to the service, and then she packed her things. It didn't take long.

36

Aggie was equal parts fear and jubilation. Luke was a mess – weeping into the dashboard and refusing to speak or look at her – but she had removed him from that terrible cult and was taking him home to get him better again. Actually, first she was taking him to the hospital to have his physical injuries taken care of, and then she was taking him home to love him into psychic and emotional health.

They had to wait for almost an hour at Casualty. During this time, Luke stopped crying but still did not respond to Aggie's presence, except to sit where she told him to and to stand when she told him to stand. If she tried to touch him, he pulled away; when she asked him questions he stared at the floor or the wall or his hands. She chatted away anyway, knowing he was traumatised by his world being turned upside down and that he was in need of some normality. 'This is a good hospital,' she told him, 'I used to work here. Not here in Casualty, but in the next building over. In Rehab.'

Luke looked her in the eye for the first time. 'This is where he works.'

'Who?'

'Your lover.'

'Luke, *you're* my lover. Right, sweetie?' She pressed her hand to his cheek but he turned from her, with a derisive grunt.

They were called in then. Luke would not tell the doctor how he'd hurt himself and Aggie could only shrug stupidly. She had no idea how he'd cut his hands so badly that nineteen stitches were needed. The damage from Greg's fists was less serious: the nose was swollen but not broken and his top lip required only two stitches. The doctor gave Aggie an ice pack and a small bottle of codeine as they were leaving. 'Don't give him any of these until he sobers up,' he said.

'He thinks I'm drunk!' Luke laughed loudly. 'No, no, Doctor. I don't drink. That's one thing I never do.'

The doctor gave Aggie a sympathetic smile. 'Whatever, he's on. Wait until it wears off.'

On the trip home, Luke was more talkative. Unfortunately. He lay back on the fully reclined seat, with the ice on his nose and started. 'You must be disappointed,' he said. 'Coming out here and not seeing your lover. Maybe we should have asked for him. Requested the services of the incomparable Dr. Keating. I wouldn't have minded, really– I mean, at least I could have seen him properly. It's impossible to tell what he really looks like from that picture; it's grainy and his face is, well, shall we say, *obscured*?'

'What picture? I don't understand what you're talking about.'

Luke snorted. It sounded thick and bloody. 'Evidence, Aggie. You didn't clean up after yourself. You left tracks. Evidence!'

'Of what? Jesus, Luke!'

He laughed. Aggie glanced at him, hoping for a clue, but the ice pack obscured most of his face. She turned the radio on and concentrated on the road.

Luke sat up, switched the radio off, lay down again. '*This is the way of an adulterous woman. She eats and wipes her mouth, and says, "I have done nothing wrong…"*'

Aggie swung the car into her driveway. 'Firstly, Luke, don't quote fucking Bible verses at me.' She turned off the ignition and pulled the ice pack off his face. 'Secondly, *adulterous?* Do you actually know the meaning of that word?'

'Do you?' He got out of the car and stalked up to her front door.

Inside, he ignored her offer of food or drink and went straight to the study. While she watched over his shoulder, he switched on her computer and opened her Internet connection. She asked him what he thought he was doing, but he ignored that question too. Aggie wondered how long the sulky, unreasonable behaviour would go on; she just wanted to take care of him, but he was making that exceedingly difficult.

On the screen in front of her, the hated words *Justice for the Unborn* had appeared, and below them, a gruesome picture Aggie recognised from the placards outside the clinic. 'What are you—?'

'Wait.' Luke scrolled down, clicking on links too fast for Aggie to see where he was going. His familiarity with the site was disturbing. 'Look.'

Aggie squinted at the screen, then laughed as the photo came into focus. 'Hah, there's Mum! She'd be thrilled about this. She's a publicity whore, you know.'

Luke looked up at her. 'You're not upset by this?'

'Not really. They can delve as deep into my life as they want. I have nothing to hide, nothing to be ashamed of. I've had worse from this lot. At least they haven't shot me yet.'

'How can you be so cavalier?' His voice cracked. 'You're in real danger.'

'Oh, sweetie,' she began, bending to embrace him, but he held up his hands to ward her off.

Aggie straightened, nodded. Luke returned his attention to the screen and scrolled past the photo of Aggie with her mother. A black and white picture of Aggie and Luke outside the clinic appeared and Aggie's stomach dropped. The fuckers had her under surveillance.

She barely had time to feel violated before Luke moved on to another picture.

Hell. Simon. The one time in her life she had spent the night with a man she wasn't in love with and it had been caught on camera. Not that she had anything to be ashamed of. Not that she had done anything wrong. Except, she remembered thinking that she hoped Luke would find out and be hurt. But that was before.

'Luke, sweetie, that was before you—'

'I can read the date. I know when it was.'

She knelt in front of him and looked up into his face. 'You know I never would have—'

'How could you do those things with him, if you loved me?'

'One doesn't have anything to do with the other.'

'It makes everything that happened this weekend meaningless.'

'No! You have it the wrong way around. The night with him was meaningless. You're everything.' Aggie pressed her face to his lap. He didn't push her away, which was enough to give her hope.

His tears fell onto the back of her head and her ears, sliding down the sides of her face until they pooled in his lap with her own. 'This is why we are told to stay pure until marriage,' Luke said. 'The pain of sexual betrayal is just so intensely awful. It's worse than anything I've ever experienced, anything I can imagine.'

'I didn't betray you.'

'You believe that, I know.'

'Is this worth all the heartache, do you think?'

'Worth? I don't know. I don't know what anything's worth any more. Everything is...' He touched her hair and face. Feather-light fingers skipping over her, fast, as if he was trying to find something, sense some answer through the tips of his fingers. 'Aggie?' he said finally. 'I think I'd really like to go to bed now.'

37

Back when Luke was first saved, he had made a commitment to get up early each morning to pray and listen to God, the way that Jesus had. Every day for fifteen years he had done exactly that, until three mornings ago. He had not thought of prayer at all when waking in her bed; he had thought only of his pleasure in her, and then, of his misery at her absence.

Now, after three days of shutting his mind and heart to the Lord, Luke found the Lord had shut His ears to Luke's prayers. His pleas and cries went out into nothingness. He thought of David, running for his life and crying *How long, O Lord? Will you forget me forever? How long will you hide your face from me?* Luke wondered if God would leave him forever too. Would he die in this pit of lust and pain and sin?

I have asked the Lord for one thing; one thing only do I want: to live in the Lord's house all my life, to marvel there at his goodness, and to ask for his guidance. Not true, not true. He had asked for the love of a woman. He had denigrated God's love by wanting more. God gave him a family and a home and a life he loved, and Luke had shaken his fist and declared God's awesome love deficient. He had thought he was lonely. But true loneliness was this, now. The absence of God.

Aggie thought he should celebrate. She said he was a lonely, confused orphan who had only turned to religion because it gave him unconditional love and a feeling of belonging and family. When he fell in love and experienced intimacy with another human being, he no longer felt emotionally needy all the time. God was the imaginary friend Luke had made because he didn't have a real one. And now He was gone.

'You have absolutely no idea what you're talking about,' he told her.

'So explain it to me.'

'Why? So you can tear it apart? Poke holes in my beliefs? Tell me I'm wrong and brainwashed and idiotic, that my life has been wasted on a delusion? That I should be happy?'

Aggie sighed and draped her hot limbs over him. 'Forget it,' she said.

So it went on. The love-making, intense and spiritual; the prayer, hysterical and unheard. It was so frightening, like being eight years old again, lying in the dark, listening to the boy in the next bed cry, holding his breath, trying not to cry himself, wondering if help would ever come. He clung to Aggie like he used to clutch his blanket: like a life preserver in cold, deep water.

He heard her heavy footsteps on the stairs, the doorbell again, Aggie shouting that she was coming. It occurred to him that Justice for the Unborn may have discovered her address. They had published Malcolm's address why not hers? She could be opening the door right now to—

'Aggie!' He ran for the stairway. 'Aggie don't open–'

'Have a seat,' he heard her say, and then she appeared below him. 'It's fine Luke, go back to bed.'

'Who is it?'

'A friend. Just give us a couple of minutes, okay?'

'What friend? Malcolm?'

'Luke, you're naked,' she said, as if that settled everything.

Luke returned to the bedroom and wrapped a towel around his waist and went down.

He expected to see Aggie's lover, the doctor, and was fully prepared to have his nose properly broken in the process of smashing in the doctor's skull. He was not prepared to find Honey and Aggie sitting on the sofa holding hands.

Honey was crying. On the floor was the navy sports bag she had carried when she first came to him and the plaid overnight case he had bought her for when she went into hospital. When she saw Luke she stopped crying, bit her lip, then sobbed and pressed her face to Aggie's chest. He felt wretched about the scene in her room yesterday. He must have been mad to think something was going on between her and Greg. To see her now – stick-like, save that small bump. Frail, fragile little bird. He *was* mad; it was indisputable.

'Can you leave us alone for a while?' Aggie asked him.

'Honey? What's wrong? Why are you here?'

'I said leave us. Please, Luke?'

He had no intention of leaving Aggie alone to corrupt Honey, but he felt ridiculous standing there in a towel. More than that, he felt it was wrong to be exposing Honey to such an obvious display of sexuality. He nodded at Aggie and returned to the bedroom, where he dressed in his blood-stained t-shirt and dusty shorts.

'Right,' he said, descending the stairs. 'What's going on?'

'Jesus Christ, Luke! Can't you just do one thing I ask you?'

He sat beside Honey, who was now sitting up straight, smoking a cigarette. 'Why did you come here, Honey?'

'To find you.'

'I guessed as much. So can I stay and talk to you, or do you want me to do what Aggie says and go away?'

Tears leaked from both eyes. 'Stay and talk.'

Aggie glared at Luke over the top of Honey's head. He glared back. 'Aggie, maybe you can make us tea?'

'Do I look like your slave?' she said, but she stomped off to the kitchen anyway.

When she was gone, Luke gently plucked the cigarette from Honey's fingers and extinguished it in the ashtray beside him. 'I'm sorry,' he said. 'I went a bit crazy and I–'

Honey threw herself at him, wrapping her arms around his back, tucking her legs under her in his lap and pressing her face into his neck. 'You can't leave me, Luke. I don't have anyone else. Me and Greg never did anything, I swear! I was just so lonely. Please, please don't leave me, Luke. I swear I'll be better.'

'Oh, Honey, oh. I didn't leave you, I left the… things are very complicated right now. It's better that I stay here for a while.'

'Let me stay with you.'

Her words and arms and body were suffocating. He tried to ease her off him but she held tight. She was stronger and heavier than she appeared, and he was injured and exhausted. 'Honey, please, you're better off at the centre. They all care about you very much and will look after you properly. I can't do that here. I have no money, no resources. I have nothing to–'

'Come back with me then. You can still come back, can't you? Luke?'

Luke closed his eyes. His legs were going numb under the weight of her. He remembered when he'd held her upright that first day outside the clinic, she was as easy to hold as a child. Now the child within her had grown and it was a woman's weight upon him.

'For God's sake, Honey, get off him. He's injured.'

'Sorry,' Honey whimpered, climbing off his knee. Luke exhaled with relief but smiled at Honey to show he was fine. Aggie put the tray she was carrying on the side table and handed them each a mug of hot tea.

'Please, Luke. I can't do this without you. I can't. I can't! You have to be with me. You promised me.'

Luke looked to Aggie for help. She raised her eyebrows at him, her lips pressed firmly together, shrugged and looked pointedly at the ceiling.

'Honey, I promised you would be safe, I never said I–'

'You never...?' Honey shook her head fiercely. 'Right, right, of course you never. How simple for you.' Her sobbing started afresh.

'For god's sake!' Aggie slammed her mug down, splashing milky tea over the table. 'Honey, you can stay here tonight. An old colleague of mine runs a shelter in Redfern. I'll take you there in the morning.'

'She is *not* going to live in a shelter.'

'Don't have much choice, do I?' Honey started crying again. 'I don't have anywhere else. Don't you get it?'

'You belong at the NCYC. That's your home now.'

'I never belonged there. I *hate* it there. I just stayed because of you. I don't even *believe* in God, you know? I don't believe any of it. It's bullshit. You're all full of mounds and mounds of utter bullshit. I don't know how I even managed to fake it for so long. Pretending to believe all that utter crap!'

Luke stood up, placed his mug on the side table and walked out of the room. He went outside and stood on the balcony, overlooking the swimming pool. His mind was a blank, or more precisely, his mind was empty of coherent thought, but the space where the thoughts should have been was not blank at all. His head was filled with black tangles, a confusion of anger and fear that started and ended nowhere at all.

He gazed at the dark shimmer of Aggie's pool and was seized

with a desire to swim. Although the night was cool, he craved the cold slap of the water. He stripped off his clothes on the way down the stairs and dived naked into the pool. For a second he was numb, then the blessed chill went through him, his eyes filled with tears, his sinuses tingled and his lungs burnt. He swam ten fast laps, then another ten slower ones. Breathless, but calmer and clearer, he rested a moment, his back against the smooth tiles of the wall.

Honey hated it at the centre. She did not believe in God. She had stayed there only because he had been taking care of her. Luke realised that he had known these things before she had told him, that his speechless rage had been at himself, at his selfishness and stupidity. She had never really been saved, had only done what was necessary to remain in his care. He had ignored the smoking and swearing, the rolled eyes, the sarcasm and impatience. He had let himself believe he had led her to salvation because he so desperately needed the distraction from his own sins.

But now the sin was the distraction from the pain of losing God. Having given in to his unholy love, he did not need Honey to assuage his guilt or keep him busy any more; he did not need her at all. She was part of that other life, the NCYC, the mission to save souls and lives, the happy surety of eternity by God's side.

The screen door squeaked open and then clanged shut. Luke turned and watched Aggie's solid calves descending the stairs, her shadow gliding over the lawn, her thick ankles crossing in front of his face. He reached out a wet hand and gripped a foot, feeling the tiny bones under his palm. She was so strong and substantial, yet so very breakable. It was the biggest mystery he had come across in a lifetime of examining mysteries. She was as unknowable as God.

'How is she?'

'A mess. She's gone to bed. I told her we'd sort something out in the morning. We, meaning me and her. Not you, obviously, since you run away as soon as someone says something you don't want to hear.'

'I don't know what to do.'

'Tell me this, Luke, and please don't lie to me. Have you slept with her?'

'What? You know I haven't!'

'Yeah.' Aggie sighed and flexed her foot. 'You haven't kissed her or… I don't know, Luke, you two seemed so intimate. When I came out of the kitchen and she was… all *on you*.'

'She's scared and thinks I can help her. And you should know me better. Goodness, Aggie, I would cut off my hands before I hurt that girl.'

'Having sex with a girl is not the only way to hurt her. She's sobbing her heart out in there.'

'It's not my– I don't know what to do.'

'Help her,' Aggie said. 'She's a teenager in trouble. Help her! It's what you do.'

'No, no. I help lead people to God, I teach them the word of the Lord, I introduce them to Jesus Christ. Without God… I have no idea what to do for her. I was only ever any use as a servant of Christ.'

'What about with me?'

He released her foot and pressed his hands to his face. He had failed so badly. Aggie, Honey, himself – all Godless and lost and doomed. 'We're all alone,' he said. 'All three of us, alone.'

'Then we're not alone at all, are we? We're together.'

'Without God, we are alone.'

'When you were with God, I was alone.'

'I need to swim some more.' Luke pushed off from the edge. He swam until he was dizzy and nauseous. He stopped in the middle of a lap and heaved, spitting up bitter chlorinated water, wiping his stinging eyes and running nose. When his vision cleared, he saw she was still there, watching.

'She loves you,' Aggie told him, in the middle of the night.

'I don't understand that.'

'Do you love her?'

'I pity her. I want her to be safe. I just don't– I can't give her any-thing.'

'Love isn't about what you can get or what you can give,' Aggie said. 'It's just wanting to try. Wanting to get through stuff together.'

He was tangled up: her long, pale limbs crushing his smaller, darker ones; her bewildering softness melting into him; the steady rhythm of her heartbeat under his ear; the gentle breeze of her breath cooling the top of his head. It didn't make sense that these bodies fit together so well, that these souls found peace only in each other's presence. It was not logical that he had come to be loved by this woman and to love her in return.

Kabbalistic Jews tell a story in which God, at the beginning of time, tries to release just a little of Himself into the world. But the jar of God shatters and shards of Godness are scattered all over creation.

Kabbalistic Jews maybe knew a thing or two.

38

'What a miserable day,' Aggie had said when Honey first came downstairs – but it wasn't true at all. Although the dark sky threatened to burst open any moment, and it was so cold that even wrapped in a quilt from Aggie's spare bed, Honey couldn't stop shivering, it was still the most wonderful, fabulous, hopeful day.

Last night, Honey had been sure that it was all over. Luke hated her and didn't want anything to do with her or the baby. Aggie, while helpful and kind, did not want to be bothered with Honey in the long term. Honey was destined for a shelter; her son would grow up on welfare, without a family, without hope. Lying in the dark, in this huge, cold house, Honey considered getting up and throwing herself out of the window. She was on the second floor, so it wouldn't kill her. Probably wouldn't. What it would do was make Luke feel guilty for abandoning her. He would be so sorry. He would bring her flowers and chocolates. He would sit beside her hospital bed and cry, begging her to forgive him. She would, after a while.

But then, a fall from the second floor would almost certainly kill the baby. She couldn't do that, even knowing that everything would be so much clearer and simpler without it. Even though she hated the bump which had repulsed Greg. Even though the thought of sharing a room with ten other pregnant girls and giving birth alone and never having a boy want to touch her again and always being alone and sad and fat – even with all that, she just couldn't do it. She kept thinking of that Bible verse: *Before I formed you in the womb I knew you.* She didn't believe that it was literally true, as if her son's spirit had always been floating about, chatting away to God and the angels, and then one day God looked down and decided that it was time for the little spirit boy to be real so he zapped his spirit into the freshly-forming zygote in Honey's womb. But there was something about that verse which really got to her. She changed it around in her mind: *Before I knew you, I formed you in my womb.* If she killed him, she would never know him. Never know who he was.

She didn't get much sleep. It was too cold, and she was too scared about what was going to happen to her. By morning, she was exhausted. She wanted to stay in bed, try and sleep some more, not face up to the day and its frightening promise of state shelters and welfare officers. But Aggie banged on her door and told her to come downstairs for breakfast, and Honey did not want to be rude since Aggie had been so nice. Also, she was hungry.

Then, as she sat at the kitchen table, looking out at the stormy sky, shivering her bum off, Luke came downstairs and made everything wonderful. 'Please forgive me,' he said. And then, 'Will you stay here with Aggie and me? Let us help you with your baby?' And then he had hugged her tight and kissed both her cheeks and pressed his head to her belly to feel the baby kick.

The three of them ate cereal and drank coffee. Aggie seemed worried. She rattled on about government agencies and child care provisions. Luke was subdued, barely eating his food, smiling only when Honey met his eyes. Honey tried to imagine what he must be feeling, having given up his career and all, but she found she couldn't concentrate on being empathetic for very long. Her happiness was so great, so complete. She wasn't afraid any more, not of anything.

'I have to get to work,' Aggie said, carrying her plate to the sink. She turned and smiled down at Luke, who was staring morosely into his coffee cup. 'Luke, baby, can you take Honey to Social Security this morning? Sort out her payments?'

He nodded. 'Yeah. Sure. I think…' He looked at Honey and gave her a pained smile. 'I think I'd better go and get my stuff from… you know.'

'That's cool. I was thinking of having a look at the maternity gear at K-mart. All my clothes are too tight.'

Luke smiled, a real one this time. 'Baby's growing fast. When's our next ultrasound?'

'Thursday. Oh and I need you on Friday morning for ante-natal group. Birth coach training starts this week.'

'You're her birth coach? That's so adorable.' Aggie ruffled Luke's hair. He smiled again and turned his head to kiss her hand. She bent and kissed him on the forehead. 'Love you,' she whispered. He murmured something back at her, kissed her lips.

It was kind of embarrassing to watch. They were so cheesy, so kissy-kissy, lovey-dovey, like couples on American sitcoms. Honey felt weird sitting across from them while they kissed. She wondered if she should just sneak out, give them some privacy. That's what she used to do, back home. Well, no, she didn't sneak out, she groaned and muttered and then ran. With her mother and Muzza you didn't have long before the disgusting stuff was in full swing; once they started pashing on, Honey was out of there.

Before she could decide to leave, the kissing was over. Aggie came around to Honey's side of the table and squatted down so her face was level with Honey's. 'Hey,' she said, smiling, 'I'm trusting you to take care of him for me.'

'Aggie, for goodness sake. I don't need looking after.'

'Humour me, Luke. I worry.' Aggie winked at Honey. 'Help him?' she mouthed.

Honey nodded. She knew what Aggie meant. Luke was like the new kid at school. He looked almost normal, although his clothes and way of talking were not quite up to the minute in these parts. Left alone he would wander around all day getting lost and asking the wrong questions. People who didn't know he was new might get angry and hurt him. He might do something he didn't know he shouldn't. He might get hurt again. Honey was an old hand at dealing with the stuff that hurt. She could steer him around the curves.

She saw that Aggie recognised this in her, and it made her proud. She saw also that Luke was smiling, pleased that Aggie and Honey were conspiring to coddle him. She felt at that moment that she belonged. She was not just a pain in both their arses; they would never make her leave the room or exclude her from their conversations. They needed her, at least a little bit.

39

L ong, long ago, before he felt the absence of a history, before
he began his search for identity, before Mai introduced him
to God and before the Christian Revolution embraced him
as a brother and son, way back then, Luke had wanted to be a policeman. As a cop, he would be respected even if he was darker than the
average Aussie. As a cop, he would be able to come down hard on
bullies and neo-Nazi thugs. As a cop, he could help people, be a real
hero. Maybe even live up to whatever heroic deeds his namesake performed. That was before.

As he placed the six cardboard boxes of his life into the boot of
his car, he thought again of that long-lost dream. It held no appeal
for him now. He had seen too much of the world, heard too many
stories of corruption and violence and prejudice. Besides, he could
never arrest a drunk for disturbing the peace or force a panhandling
hobo to move on. He could never charge a prostitute or a pick-
pocket. He could never blame a person for failing to be good.

He was, technically, a trained social worker, but he had never
practised, never even registered to practise, and he had no confidence
in his ability to be either impartial or perceptive. What else could he
do? He was quite good at gardening and cleaning. He could run
really fast. Recent reports indicated he was a talented kisser, but he
doubted one could make a living from that. Public speaking used to

be his forte, but he had nothing left to say. All his speaking and teaching and leading and counselling, all his everything, had been for God. Nothing seemed worth doing if not for His glory. Nothing seemed worth striving for now He had turned away.

Luke closed the car boot and leant against it, taking a last look at the cabin he used to call home. It looked so small and disconnected. He found he was not sad about leaving it behind. He had an inkling that some time in the future he might be happy with Aggie and Honey and the child. That the large, sad house could one day feel crowded and joyous. He understood that God was not in the faux-timber cabin. If Luke was ever to find Him again, it would not be here.

He was meeting his family for lunch. He parked his car next to Aggie's and did not turn his head toward his former life as he walked towards the clinic. As soon as he saw her, slouching against the edge of her desk, twisting the phone cord around her hand, laughing, he felt stronger, surer. He must have something wonderful to offer the world if this woman loved him.

'Butler.' Mal stepped in front of Luke and held a meaty hand up in front of his face. 'Just a sec.'

'Hello, Malcolm. How was your holiday?'

'Notice all those protesters outside?'

'There aren't any protesters outside, Malcolm.'

'Exactly. First day in over a month the footpath hasn't been crawling with them. At first I was thinking, fan-bloody-tastic, you know?'

Luke looked over Mal's shoulder and caught Aggie's eyes. She rolled them and gestured to the phone. 'One minute,' she mouthed.

'But then Aggie comes in and tells me that you've moved out of the fundy house and into hers and I can't help thinking–' Mal stepped forwards so his chin was level with Luke's nose, '–that maybe the two are somehow linked.'

Luke took three steps backwards. 'Your logic escapes me.'

'Well, logic isn't a minister's strong point is it? I'll spell it out. You called off the attack dogs because you and Aggie are fucking. Sent 'em to harass some other poor health worker.'

'Listen to me for a minute. I—'

'Hey, baby, how'd you go?' Aggie slid into the space between the two men. She kissed Luke and ruffled his hair, then before he could answer she turned and slapped Mal's arm. 'I heard everything you said, you big bully. You know he had nothing to do with all that.'

'It's a big coincidence. That's all I was saying.'

'Why d'ya have to be so bloody negative? It's a happy day, Mal! Luke and Honey are free. I've got all the company I could want and – icing on the cake – the protesters have gone away. It's a happy, happy, happy day. Right? Right?'

Mal shrugged, grumbled, turned away. Aggie laughed and threw her arms around Luke. 'He'll come around. I was worried about you. I thought they might talk you into staying.'

'No.' Luke did not tell her that not one of them had spoken to him. That they all stood in a line and watched him pack his things and when he had finished, they went inside and closed the door.

'Brave boy.' Aggie kissed him again. 'Everything's going to be okay, you know that, right?'

'I don't know it, not for certain, anyway. But I… I love you and I think that if I can—'

'This is a place of business.' Mal barked. 'Go and emote elsewhere.'

Aggie stuck her tongue out. 'Fine. Come on, baby, let's leave grumpy bum here alone.'

'Honey's meeting us here. She should be along any minute now.'

'We'll wait in the park. All the cool kids go there to make out with their boyfriends, you know.' Aggie grabbed her bag from the hook near the back door, ran to Mal's desk and kissed his forehead, then grabbed Luke's hand.

With the money Luke gave her, Honey bought a black plaid baby-doll dress, a red miniskirt with a stretchy tummy panel, a black sleeveless t-shirt, an electric blue stretch jacket and a big bucket of chocolate-coated honeycomb. When she got her first Social Security cheque, she would buy something for Aggie and Luke, to thank them. She wondered if they would get married and have children of their own. That would be very cool. Then Honey's son would have some friends, more than friends really. If she was living with Aggie and Luke, she would be sort of like their daughter – no, more like their little sister – and so her son and their kids would be like cousins or something. He would never be lonely, that's for sure. And that was important.

The other thing she bought at K-mart was a little hardcover book of baby names. She read it as she walked up Koloona Street, trying to imagine what her son would look like, what name would suit him. She would like to call him Luke, because that was the name of the only really nice man she had ever known, and she really, really wanted her boy to be a nice man one day. But it would be embarrassing for Luke to have a baby named after him; some dirty-minded people already thought he was the father, because of how he took care of Honey so much.

So not *Luke*. And not *Steve*, because then he would *definitely* turn out to be a creep. Honey considered her own father's name, *Estefan*, but worried the poor kid would get hassled at school. Bad enough he would have a woggy surname like Allende. No, his first name would have to be something Aussie and gentle sounding, but not wussy or girlish. *Adam* was nice and Biblical so Luke would approve, but then the poor kid's initials would be AA, which, with Honey's family history, was just asking for trouble. *Caleb* was a definite possibility. It meant *dog* which was good, because dogs were cute and cuddly but could be fierce and tough when they needed to be. She would have to check with Luke though, because she was sure Caleb was a Bible character. She couldn't remember whether he was good or not.

Anyway, she was almost at the clinic. She would ask Luke and Aggie what they thought and the three of them could decide on it together.

The park bench was dripping wet, so Aggie and Luke could not sit on it and make out like teenagers. Instead they held hands and walked around the circumference of the little park, talking softly about the future, reassuring each other that everything was going to be wonderful. They talked about taking a trip together. Aggie was horrified to learn that Luke had never left the country. She told him she would take him anywhere he wanted to go.

'I've always wanted to visit Jerusalem,' he said.

She felt the tickle of fear which in the past she had felt when her married lover mentioned his wife or children. The man she loved had an older, deeper love; she was an adventure, a holiday, and one day, he would return to the world of his heart.

'Jerusalem it is.' She knew how to be the other woman. She would make sure his thoughts of Jerusalem were forever entwined with thoughts of her. Like making friend's with Simon's daughters so they would forever remind him of how cool she was.

'No.' Luke caught her around the waist and pulled her close to him. 'Let's go somewhere else. Somewhere we won't have to worry about getting blown up the whole time. Canada or Greece, maybe. We'll go to Jerusalem when things settle down. That's if you still want to take me in fifty years or so.'

They walked, made plans, kissed. The world smelt new and earthy, like trampled Autumn leaves and freshly-turned soil. As they passed under a low-hanging branch, a gust of wind sprinkled them with rain drops which clung to Aggie's curls and slid over Luke's cheeks like tears.

Aggie saw Honey first. She waved, but the girl had her head stuck in a book and did not see. 'She's gone in. We'd better go save her from Mal's bad mood.'

'I'll wait here, thank you very much. I have no desire to tempt fate by placing myself within striking distance a second time.'

Aggie laughed and kissed his lips. 'Back in a sec, you big wuss.'

She was barely out of the park and onto the footpath, when an ear-splitting noise lifted her into the air, which was suddenly not fresh and clear, but opaque, choking. Landing hard she swallowed blood and spat out teeth. She tried to see but there was only smoke, black and thick. Bands of pain squeezed her chest and ribcage. There was a terrible, inhuman roar, which might only have been the sound of her own shattered ear drums. She tried to breathe, but the pain in her chest stopped her lungs from expanding. Her mouth and nostrils filled with smoke and grit and soot and God knew what else, but not air. There wasn't any air.

She tried to determine where she was. She knew she had covered some distance in the air and landed somewhere hard and blood making. So could be the footpath or the road. So someone, surely, would be along soon to pick her up. She could stop trying to move, stop trying to scream, stop trying to breathe. She could stop.

40

The service was held in the Castle Hill church, the sermon conducted by Pastor Riley, with a reading by Belinda and a song from Leticia. Luke did not cry. It wasn't real. The God they claimed had wanted this did not exist. The Jesus who was allegedly walking beside Honey, holding her baby in his arms was a fiction. Luke stared and stared at the cross over the pulpit. He stared at the cross and its only meaning was in its resemblance to the one Honey had worn around her neck. It was a symbol and a young girl's throat was what it symbolised.

The funeral was well-attended. Two, maybe three hundred people, most of them under twenty, about half of them from the NCYC. Luke picked Honey's mother straight away; she looked just like Honey never would. Luke did not speak to her or to anyone else except Will, who was there to support him, just as Luke had supported Will through Malcolm's funeral yesterday. Each man would have preferred Aggie there to hold his hand, but she was a barely-living mummy, unreachable because of a wall of doctors and a pump filled with morphine.

They went to St John's after the funeral, to sit and drink weak coffee and wait for Aggie to wake or worsen or improve. Selfishly, Luke wished for her improvement so he could tell her about the terrible thing that had happened. He wanted her to share his suffering, quiet his spirit. 'We can't burden her with it until she's strong,' said Will and the doctors and the mother who had appeared in heels, with an entourage, like a film star. Luke nodded his agreement. How could he not? But he wanted Aggie to know, to feel this, to help him understand.

Will had kept the world turning in the days and nights that had passed since the explosion. He had arranged the funerals, contacted the relatives, slept at Aggie's place so he would be there to cook for Luke and to drive him to and from the hospital. And he had talked and talked and talked. 'My way of grieving,' he explained, 'is to articulate every last damn thing that I'm feeling and thinking. You, on the other hand, grieve by going into a coma. That's cool. We've each got to deal in our own way.'

This afternoon though, having seen the coffin containing what was left of Honey and the (according-to-the-government) non-person in her womb lowered into the earth, Luke was troubled by a question so large that it forced him out of his silence. 'How am I supposed to live another thirty or forty years,' he asked Will, 'when it takes everything I've got in me just to keep breathing from one minute to the next?'

'Oh, man, I know, I know.' Will reached across the table and grasped Luke's hands, wrapping them up in his own. 'I've been pummelled by death, Luke, *hammered* by it. There was a time it seemed I had a funeral to go to every month. With each one I felt I couldn't take another death, not one more. Every time I had to put on my damn black suit and tie again, I thought: *this is it; this is the absolute limit of my endurance.* So many times, I felt I couldn't go on. But I did. I'm still here and I'm still living large, falling in love and getting hurt so badly that if I talked for twenty years without stopping, I still wouldn't be able to describe it.' He stopped and closed his eyes, working his lips in a silent prayer for strength. Luke had noticed that he did that from time to time. He had a faint curiosity about who Will was praying too, what God he thought gave a hoot about a grieving homosexual. Which God gave a damn about any of it?

Will swallowed loudly and opened his eyes. 'The world is unbearably sad, Luke, but you will survive it. You just have to keep going. Concentrate on breathing. Just focus on that one thing. Just keep on breathing.'

Luke breathed in and out. His lungs expanded and contracted. His chest rose and fell. Honey would not have felt a thing, they said. She (and her baby that wasn't one, not yet, not officially) would have been dead within half a second of detonation. Her body was barely recognisable. The baby (which wasn't one) was shielded from the direct blast by Honey's flesh, so there was something of it to bury with her. A body which wasn't one. Luke breathed in and out, easy as anything.

'Luke, precious?'

He looked up at Carrie Grey, the strange mother whom he had imagined as cold and loveless, but who had not left Aggie's side for more than a minute at a time, and who showered alcohol-scented kisses on him at every opportunity.

'Darlin', she's awake. She's asking for you.'

She was propped up on a pile of pillows, a big, bald Frankenstein's monster. She smiled a crazy smile. 'They shaved my head.'

'Looks like someone slipped with the razor.' Luke followed the line of thick black stitches with his eyes. It started above her left eyebrow and zigzagged its way across her forehead and up over her skull, ending at the nape of her neck. Small patches of three or four stitches were sprinkled over her shiny, tight-skinned face. The right eye was swollen shut, the left remarkably clear and undamaged. He kissed her there, on the tiny miracle of her unharmed eyelid.

'Are you in a lot of pain?'

'Not so much. I assume I'm heavily medicated, because I snuck a look at my stomach just now and half of it seems to be missing. But all I can feel is the itching of my damn leg under the plaster.'

He was glad to hear it. He said so, tried to smile, took a deep breath and began. 'Aggie, I–'

'Sit down, Luke. Here, next to me. Hold my hand while you tell me.' He did as she asked, being careful not to touch the sticky plaster attaching the drip to the top of her hand. She looked at him directly, with her one good eye. 'The clinic blew up, didn't it?'

'Rubbish bin full of explosives. There was another one due to go off in Liverpool but the police got tipped off in time. The girl who rang them had helped blow your place up and was freaked out by what… apparently, she thought the explosion would just shut the clinic down. She said she hadn't wanted to–'

'–kill anyone?'

He nodded.

She closed her eye for a second, then nodded back at him. 'Mal?'

'I'm so sorry, Ag.'

She sucked her breath in through her nose. Her open eye filled with water, and she gasped as a tear dropped onto a patch of stitches. 'How's Will?'

'He's okay. He's here if you want to see him.'

'Yeah. Soon. Can you wipe my face for me?'

Luke took a tissue from the box by the bedside and slowly, carefully mopped up the tears. She didn't wince when he accidentally touched her stitches, but she did gulp when he kissed her eyelid again.

'Is that it?' she said when he was beside her again.

He looked at her. Bald, broken little thing, criss-crossed with black lines, glassy-eyed from tears and morphine. His need to share his pain with her was gone. His back was unbroken; he could carry the load a while longer.

'You should rest.'

She closed her eye, sighed. 'How long have I been in here?'

'Almost five days.'

'That's a lot of rest.'

'Ag, I–'

'Luke, please, I'm fine. Well, okay, not fine, but I'm here and I'm going to recover– but I can't do that until the injuries have all been inflicted. You know?'

'Yes. Okay.' He inhaled deeply, filling his lungs with antiseptic. 'Honey was right in the doorway when it… She's dead Ag, her and the boy. How's that for wicked irony, heh?'

'Oh, God, Luke, she was– Oh, God, baby, I'm so sorry.'

He began to cry. The first tears he had shed since it happened. He knew Aggie would do that for him, crack him open and take on some of his pain and grief. He pressed his head to her bandaged chest and wept and wept. By the time the nurse came to tell him he had to go, he knew that Will was right, that he could survive. Grieving with her had put him into an entirely different universe from where he had been stuck all week. In this new place, there was hope. There had been no way for him to get here alone.

He drove Will's car back to the big sad house and gathered together Aggie's yellow slippers, her favourite pyjamas and some books. He made a bouquet of red and yellow roses from her garden and wrapped the stems in the yellow headband she used to wear. He wanted her to see how her roses were thriving, how last week's rain had caused the garden to explode in colour. He was beginning to understand something. It had to do with the garden and the grass and the little tufts of hair sprouting from Aggie's shaved scalp. It had to do with resurrection.